KILL
SWITCH

NOTES OF NECROSOPH

AL K. LINE

Copyright © 2022 Al K. Line

On Guard

"What are you doing?" asked Phage as she raised an eyebrow and tilted her head. She looked like an angel. Her hair shone, she was wearing bright crimson lipstick, and had a mischievous smile. I could smell the scent of shampoo mixed with the tang of silage because she'd just been feeding some of the animals. Divine. Heaven on earth.

I lifted the visor and said, "I'm not getting caught out this year. No fucking way. Have at it, you bastards. I'm ready for you." I shook my fist at the ceiling. My armor rattled.

"Where on earth did you get all that stuff?" Phage stifled a chuckle.

"Don't you dare laugh!" I warned. "I got it from a guy. I refuse to be cut, bruised, burned, or stabbed when the note arrives this year. It's the same every bloody time. Daemons coming out of your kettle. Wraiths down the chimney. Damn critters under the floors. Necronotes poking you in the eye. Nope, I'm done with it. Come on, you buggers."

"So, you thought a helmet, a breastplate, a shield, and a bloody sword would be the answer?" Phage stepped into the room, a pity smile now firmly planted on her sexy face.

There was a hint of perfume. It stirred things under the armor, even at such a stressful time.

"Yes. I did."

"Why didn't you just get a phone box? You could have stood in it and waited for the note."

"Don't be silly. I... Actually, that's not a bad idea!"

"Yes, Soph, it is. It's a terrible idea. So is all that gear. It won't work," she sang, then wandered off into the kitchen, her hips swaying. I noticed she wore very tight black jeans.

What was with her today? Did we have something planned? Was there an anniversary? Nope, just my yearly birthday and all the crap that went with such an ominous date for a poor, weary Necro.

"Have I got a cake? Can we do our special thing?" I called after her.

She returned, smiling. "Look, I'm sorry I forgot your birthday that one time, but you don't have to keep reminding me."

"I didn't say a word."

"You implied it."

"Did not."

"Did too. And yes, we will do your special thing. But no, there isn't a cake."

"Aw, why not?"

"Because there's no butter. There isn't enough flour. The thing they call sugar nowadays tastes like chemicals in a bag, and that's why I was crying and upset and thoroughly pissed off. There isn't enough of anything."

"When were you crying?" Had she been?

"Men," she tutted.

"Just like the war, but with a shitload of cereal, and loads of meat and carrots and veg, and..."

"Shut up! Oh, and happy bloody birthday." Phage stormed off.

"Can we do my favorite thing now?" I shouted hopefully. She slammed a pan on the counter in the kitchen. Guess that was a no.

There was a rustle of paper, a sharp breeze, and then my yearly note shot through the letterbox, whizzed down the hall, and darted straight through the open visor of the helmet. Fuck, didn't think this through. I fell to my knees, choking, as my breathing holes were blocked. I needed them clear. It helped me stay alive.

Mr. Wonderful's head appeared through the catflap. He looked around cautiously, same as always, then his pristine, sleek white body poured through the opening. As I spluttered and choked to death, he glanced my way with blank, bored, cold eyes, then sauntered past.

"I own that catflap. I own the door. I own this hallway. That helmet's mine. That dying man is mine. I don't like swords, but it's mine."

"Help me," I pleaded, communicating mentally with my evil, twisted fuck of a cat.

"I thought we weren't playing our game with the Necronote any more? You said it was stupid."

"But I'm dying. And we didn't play the game. You didn't bring it to me, and I didn't pretend I didn't know what it was. Help me." I tore at the helmet, yanked it off my head, almost tearing my ears off, and locked eyes ready to burst from their sockets with Mr. Wonderful. I choked. My time was nigh. Just my luck. I'd die on the doormat with a cat waiting to suck on my eye juice.

"Fine," sighed Mr. Wonderful, acting like this really was too much bother, because it was. With a glance into the living room where he wanted to curl up and dream of doing evil things to innocent voles, the twisted bastard cat strolled lazily over, hopped up onto my shoulder, and purred.

"What are you doing?"

"Just go with it," he rumbled contentedly.

I turned my head in utter shock at his twisted callousness, then my eyes widened as he grinned and the claws on his right paw extended with an audible snick.

"No, don't!" I pleaded, even as the note fattened in my mouth and the sharp edges stuck fast into my cheeks. I tasted the familiar tang of iron as my gums were torn, then Mr. Wonderful, glint of pure menace and unconcealed delight in his eyes, and a ton of glee, swiped lazily at the soft tissue inside my nostril.

I sneezed, and the note shot from my mouth and slapped soggily into the door. It slid down, landed on the tiles, then jumped like it was in the throes of a seizure. The murderous paper shook itself clean of my pink mouth juices, then sprang up, all the creases and wet gone. Seemingly satisfied, it settled back down, dry as a bone, crisp as the moment it was birthed in the vast, endless Necroverse.

Mr. Wonderful hopped off, stared at me, and said, "You're welcome," before sauntering off into the living room while I gasped and clattered about in my damn armor.

"I need a new plan," I muttered, as I scowled first at the cat, then the note.

"Happy bloody birthday, Soph," I sighed. Pissed, I got to my feet shakily and peered at the docile note. Because of the armor, movement was awkward, so I bent at the waist, legs straight, and as blood poured from my mouth onto the tiles I snatched it up and read the name.

Necrosoph.

Yep, it was for me alright.

With my guts squirming, my chest hammering, and the usual need to go sit on the toilet for several hours overtaking me, I nevertheless unfolded the crisp paper and read the two words it contained.

At least I would have, if I'd been wearing my glasses. All I saw were squiggles, and it appeared like there were more than usual.

I dashed into the living room like the Tin Man from Wizard of Oz, nearly tripped over Mr. Wonderful, who was curled up on the murder rug, and grabbed my glasses.

I gawked at the note, confused. It was coordinates. For years now it had been the stupid two bloody words that you had to open the Necroapp to decipher. This was different. How it used to be. A series of coordinates that pinpointed the location, but not as accurately as the app.

Despite myself, I smiled. It was like old times. I nevertheless pulled my phone from its protective case and input the details.

Nothing.

The colored wheel of death spun around and around, then my phone just died. It shut off completely. Ah well, not like technology hadn't let me down before. I turned it back on, then tried again. That's how you fix things.

Nothing.

No phone signal. No data. No wi-fi. No way to make a call, send a message, or get online. Not to worry, these things happened. We were pretty remote, after all, and sometimes we lost our connection. It'd be back later on. But wanting to know, I searched through the books on the shelf and found the map of the UK, then checked the coordinates that way.

"Oh dear," I said, because I'd promised I'd stop swearing as much. Then added a quiet, "Fuck," under my breath, and looked around guiltily in case anyone but Mr. Wonderful had heard, because screw him. I was in the clear.

Before anything nasty happened, I pocketed the note securely, put a ring around the location on the map, then went into the hall and stuffed the map into my inner jacket pocket and zipped it shut. I wasn't even sure why, but it felt like the right thing to do.

"Soph, have you got a signal?" asked Phage as she sashayed into the hall. Still sexy as hell, I couldn't help but notice, because even under such stress I was still a man.

"Nope, just lost it. Oh, and my note arrived. And I nearly choked to death. Didn't you hear?"

"I thought you were just trying to get all that stupid stuff off. Sorry about earlier, and sorry about the note. Did you get the location?"

"Yeah, it was the weirdest thing, though. It was properly old coordinates, like it used to be before your time. No need for the app."

"That's odd. Nothing too far, I hope?"

"You know I can't say. Or can I? We've shared locations before, right?"

"A few times. But best not to. I can't keep track of what we're allowed to do and aren't. Sorry, I wish you didn't get it. "

"Yeah, me too. But it's so bloody familiar now. Just another birthday."

"Just another birthday," Phage agreed. "Um, my name wasn't on it, was it?"

"No, and don't look embarrassed for asking."

"Phew. Sorry, that sounds callous, but I don't think I could handle that again."

"No, me neither."

"Now, about your present."

My wife smiled lasciviously. I ripped the gear off and chased her upstairs.

Not everything about a Necro's birthday is bad. Some things are very, very good indeed.

Showered, dressed, yet still sweaty, and with a huge grin on my face, I raced downstairs while Phage hopped out of bed and took her turn in the bathroom. With a quick check I was alone, I fired up the laptop and was pleased to discover that the signal was back up and running. Must have been the turn-it-off-and-on-again fix. That's the only way to fix technology, all the rest is just a conspiracy.

I surreptitiously performed a task I had done hundreds of times over the last few months, and clicked and passworded my way to the Necronet. Jen had turned me on to it when she'd spilled the beans about Tyr's power pellets, a.k.a. his poo. She'd been banned from using it as she already knew more than she should, but I couldn't help but wonder what else was there.

Soon, I was utterly addicted. I read and I read and I read. I gasped, I shook my head, and I kept on delving deeper and deeper into the dark underbelly of the Necronet, reading about anything and everything to do with the life of a Necro, and the Necroverse itself. The sad thing was, just like the regular internet, most of it was utter garbage. Full of half-truths or outright lies. I would shake my head, mutter to myself, and keep on clicking.

There was just so much of it. I became consumed. I learned more about Tyr and dragons in general, and seemingly what he'd got up to was entirely to be expected. In fact, I'd go so far as to say I did rather well controlling him the way I had for as long as I had. At least, that's what some guy said on the Necronet, so it must have been true. Why? Because it suited me.

I read about Necronotes, even though I knew I shouldn't, but it was pointless as there was no information, just conjecture, and most of that vague as hell. Seems everyone knew to stick to the rules, and nobody had risked talking too openly about details. And yet I continued to search. To click, to read, and I would be lost for hours in this virtual world.

It was all so new to me. I kind of knew how the web worked, had seen it progress and kept up-to-date with things like smart phones and all the new stuff that came along, but only just. I had never spent much time on the internet as I was a busy guy, and when I wasn't busy I liked to sleep in my chair, devise cunning ways to eliminate Mr. Wonderful, or call Bernard names. A guy only has so many hours in the day, and I needed to fill some of them with insults.

And then we had downtime after the winter killing spree. Phage was done for, Jen was moody, I was still trying to recover from the time before. We toiled away in the garden. I fixed fences, cut hedges, looked after the animals, but instead of sleeping when I could, I stared at a damn screen. I got more into it after our winter and spring work was done, and as the weather warmed and the jobs eased, I had plenty of free time. I spent it on the Necronet. It became almost all-consuming. I was an addict.

It beat killing strangers, but it left me strangely jittery and disassociated from reality. I knew I should go cold turkey, but it seemed like there was always one more thing to check, one more search query to make. And the end result, months down the line on my birthday? I knew hardly fuck all more than I did before, apart from that the Necros who posted online were a bunch of mindless, twatheaded fucks.

And I still hadn't quit.

I sighed, and I clicked. Then the power went out and the connection died too.

"Not again."

I waited for the power to return, tapping my foot impatiently. Everything jumped back to life. But there was no internet connection. I checked my phone. Same thing.

"Hey, what you doing? Like I don't already know." Page smiled sadly at me and licked her lips.

I turned further in my chair and nestled into her belly. "You smell amazing. And I like the new look, with the make-up. Very sexy."

"Thanks. Thought I'd try something different. You honestly like it?"

"Very much. The signal's gone again."

"Take a break then. You have to stop this. You're obsessed."

"I know. I can't help it. It keeps dragging me back in. I'm weak. Nearly as weak as you make me feel every time I look at you or think about you."

"You are such a charmer. So just quit. You already said you've learned next to nothing. And you aren't setting a good example for Jen."

"Hmm, you're right. I should quit." I glanced back at the screen. "Still no signal."

"Come on, shoo. I'm going to make lunch. Can you go get Jen?"

"Sure. No prizes for guessing where she is. She loves it up there with those guys."

"Sure does. And Soph?"

"Yes."

"Stay safe. Be careful. Don't do anything rash this year. It's been a weird time for us lately. We both know there's something going on, but please just do what you have to do and come back to us. Don't go trying to find things out."

"I won't. I promise. I don't want to know, and that's the truth."

"So why the Necronet?"

"Honestly? I don't know. Because it's there? Because the internet is still new and mysterious to me. Because I'm an idiot." I got up and pecked Phage on the cheek, then went to get my daughter.

Besties

I cupped my hands around my mouth and hollered, "Hey guys. How's everyone doing?" up into Sanctuary, the incredible build my friend and neighbor Job—always say Jobe, but never spell it that way or he'll kick your arse—had spent years building for Tyr and Jen.

Three heads peered over the edge of the topmost platform and smiled. One daughter, one tiger, one dragon, all present and correct. I'd like to say it felt strange seeing them up there, but it was absolutely normal. For a Necro.

"Hey Dad. You coming up?" shouted Jen. She hopped to her feet, then with an acrobatic twist she spun her body around then plopped herself down with her legs dangling over the edge.

My heart skipped a beat, same as always, but I kept the smile on my face even though my upper lip was sweating, and waved. "Um, not today. Just checking you're okay. You coming down for lunch?"

"Sure. Ready to catch me?"

"What!? No, don't jump!" I bellowed.

Jen spun around again, then lay flat on her stomach and hung her head over the side. "Haha, got you."

"You sure did. Tyr, Rocky, you guys good?"

"Tyr happy. With best friends."

"I feel happy too," said Rocky.

"Good, that's good." Damn, there were more teeth up there than in a dentist's bin. I tried not to think about it, that my twelve-year-old was hanging out with creatures able to rip her head off without it being a struggle.

But they were her friends. Her companions. And also her guardians. Tyr loved her dearly, and still wanted to marry her, which was not going to happen. And Rocky had quickly become part of the family. Whereas most of the animals at the zoo liked to live quiet, relaxed lives, Rocky was keen to be outside and explore the world as much as possible. Not surprising when he'd spent his entire life locked up and mistreated, hardly ever leaving a cell of one form or another. Now he hung out with Tyr and Jen, but never roamed, as he understood it wasn't possible for tigers to be seen wandering the Shropshire countryside. There would be questions.

Rocky had struck up a very intense friendship with Tyr, and the two were now pretty much inseparable. They just clicked. Both now lived outdoors in Sanctuary. You would often see them curled up next to each other, Rocky snuggled up to Tyr's belly while they snored away. Sleep was their absolute favorite thing. That, and eating. And Tyr loved a bit of killing and frazzling, as you'd expect of a hormonal, basically teenage dragon.

All three of them climbed down from the top level to a series of platforms below. Via trees, girders, and various planks and even ropes for Jen, they either flapped, climbed, jumped, or swung like three monkeys. This was second nature to them all now. Jen was strong and agile thanks to Job's feat of engineering, and utterly at home at height.

Job's construction was not only perfect for Tyr, but Jen too. I wondered if he'd had that in mind when he built it. Knowing it would make her so strong, and at ease being up high. Something that she'd need to accomplish if she was to fly Tyr when she, and he, were older? I wouldn't put it past him, the wily, grumpy old bastard.

The more I'd come here and investigated it, even climbed up to the third level once, the more impressed I was by Sanctuary. It truly was an incredible achievement.

Turns out, Job had once spent a decade as a very valued engineer back in the day, and was responsible for teams who built some of the most impressive Victorian bridges in the land. He'd even gone to America back when it was a months-long passage, just because he loved it so much.

No surprise then that he'd been able to build Tyr an awesome new home, and a place for Jen to hide from her parents when she wanted to act all grown up.

Not that she was. She was still my little girl and would remain so for the rest of her hopefully very long life. She loved it here, hanging out with Tyr, even sleeping out when the weather was fine, which was a lot of the time. But ever since we'd first seen the finished Sanctuary, it had become a place not just for Jen and Tyr, but for a new friend too.

"Hey Dad." Jen waved as she landed on the platform. The whole thing swayed slightly as they bounced about, utterly unperturbed. "You sure you aren't coming up?"

"Not today. I'm taking a break from doing terrifying stuff."

"You're so funny. There's nothing to be scared of."

"I know. Right, little Miss Monkey, you coming for lunch or not? I'll eat your food if you don't hurry."

"Okay, be right there." Jen dropped down, then hung by her hands from the side of the platform and swung herself out into space. I couldn't look, just breathed again when I heard her land on the lower level.

I left her to it, knowing she'd be safe. But a tight knot in the pit of my stomach remained, because I was her father, and I always worried. I knew this was a good time, that the future was when I would really stress, so I lived with it. I wasn't unique in my concern. It's what parents did best. Always had. Always would. We try to keep them safe, but we cannot protect our children from the big, bad world. Merely show them ways to deal with it, to cope with what might be out there waiting. Even that's never enough. They have to find out for themselves. And that truly is a terrifying proposition.

I checked my phone again, slave to the tech. Still no phone or internet signal. This was getting weird.

"Come on, Woofer, let's go have our birthday lunch. It's the weekend. I love it when my birthday is on a weekend."

"Why? When is Woofer's birthday?"

"Yours? Um, not sure. Do you have a birthday?"

"No. Woofer never had birthday."

"I think you're right. Would you like to share mine? We could have it together."

"Yes. Woofer want birthday. How old is Woofer now?"

"Well, um, this will get confusing. You're about eight, and, er, I guess maybe we should stick to celebrating when it is your birthday. We don't have an exact date, but it's around April time, I think. We never knew for sure, so I think we just decided you looked like the kind of dog to be born in April." I shrugged.

"So Woofer will die soon? He really will?"

"You will die when I tell you it's okay to. Not before."

"Soph makes a joke about Woofer being dead?" The poor guy hung his head low and stared at me pitifully.

"No, of course not. I love you dearly and never want to lose you." I squatted and hugged him. I adored hugging Woofer. It was like a stinky old blanket, but with extra drool. He did love to drool.

"Play ball with poor, sad, old Woofer?" he whined.

"Sure boy. Where's your ball?"

Woofer dashed off, anxiety gone, ears high, tail higher, flapping as he ran around Job's beautiful meadow in search of a ball that was most likely up by the house in our garden. Still, it kept him trim.

It reminded me that I needed to talk to Phage about something I'd discovered on the Necronet concerning the power pellets.

Woofer followed me through the gate we'd all decided was a good idea when I fixed the fences. It made access easy and nobody would ruin the new fencing.

Woofer raced up to the house, and when I got there he was sitting and panting happily, bright orange ball in his mouth.

I took a deep breath, smiled, and said, "Drop the ball, Woofer. I said, drop!"

Woofer ran off. With the ball. I left the nutter to it and headed back inside.

Phage wasn't in the kitchen, and the TV was blaring, which was unusual, as we weren't big on TV in the day and hardly even watched it at night.

"What you doing? Watching daytime TV? Is it about people selling houses? Or buying stuff from an antiques shop then trying to make more money by putting it into an auction? Never seemed to make much sense to me. I mean —"

"Quiet! This is important."

I moved beside Phage where she was sitting cross-legged in front of the TV on the murder rug. I sat beside her and listened.

"...worldwide phenomenon. Every country in the world has lost all internet signal, most TV stations and radio stations are unable to broadcast, and there is currently no way to make a telephone call. Early indications report the current death toll from accidents and the inability to call emergency services is in the millions. Crime is expected to skyrocket as criminals will be able to do as they wish and not fear the police, and it is believed that martial law worldwide will be announced within the hour unless service is resumed. We may lose this broadcast at any moment as we are currently running on—"

The screen went blank. Phage tried all the channels with the remote. The world had truly gone dark.

"Those bastards," I moaned.

"Who? Who's responsible?"

"I knew this was coming. Everyone did."

"I didn't. Saw what coming? What are you talking about?" asked Phage, looking worried.

"It's them," I told her, waving my hand around.

"Who? You're making no sense."

"The bloody government. Or, you know, not our government, the worldwide order. The ones really in charge. Our overlords."

"You mean the Necros? Those making our lives a misery?"

"No, not them. Now it makes sense why my note didn't need the app. They knew this would happen. But it isn't them, it's the powers-that-be. Just another way to control everyone. They want us locked up, not asking questions, not causing trouble."

"Soph, you're talking nonsense. This isn't some big, worldwide conspiracy. Why would those running the world want all communication turned off?"

"So they can do whatever the fuck they want. That's why. Think about it. They could be doing anything. You just wait. It'll be carnage. Like she said on the TV, crime will skyrocket. No police, no firemen, no ambulance. God, imagine what it's like in hospitals."

"Hospitals don't need the internet."

"No, but they need phones. They need ambulances. People will just be turning up in their cars. It'll be mental. Out of control. And how will we know what's happening? They could be changing everything."

"They? You keep saying they. Who are *they*?" We both stood, then headed into the kitchen.

"Is lunch ready?" I asked, looking at the mess on the counter.

"Soph, how can you think about that at a time like this? And no, I was halfway through when the radio died, so I turned the TV on. Right, so what do you really think is happening?"

My stomach rumbled. "I think that the megacorps in charge, the ones behind basically everything we now buy, have shut the world down."

"For what possible reason? I'm sure it's just a glitch."

"A glitch? How can it be a glitch? There's like a gazillion satellites and whatnot for phones, and there are digital signals and, er, internet switchboard thingies that mean you can't just flip a switch and shut it off. It's all different for every country."

Phage laughed. "You idiot. You have absolutely no idea how any of it works, do you?"

"Um, no," I admitted. "None whatsoever. Do you?"

"No. Not a clue. I know phones work via relay stations and satellites. But the internet? No idea. And TV. That's transmitters, I think. Gosh, how does any of it work?"

"It works because we believe it does."

"That is by far one of the most stupid things you have ever said," laughed my beautiful-smelling wife.

"Aha, but not the most stupid."

"No," she conceded, "you've said much more stupid things in the past. So, what now?"

"Lunch?" I suggested.

"Yes, lunch. I bet it will all be fixed by the time we've eaten."

"I wouldn't bet on it. I wonder if this is happening everywhere? I mean every single country? That's what the woman just said, right?"

"Doubt it. It's impossible to do that."

"Ah, I remember. It's called a kill switch."

"What, an actual switch? A way to just flip all communication off? Seriously?" Phage waved the bread knife as she spoke.

"Hey, don't shoot the messenger," I told her, backing away to the other side of the table.

Phage looked at the knife. "Sorry. But seriously?"

"I heard about it. I'm sure. Actually, it was probably back when you were a little baby. I remember they turned off the internet in numerous places. Egypt, Myanmar, when the military took over. Lots of other countries. They called it a kill switch. I don't think it really is, but the governments can do it. They just stop the service providers from running."

"Kill switch. Sounds made up to me."

"What's that about a kill switch?" asked Jen as she skipped into the kitchen. She was covered in dirt and her hands were filthy. I was so proud.

"The internet is dead. And there's no mobile signal. No messaging, no phone calls, no TV, not even radio. We have officially stepped back in time. You wait, you'll be getting the jitters within the hour," I told my princess.

Jen just shrugged. "Probably just a sun spot or something. It'll be back on. And besides, we can just use the landline."

"Nope," I said smugly. "It's the same thing. You won't be able to speak to anyone. The phone runs via the internet now. They did that years ago. So do traffic lights, cash machines, just about everything. It's all digital stuff now. Nothing will work. Nothing at all. Think what the roads would be like if everyone was driving."

Jen frowned, then picked up the handset from the charging cradle. I wasn't even sure why we still had it. I couldn't recall it ever being used, and it had certainly never rung. I wondered what our number was.

"It's dead," said Jen, the handset at her ear. She put it back down and checked her phone, then glared at it. She wandered off then came back and confirmed, "No TV. What's going on?"

"Like I just told Phage, it's the kill switch."

"We learned about that for a project," said Jen. "We had to see if it was possible to turn off all worldwide communication."

"And was it?" asked Phage.

"Sure," she said breezily. "Most countries have laws they can enact if we're under cyber attack or something. They can force all the companies to turn stuff off. Then that's it, done. Or you cut the big cables. Most internet works via these massive cables running for thousands of miles along the ocean floor. You can just cut one end, then that's that."

"Shut up! Big cables under the sea? That doesn't sound right," I said.

Jen shrugged. "Look it up."

We were all silent for a moment, then laughed. Because we couldn't look it up. We couldn't check any facts, phone a friend, or even ask the audience, because we weren't in a game show, although it certainly felt like it at times. A game show to the death. Now it was just us. It suddenly felt very real, and really rather lonely.

Damn. No Necronet. Maybe it was a blessing in disguise. Nothing like someone turning off the world to make you realize you have issues.

"So, what's for lunch?" asked Jen breezily.

"Aren't you worried?" asked Phage.

"Mum, it's just the internet."

"And phones. And TV," I reminded her.

"Yeah, so? It'll get sorted. Anyway, we can just use catch-up." Even as she spoke, she realized what she was saying. "Um, no, guess not."

"They'll turn it back on again. Won't they?" asked Phage.

I wasn't so sure.

Woofer Will Die?

"Woofer will live for short time now?"

"What was that, buddy?" I turned to Woofer, sitting beside Jen on the sumptuous new lawn that seemed to need mowing constantly, as she tapped at the phone we'd finally caved in and got her.

"Want to stay with Jen and Soph and Phage and all friends. Not want to die." Woofer hung his head low and leaned against Jen.

"Don't be sad. You're still young," she told him. Jen put her phone away with a frown then cuddled Woofer. He whined quietly.

"Why do you keep thinking such dark thoughts, Woofer?" I asked him.

"Everyone else not need to worry. Woofer is getting old. Feel old. Sad. Don't want to leave everyone. Don't want to hurt and be alone. Be dead in ground."

I caught Jen's eye as she brushed away a tear. I did the same. He'd got worse, talking about his mortality more than ever lately. The poor guy was really hung up about it. Was it because he'd come along with me to Liverpool? Actually seen how brutal the world could be? But hadn't I taken him because he was worried about dying?

Was it because of Tyr's multitudinous changes? Woofer had certainly been concerned about the shift from wyrmling to the massive creature he now was. He couldn't keep up; Tyr changed so fast. Or was it because Jen herself was growing quickly, too? She was different now, a true young lady. Still full of the joy of youth, but like Tyr there was a clear change.

More serious, less keen to play silly games, and thus, less fun times for Woofer. He was, like all dogs, a forever child. They didn't grow up and turn into a grumpy, serious adult, stressing about bills and jobs and why things had always been better in the good ol' days. Dogs always wanted to play and be daft until they were unable to.

Woofer was a long way from that. He was healthy, fit, if a little solid on the rear end like most Labradors, so what was it?

"Woofer, let's have a serious talk," I told him. I scooted over to him and Jen and looked into his deep brown eyes. "You look so unhappy, boy. Why do you keep dwelling on this?"

"Woofer is sad. Want to play for all times. Don't want to miss out on fun and must see Jen grow into woman. Maybe because of Tyr? Tyr grows, is different. Now Woofer realizes Jen won't always be same. Woofer tries to think about her before, but is hard."

"I know it is. You're a dog, and dogs live in the present. Not the past. But they don't normally think about the future, either."

"It's because of us," said Jen. "Woofer, you can talk and think more than other dogs because you've been around us, so you pick up some of the magic that comes from us and all the other gifted animals. It's made you smart." Jen hugged him again then rubbed his head.

"Woofer knows not smart. Just dog. Dumb dog." His ears were flat against his head again. I don't think I'd seen a sadder sight in my life.

Over the years, I'd had the pleasure of having numerous dogs as my companions, and conversations similar to this had come up a few times. But Jen was right. Although not the brightest spark, by dog standards Woofer was a clever fellow. Talking with the other dogs I'd known wasn't like this. It was very basic, more about what they wanted to do, what they wanted to eat, where to go for a walk, their desires and urges made real. There wasn't much actual chat because dogs were just that. Dogs.

"Woofer, you are very different to others, Jen is right. You are smart. We have proper conversations. That's rare. You weren't like this when I first brought you home. You didn't talk like this."

"Yes, you're a true Necro already," Jen told him.

"Woofer dumb. Knows he's dumb. Talks funny. Don't know how to say things different."

"You're perfect just the way you are. Isn't he, Jen?" I nodded my encouragement to her.

"Absolutely! Just about perfect." Jen rested her head against Woofer's side and stroked his back while I rubbed his ear. Woofer whined.

"Oh, Woofer, don't be so sad. You are still young. You're what? Eight, isn't it?"

"Woofer not know. Too dumb. Can only count to one. One."

"Oh, Woofer." Jen burst out crying and squeezed him tightly.

Woofer whined and lay down on the grass, utterly depressed. My heart felt like it was breaking. The toughest thing in the world about living with animals is that they die so soon. It felt like only yesterday I'd brought Woofer home. Jen was a tiny girl, and she adored Woofer from the moment she set eyes on him. We all did. We all loved him.

"Jen, go and get Phage for me, please. There is something we all need to discuss as a family. Tell her to eat a little of the power pellet, just enough so she can understand Woofer, okay?"

"Okay. What's this about?"

"Just go get her, please. I'll explain in a while. And be quick." I angled my head to Woofer. Jen nodded, knowing that Woofer was about as sad as any dog in the whole world had ever been.

"Don't worry, we'll sort something out."

"Woofer won't die?" he asked with a glimmer of hope in his eyes. His tail thudded slowly.

"Who knows? Maybe you will live a very long time. I sure hope so."

"Woofer won't. He will be dead soon and miss Jen becoming a grown woman. Knows will be dead before then. Don't know how many years until Jen is grown, but too many for Woofer to see." Woofer turned away from me and curled his head into his legs to hide his sadness.

I felt like the worst person alive. This was the problem with the Necro life rubbing off on poor creatures like Woofer. Unlike other animals, he knew what he was, that he would die, and what that meant. Your regular dog doesn't understand such concepts. They aren't wired that way.

We had done this to him. Made him what he was because we loved him so much and he spent so much time around us. And now look at him. This was entirely our fault. And the only one paying the price was this despondent dog before me. Hiding his fear and sadness when he should be running around with his favorite ball in his mouth.

Yet another reason why I hated this Necro life.

All it brought was pain. Pain and suffering.

"What's this about?" asked Phage as she strolled down the garden, holding hands with Jen. My daughter's face was red and her eyes were puffy and swollen. She'd clearly had a good cry where Woofer couldn't see.

Living with animals was so hard. We had so many that depended on us, but it was different with some. Woofer was family. True family.

This was tough on Jen, too. Just like Tyr, he and Jen had grown up together. She hadn't lost anyone yet, and now she knew how long we'd all live, that Mr. Wonderful was over fifty, well, it made it doubly hard to accept Woofer's short lifespan.

Should I tell them what I had learned? Dare I? Was it wrong? Was it worth the risk? Was it my place to decide? As Phage watched me with concern, I decided I had to share this important information.

"Did you take the power pellet?"

"Yes, I took a little like Jen said. What's this about?"

"Great, that's great. Can you sit down? You too, Jen. Damn, it's hot."

"Did you use sunscreen?" Phage asked Jen.

Jen rolled her eyes. "Don't I always?"

"Less of the eye-rolling, missy," I told her.

"Sorry."

"Woofer, are you listening? I have something very important that we all need to agree on." Was I doing the right thing? Maybe this should wait and we could talk it over without Woofer. Too late now. I was all geared up, so it was now or never.

"Woofer listening." He made a show of struggling to his feet, groaning like an old man.

"What's the matter?" Phage asked.

"Woofer very sad. Never see Jen be woman. Never play with Jen's children. Never go on adventures with Soph or Phage. Just die." He howled with sadness.

"Oh, Woofer, please don't talk like that." Phage and Jen both sat and tried to console him, but he was beyond depressed now.

"You guys know I've been spending some time on the Necronet, right?"

"More like all the time. It's so unfair," complained Jen. "I bet it's you who broke the internet. Probably used it all up, the amount of time you've been on there. And I'm not allowed, so why are you?"

"Because I'm an adult and know all the horrible things that happen in the world. You don't. But look, part of the reason I've been on there so much is because I learned things about the, er, power pellets."

"The poo of power, I like to call it."

"Can we please not mention poo when discussing something I have just ingested," said Phage as she rubbed at her ruby lips like that would make a difference now.

"As I was saying, I learned more about it and what it can do. I told you guys that if you got very old dragon poo it could make the changes that occur permanent, and it could do a lot of stuff that Tyr's can't, right?"

"You did," said Phage.

"According to some guy on the Necronet, you can get similar effects if you basically overdose on a younger dragon's pellets. Not dragon powers like invisibility, or not for certain, but things like Tyr's ability to camouflage himself is a possibility, and morphing, maybe even something new. It's not guaranteed, any of it, but it can work."

"Woofer could be invisible? Woofer could play hide and seek. Be very good." He perked up a little at that, but he soon hung his head again.

"That's just side-effects. The main outcome, and I must stress that this is extremely dangerous and it might not even work, or it could kill you if we get it wrong, is that if you basically take a massive dose of it, and it would mean the dry stuff as it's more potent and you can make powder, it can make you semi-immortal like some Necros. Like us, Woofer. And Tyr."

"Soph, that's nonsense," said Phage. "You read it online and think it's true? Come on."

"Yeah, Dad, even I know you can't trust the things people write online."

"This wasn't just a random nutjob spewing ideas. The guy wrote this whole long piece on it. But more importantly, he scanned pages of a book. An old book, like the one I read about dragons. This was even older, and no, I don't know where he got it from, what it was called, or even if it was genuine. But it looked like the real deal. I don't know what the guy had to lose by showing the pages of the book, and he said that it made sense. I know it sounds daft, but we only found out about the poo because of Woofer eating it and then Jen looking it up and doing the same thing, so why not this?"

Everyone stared at me, mouths agape.

"You're serious?" asked Phage.

"Deadly. Excuse the pun. What do you think?"

"I think it's awesome!" Jen smiled, then leaned forward and flung her arms around me. "Thank you, thank you, thank you. We can save Woofer."

Woofer barked excitedly and ran laps around the garden, seemingly cured of all that ailed him. It was some kind of a miracle.

I turned to Phage and told her, "Sorry, I know we should have discussed this in private first. I was going to do more checking, but what with everything offline and Woofer being so miserable, well, I just couldn't take it any more."

"I understand. Soph, it's fine. I know that he's the way he is because of us, that he shouldn't have to know these things, be worried like he is. It's been going on for years now and it breaks all our hearts. It's fine." Phage pecked me on the cheek and smiled sweetly.

"You're so understanding. What did I do to deserve you?"

"Ugh, you guys are so gross. Why can't you be like other parents and argue and just pretend everything's okay when really it isn't?"

"Come here," I laughed, then grabbed Jen and tickled her tummy. She squealed, much to everyone's delight, and it sent Woofer into a fun-induced mad sprint back and forth, utterly trashing the new lawn.

"Woofer, come here, please. We need to finish discussing this and form a plan." Woofer came and flopped down beside us, panting. His eyes were wild, like he was already quasi-immortal.

"Woofer can be with everyone for all time now. Hooray." His tail thumped madly, his chest heaved, his eyes danced.

"Now look, this is a serious business. Don't anyone get too excited because, like I said, there are some big risks involved. If you take too much, it could kill you. You could die today if we do this and it goes wrong. But the best chance of it working is when you are still young, fit, and healthy. If you are old and frail, then it most definitely will kill you. Even so, we're taking a huge gamble. You need to eat a lot of it, I mean a lot, and you are going to feel absolutely awful. The sickest you have ever been in your life. Do you understand me?"

"Understand. But if Woofer doesn't try, Woofer dead soon anyway. Will be able to fly?"

"No, you won't be able to fly," Phage told him. She turned to me. "He won't, will he? Can you imagine? A flying dog!"

"Flying is for birds and dragons only. But you will be able to live a long time, be able to regenerate unless something catastrophic happens, and basically be more like Mr. Wonderful. I mean, Bernard's always accidentally killing that cat, and he always comes back."

"Woofer will be cat?" he asked, cocking his head to the side.

"No, you will most definitely still be you. A dog. A great dog. The best dog. Just with some of the abilities like Mr. Wonderful. Like all Necros. But listen everyone, and I can't emphasize this enough, there is a risk. Anything could go wrong. It might not even work at all. So what do we all think? We have to accept that we could lose Woofer today if we do this. And you must understand that, Woofer. This could be your last day with us. So there it is. Well?"

"Woofer can have sausages?"

"Huh?"

"Can eat the power pellets with sausages?"

"I guess." I shrugged.

"Woofer love sausages."

"You sure do," laughed Jen as she cuddled him and nodded her head to say she agreed we should do it.

"I think if Woofer wants to try, then we should do it. But are you sure about this?" Phage asked.

"Honestly? I don't know. I can't bear to think of losing the daft lump. But I know you aren't happy," I told the smiling dog. "Okay, let's force feed the dog sausages and dragon poo!"

And thus began another strange episode in this poor Necro's life. One of many over the years. But this was the first one that involved quite as many sausages.

Dog OD

"Wait," I told the excitable mutt sitting on the lawn, using all his self-control while I held a large bowl of perfectly cooked sausages.

"Woofer so hungry. Will faint soon. Maybe even die of hunger. Feel so empty." He licked his lips and stared at the sausages mournfully.

"You had your breakfast, and a chewy," I lectured. "*And* a handful of biscuits. *Plus* half a sandwich. I think you can hold out a while longer," I laughed.

"Just give the poor thing his sausages," Phage chortled. She gave me a cheeky wink.

"I just want to be sure. Woofer, I made these myself. I mixed all the lovely meat in with the power pellet powder so there is an awful lot in here. Once you do this, there is no turning back. So, are you absolutely, one hundred percent sure?" I knew it was pointless to ask. If I'd told him I'd laced them with arsenic and he would definitely die if he ate them, I think he'd risk it. Because. Sausages.

"Woofer want to be like Tyr. Can eat now? Then play ball with Woofer?"

"Dad, it'll be fine. I just know it will." Jen beamed at me and her mother; both nodded that I should do this.

I placed the bowl down on the lawn. Woofer began to drool like a mad thing, and then I said, "Take."

He raced over and tucked straight in, what few manners he had utterly gone. We huddled close and watched the sausage assault as the sun beat down while Woofer inhaled what was possibly his last ever meal. At least he'd go out with a smile on his face.

"Dad, I'm scared."

I put my arm around Jen and told her, "Me too. Very. But we have to think positive and we mustn't let him see us worried. Stay strong. According to my research, this will happen pretty fast. We'll know soon enough if it worked or not."

"He's a fighter. He'll pull through, and then he'll be Woofer the Wonder Dog," said Phage. She frowned, and all three of us sniffed and rubbed at our eyes.

Several seconds later, which was a record for Woofer as he'd never taken so long to eat a meal in his entire life, the bowl had been licked clean repeatedly just in case he'd somehow missed a sausage, and then he waddled over to us, sat down, and beamed.

"You got a full tummy?"

"Woofer not know what it feels like to have full tummy. Is it nice?"

"Yes. It means you've had enough to eat. And you, my friend, most definitely have."

"Have more sausages? Woofer could eat."

I smiled down at my faithful companion and shook my head in wonder. "Afraid not. How are you feeling?"

"Feel fine. Play ball with Woofer?"

"Sure, we can all play if you'd like." I turned to the others. They nodded their heads, all of us relieved.

Woofer stood, and then he did the loudest fart I had ever heard. And being so old, I'd heard many a fart from many a creature.

Woofer jumped three feet in the air in shock. He landed, then turned to investigate the noise, then stood stock still as he sniffed the air. I made the fatal mistake of doing the same.

The freaked-out mutt whined, then ran to the herbaceous border. I coughed, choked, gagged, and put out a hand to Phage's shoulder to steady myself, but she spluttered as the noxious fumes hit, so ran in the opposite direction to Woofer, leaving me leaning towards thin air and keeling over sideways.

It was worse closer to the source. Much worse. Panicked, I crawled across the lawn like a soldier in battle as invisible missiles assaulted me from every side. Jen laughed, then it got her too, and she coughed before legging it down the garden.

Woofer, unable to escape the source of the foul emanations, whined as he let rip again. Then it became really bad. A noxious war zone. Fart after fart after fart. They kept coming.

Parp. Parp. Paaaaarp.

He dashed around in a panic, whining, howling, coughing, and pleading for assistance.

From a safe distance, and after greedily inhaling fresh air, I called, "Sorry, didn't I mention this bit? Woofer, I think it best if you follow me to the paddock. Because if you aren't enjoying this bit, then you are gonna hate what comes next."

"Hey, what are you looking so happy about?" asked Phage as she nudged me in the ribs with her elbow.

"He might be the stinkiest creature on the planet, but he's still alive. Come on everyone, let's get Woofer where he can't make a mess of the lawn." I opened the gate and we headed past the chickens, the zoo, and Tyr's old barn, then into the rough land at the bottom of our property. Hopefully, the smell wouldn't make it back up to the house from here.

Woofer stormed ahead, keener than us to escape the malodorous fumes, but standing no chance. We grouped together, with Woofer standing in front of us looking panicked, and Phage told him, "It's okay. It'll be over soon. It's just gas."

"Woofer not like smell. Woofer like all smells. Very bad."

"It is quite atrocious," I agreed merrily. "Now, you're going to experience—"

Fpliiiiiiiiiiit. Fplit, fplit, fpliiiiiiiiiiiiiiiiiiit.

Woofer's backside not so much let loose as exploded. Liquid excrement, utterly gross and volatile, erupted from his rear with the force of a slick new train. He moaned as his back arched and the foulness was evacuated over and over. He could do nothing but stand there and let it happen.

We took several steps away until stopped by the new fence.

"Dad, is this normal?"

"Apparently, but it should be over soon. Then things are going to get very bad indeed."

"Like how?"

"He'll puke, he might have several seizures, and if he gets through that then it'll start to get worse. I mean truly horrible."

"What!? Why didn't you say?"

"I didn't want to make you worry even more. Ah, here we go."

All eyes were on Woofer as he purged a dark liquid in one continues stream while the other end continued about its disgusting business.

On and on it went. The smell downright insulting to flowers all over England.

And then, with a final rip of doom, it was over. Woofer was motionless, too afraid to move in case it began again, but this was textbook dragon poo overdose according to some bloke on the internet. Meaning, so far, so good.

"Right, now move away from all that nastiness and settle yourself down. I know this is horrible, but think about the future. You might be immortal," I told my panting, wheezing, terrified dog.

"Woofer lost all his sausages," he complained.

Jen turned to me, amazed. "Wow, even at a time like this he's concerned about his sausages."

"You'll be fine, boy. Just ease over there, slowly does it, and then lie down. You might start shaking, but it's part of it."

Woofer walked over, unsteady, then collapsed in an exhausted heap and rolled onto his side. His ribcage rose and fell rapidly, but he seemed kinda okay.

I pulled Jen close and told her, "Don't be scared. This is meant to happen. He'll probably start shaking in a moment, so be brave for him."

"I will." Jen smiled weakly, then called to our stressed dog, "You're doing awesome. Way to go, Woofer."

"Yes, come on, you can do it," shouted Phage.

"That's my boy," I told him. "You're going to live for so long now. Think of all the sausages."

Woofer's tale thumped dejectedly, then his eyes rolled up in his head and his entire body convulsed. I ran over, really concerned, as the side-effects escalated. He spasmed violently. His tongue lolled out and the next seizure caused him to clamp down on it. I worried he'd bite it in two, so as the shaking slowed I pushed it back into his mouth, ignoring the foulness on my hands.

He shook so intensely that he turned over completely and I feared he'd snap a leg, so I had to hold him down forcibly as his body jerked repeatedly, each convulsion worse than the last. Foam bubbled from between his teeth, tinged red, which I knew was not a good sign. What had I been thinking? Why had I suggested this? We were going to lose Woofer and it was all my stupid, smug fault.

The stiff jerking slowed and then stopped. I released him and wiped away the bloody foam with a tuft of grass. As I stood back, Woofer's chest rattled. He was still.

Woofer was dead.

"Dad! Oh no, poor Woofer," cried Jen.

"Stay back," I warned.

With an almighty thunderclap of anguish and pain, Woofer screamed into the bright, clear day as air rushed back into his now immortal lungs. He tore at the ground with his claws to find purchase. Our beloved friend stood there, eyes burning with ferocious life born of a deep-seated desire to live forever and remain with his family, and he leapt into my arms in one utterly un-acrobatic leap.

I found myself crying and laughing for joy as I cuddled an utterly filthy, beyond sticky, immortal dog. My dog. Our dog. Woofer the immortal.

"How you feeling?" I asked with a smile as I lowered him. My back screamed with pain. He felt like he'd doubled in weight. Was that a thing?

"Woofer feel..."

We waited, and we waited, and we waited, and then Jen blurted, "Woofer, you're alive! I'm so happy."

"Invincible!" Woofer's tail was erect, his ears were up, and his eyes shone.

Then something truly miraculous happened. His coat kind of bristled, he shook out like he'd just been locked out in the rain, and all the dirt, the puke, the shit, the piss, and even the smell, was flung away from our beloved companion. His coat was now so shiny the light bounced off it, making him look almost white, the black was so intense. We shielded our eyes against the glare, which gradually dimmed, and there before us was a new creature. Something born of the Necroverse. Necrowoofer.

"I can't believe it," gasped Phage. "It actually worked! You did it! He did it. Look at you."

Jen hugged me tight then we all ran to Woofer and made the biggest fuss of him ever. He stood there, lapping it up, proud and happy. And immortal.

"Play ball with Woofer?" he asked hopefully.

"Sure, buddy. And you can even have more sausages." Phage glared at me. "What? I meant normal ones, nothing added."

"Can I have some too?" asked Jen. "I'm starving."

"Me too," agreed Phage.

"Hmm, I could eat."

And so it was, on the day Woofer became a true Necro, we sat at our picnic bench on the lawn and ate a ridiculous number of sausages.

By the time we'd finished, I was having second thoughts about the whole thing. Woofer had become something else. Something other. Every owner's worst nightmare. Unstoppable.

He was faster than a speeding goblin, could become invisible at will, could seemingly morph without pain, and I was pretty sure he could fly, although he was so damn speedy I couldn't tell.

It made for a lot of ball throwing.

I had an eternity of this to look forward to.

Honestly? I didn't mind.

Much.

Until he nicked my last sausage. Then things got nasty.

A Nice Note

Relieved, and buoyed by the "experiment" succeeding, I whistled my way along the hallway, still buzzing from the knowledge that Woofer would be our companion through the ages. He was happy, and full of sausages. I grabbed the shiny, well-worn newel post at the foot of the stairs, ready to hop up a few steps and get things sorted for the inevitable misery of the next day when I'd have to leave and go fulfill my note.

The letterbox snapped open just as Phage came down the hallway behind me. A crisp white note shot through, angling right for her.

She dodged aside, the note shot up, spun, then tore at me with the intention of seemingly ending my days by way of decapitation.

I ducked, stumbled on the stair, slipped and fell onto my arse, then banged my head on the newel post.

The note circled me three times then dove down and fluttered gently to land on the rug by the front door, so dark with years of dirty boots that I honestly couldn't recall the original color.

"Will they never leave us alone?" I screamed, so utterly beyond pissed off I didn't even try to keep my voice low.

"It can't be. Not another note," whispered Phage, checking the hallway to see if Jen was about to come running.

"Sorry, didn't mean to shout. But what now? Could it be for you? Or is this another job for me? I can't bloody believe this."

"We were having such a nice afternoon, too. Soph, I'm so sorry."

Phage helped me to my feet then we both stood there, staring at the folded piece of paper on the filthy rug.

Unbelievable.

I could not handle this.

I knew I would have to.

But last year had been too much, one of the worst ever. Too much death. Not only had I gone to Liverpool and nearly been broken, but then having to accompany Phage after the hit-and-run, and all that with Shae, not to mention the assault on our home, it was simply too much death. Too much slaying, too much blood. Too much cruelty. Now this?

They were trying to break me. They wanted me destroyed. This was it, they would finally have their way. They'd clap their hands with glee as I unraveled before their eyes and finally succumbed to this utter cruelty.

"It's okay, I'll handle it," I told Phage with a grim nod. I had to be strong in front of her. She would worry otherwise. Sure, she would anyway, but at least if I acted like I could cope, her concern might be minimized.

With a sigh, I bent to retrieve the note, so angry I didn't even think about what it might do. The letterbox snapped open again and another sheet sped through, then another.

"What is happening?" I hissed, not quite believing it.

The two new notes landed perfectly on top of the first, forming a neat stack. I snatched all three then backed up to the stairs and sat, numb with shock.

With a glance to Phage, I reluctantly unfolded the first, then the second and third, and squinted at them. Phage coughed discreetly and smiled with sympathy as she handed me my glasses.

"Thanks."

I read the notes in silence, not believing what I was reading. When I was done, I folded and stowed them in my shirt pocket where they wriggled for a moment as if getting comfortable, then were still.

I turned to Phage and smiled, really smiled.

"What? What is it? Why are you happy? Is it for me? Do I have to come? Oh, Soph, I'm sorry, but I don't want to. I can't. I just can't."

Phage burst into tears so I heaved up then wrapped my shaking arms around her and whispered into her sweet, peach and apple-smelling hair, "It's okay. No, you aren't coming. You stay and look after Jen and play ball with Woofer. This is, er, well, it's actually good news."

Phage sniffled then moved away so she could see my face. "You mean it? Can you tell me?"

"Sure I can. At least, I guess so. It's permits. I just got given permits so I can drive! Yes, that's right, I can use the car. Go anywhere, use the pass, not be bothered. How about that?"

"That's wonderful. Do we have enough fuel?"

"Um, not sure. We were getting a tiny quota for years, but never enough to go far, and we never had permits to allow us to. I think we've probably used most of it just on short runs. And damn, that was years ago anyway. It won't be good now."

"Wait! Let me check. I've got a feeling about this." Phage fumbled with the handle, her fingers shaking, and opened the front door. There, on the front step, was a large fuel canister, easily enough to get me where I needed to go and back again.

"No way," was all I could say.

Phage turned, beaming. "I had a feeling. So you can drive? You can really drive?"

"Looks that way," I said, still nonplussed by this peculiar turn of events.

"You're so lucky." Phage hugged me and I gripped her tight.

What had been done to us that we were both genuinely excited that I was able to drive to go kill a stranger rather than it be any effort at all?

We truly were servants of our hidden masters.

After milling about and getting gear packed in the car, I went to find the others. They were all outside in the garden, enjoying the ridiculous heat. Phage, Jen, and Woofer the Sausage Thief were all laughing and joking about in the small paddling pool under the shade of a massive umbrella. I smiled as I wandered through the garden, then stopped dead in my tracks as I got that funny tingle at the base of my neck. I turned this way and that, but couldn't see anything untoward. No daemons, no Necros, apart from the ones I loved, and no weirdness at all.

Which was weird.

"Hey," shouted Jen as she waved.

"Hey," I called back, happy to see her so full of life. It had been tough on her lately, and she knew more than she should, but after her initial meltdown and refusal to believe it, there came understanding of a sort.

She gradually came back to herself and grew close to us again. Things were different, there was no denying it, and I saw the way she looked at me sometimes when she thought I couldn't see her. Full of doubt and concern. Not fear, never fear, but something akin to it. Wonder? Disbelief? Outright denial. Scared it was all true? Maybe a little of all of it. She couldn't reconcile the things she'd been told with the way we were at home.

How could you?

Yes, honey, I love you very much, but excuse me while I go stab some bastard in his face. I'll be right back, promise. Don't do the cake without me.

In the end, we let it go. Or tried to. The topic of Necronotes came up more often than I'd have liked, and we explained a little about what would happen. But again, she didn't quite believe it. Not deep down inside. She was too young, too innocent, and I wanted to keep it that way.

She could not accept she would have a new name and have to do these things. She shouldn't have to accept it. But she would.

"Come on, slow coach. Come and cool down," Jen called.

"I bet that water's warmer than the air," I told her as I pulled off my flip-flops and stepped in. "Yep, I was right."

"Woofer like it."

I panicked. "Um, should he be in here after, you know?"

"Don't worry, we hosed him down. Although somebody drank more of the water than he let us use to shampoo him," laughed Phage.

"Woofer not like smell."

I bent and sniffed his fur. "You smell wonderful," I told him. Truth was, like all dogs after a thorough shampoo and rinse, he smelled like a stinky dog with a load of shampoo poured over him. I liked it. It was familiar, safe, honest. "Right, that's me done," I told them. "I'm just going to relax before dinner. Um, what's for dinner?"

"Are you serious?" Phage stood with her hands on her hips and glared at me.

"What?"

"Dinner? We had lunch, then all the sausages in Shropshire. You're still hungry?"

"I could eat. I mean, that was a snack, right? It wasn't *dinner* dinner." I winked at Jen; she stifled a giggle.

"He's right, Mum. It wasn't *dinner* dinner." Jen burst out laughing, and Woofer, not needing much encouragement to go mental if something even approaching exciting happened, sloshed out of the pool and ran around barking happily.

"What's he saying? I think the pellets have worn off."

"He's not saying anything. He's just barking. Just being a regular nutty pooch. Now, about dinner."

"Oh, you mean *dinner* dinner. Not just dinner?"

"Yeah. Can we have some?"

"I am hungry," said Jen.

"Seriously?"

"Well, maybe later on?"

"In an hour or so?" I asked optimistically.

"You two are killing me." Phage looked divine as she smiled. I wished we could stay like this forever.

I turned as my neck hairs bristled again. What was it?

"Anyone getting a funny feeling?"

"Like what?" asked Phage, instantly serious and looking sexy in that dangerous, I will rip your face off and make you eat it even though you haven't got a mouth because I smashed it, way.

"Dunno. Just a feeling. Something isn't right. Jen, I think you should go inside. Woofer, protect Jen. You are now the official guard for our home."

"Woofer was already guard. Always save everyone from harm."

"Oh, yes, um, right. Well, now you are the extra, super important guard with dragon powers. So look after her." I'm sure he tried to salute, but either way, he fell over.

I took in the garden methodically, checking every bush, every shadow, even the hedge and the trees. Nothing weird. What was it? Phage came beside me while Jen absolutely did not do what her father asked, although Woofer was beside her, teeth bared. He looked like he was smiling, not snarling.

"Um, did anyone move Wonjin?" I asked, staring up at the big guy with a frown. "Does he usually look like that? Is it me, or has he got bigger? Or moved? Something is different."

We gathered around the troll, who still stood in pride of place in the middle of the lawn. We'd pretended he was a statue for so many years that it came as quite a shock when he basically mushed the head of an intruder then spilled the beans to Jen about what awaited her when she was older. We'd also learned he was here to look out for her, and was biding his time while he waited to fulfill his own Necronote that was received once every troll year, akin to a hundred human years.

"Has he moved?" asked Phage. "I can't remember what position he was in before."

"Looks like big rock to Woofer. Troll can move?"

"Yes. His name's Wonjin," I told Woofer.

"Oh, yes, Woofer remember now."

"Do you really?" I asked.

"No."

"Didn't think so. You were about to pee on him. He threw the ball for you. You had a great time."

"Woofer like playing ball."

"Really? You should have said."

"When? Now?" he asked, tail swishing like it was sausage time again.

"What? No, not now. Can we please stay on topic?" I looked up into Wonjin's blank features and asked, "Hey. Have you moved? Are you about to go somewhere? You haven't said a word since you last spoke." I considered what I'd just said and tried again. "What I mean is, that since you last spoke you... No, hang on. It's been ages since you said anything."

"Well done, Dad. You used words then. Too many, but at least they made sense this time."

"Thanks," I said, grinning. I held up my palm for a high-five. Jen left me hanging. I turned to Phage. She shook her head. Guess I didn't deserve one.

We stared, we waited, we got bored eventually. Woofer wandered off to "have a play" with Mr. Wonderful, which always went so well, and we were about to leave when Wonjin sighed.

"You tired, big guy?" I asked.

"Wonjin need rest before he moves. Feel warm and ready. Crystals activated."

"Oh, the old brain, right?" I said with a knowing nod.

"Yes. Needs cold and heat, like plants. Dormant then active. Wonjin moved in night, caught note. All warm in head, like Wonjin said. Crystals activated."

"What's he talking about?' asked Jen.

"Trolls have crystal brains," I told her. "Seems his is up and running." I asked him, "So, you got your note? Far to go?"

"Very far. But not matter. Wonjin is fast. Take maybe... few minutes?" he mused.

"Um, that must be very close then," said Phage, looking a bit worried.

I was concerned too. It couldn't be one of us, could it? No, he'd said he was here to protect us. Could trolls lie? I supposed they could. I was no troll scholar, knew next to nothing about them.

"Close for Wonjin, not close for humans. Go through... What is word? For rip in air, like eye? Like gap in this world leading to other place. Wonjin use that. Much quicker. Take Wonjin maybe few troll minutes. Few human hours. Is hard to think on human time, so tiny."

"I guess we all have our own perspective," I told him. "So, you got your note. Are you worried?"

Wonjin lifted his arm and opened his palm to reveal a slab of flat stone maybe the size of an A4 sheet of paper. It was carved with indecipherable glyphs—the troll language, I assumed.

"Not worried. Either win or not win. Is the same. One troll live. One troll die." He shrugged.

"But you want to win, right? You don't want to die, do you?" asked Jen, full of concern.

"Want to win. For pride of lineage. But all trolls same really. Know same history. All connected. Now not many. Troll kill troll. But all history remain as long as one troll live. But need baby trolls. Need mate."

"Yes, that would be nice," I said. "Someone to stand next to in the garden. So you don't see yourself as more important than the troll you must fight?"

"No. Why would Wonjin think that? Other troll, he be thinking want to win. Same as Wonjin."

"That's a nice way to think about it," said Phage, smiling up at the sentient mountain. "Good luck. Hopefully we'll see you soon."

"Yes, be back in few hours maybe."

"Stay strong, and be well," I told him.

"How about a hug?" asked Jen, holding out her arms. She looked like a doll next to a giant, which I guess is what she would seem like to him.

"Not want to crush the Jen."

"Then be careful," she told him, putting her arms out again.

Phage and I exchanged a nervous glance, but what are you gonna do? If he wanted to hurt us, he could.

Slowly, and very carefully, Wonjin reached down and scooped Jen up with his free hand then lifted her up so they were eye to eye. He smiled slowly, then pulled her in to his chest and said, "Hug is nice. The Jen is warm and squishy. Not hurt?"

"No, not at all," she told him. "And a hug is always nice."

Wonjin lowered Jen and then straightened up. He nodded to us then snapped his fingers with a crack like thunder.

The world was emptied of sound like the after-effects of a gunshot at close range. Everything was still and silent as the air simply parted to reveal a barren, snow-covered landscape of rocky mountains. A blizzard howled through the rend in our world, the snow hissing as it melted instantly.

Wonjin turned from us then stepped through. On the other side, he faced us and nodded once. He snapped his fingers and the eye into another place shrank, then sealed shut.

Sound returned like an assault to the senses. Birds chattered, animals grunted, Mr. Wonderful hissed at Woofer from up a tree, chickens clucked, and the cockerel let loose with a barrage of complaints about not enough fresh sawdust for his ladies.

"So, can we have dinner now?" I asked.

"Dad!"

"What?"

"That was... He was... Aren't you a little bit...? Ah, forget it. What's for tea, Mum? Can we have sausages?"

"No!" we both shouted simultaneously. But it was too late. Woofer came tearing down the lawn, skidded to a halt, and sat, tail wagging, eyes gleaming, as he said, "Sausages?"

We laughed and joked as we headed to the house. I hoped Wonjin would be okay. I'd got used to the big lump on my lawn. It looked barren without it.

Missing Misfits

We didn't do adult birthday celebrations for obvious reasons. Ever since Jen was little, we simply told her that it was for children, and adults liked to just have a normal day. Jen would often bring me a little gift, though. She even brought me a frog once. The frog was not happy about having been stuck up her jumper for several hours, although Jen thought it was ace.

Now Jen had learned what it signified, she had been very quiet about the whole thing. She was trying to avoid the inevitable. That I had to leave and do what I had to do. She had been wanting to talk to me all day about it, that was clear, but had decided not to ask. I guess she didn't want to know, which was fair enough.

She'd wished me happy birthday that morning, but for the first time ever since she was old enough to understand birthdays, she hadn't given me a card. There was this weight hanging over us all, an unspoken tension, no matter that we'd had a pretty amazing day full of surprises and mystery. Trolls and sausages and immortal Woofers and cans of fuel and what have you.

Dinner was over, a nice light pasta dish, the kitchen was cleaned, Jen was drying what didn't fit in the dishwasher, and I was wiping down the counter while Phage relaxed in the living room.

I could feel her eyes boring into the back of my skull as I rinsed the rag then folded it neatly over the sink.

"Go on then, ask."

"Ask what?" Jen frowned, then bent to the cupboard and put the plates away. When she stood, her face was a little red and her eyes sparkled as she held back tears.

"Honey, I am so sorry. We didn't want you to know. We tried to keep you from this. I'm so sorry."

Jen lost it completely and burst into tears, then wrapped her arms around me, clinging as tight as she could. She was so tall now, up to my chin. I couldn't quite believe it.

"Do you have to go? Do you have to do it?" she sobbed.

"I do have to. But no, I don't want to. With all my heart, I want to stay here with you guys and never have to leave, ever. But I have to do this. It's the way."

"What way? Why do you say that? How can you say that? You just accept this? I still can't believe you're so old, and know so much. Have seen so much. It doesn't seem real."

"I understand. It's a pretty big thing to wrap your head around. All you need to know is I love you. And that I would never hurt anyone unless I had to. These notes, they are the worst thing in the world, but it's part of who I am. And unfortunately, part of who you are. Who you will be. Never enjoy it, always know it is a terrible thing, but you must decide what you do and you must do it with every ounce of your ability. I'll teach you things over the years, so you're ready, but no, it's never easy. It shouldn't be."

"So how can you do it? You know, actually kill a person?"

I swallowed a lump in my throat and motioned for her to sit down.

Jen snuffled, and cleared her face, then when we were both sitting I took her delicate, small hands in mine, although I noticed the callouses from all the climbing, which was good, and I told her, "Although I abhor what I do, I am a very dangerous man to my enemies. I hate killing and it takes something from you, Jen, but I am capable of it. Those of us who survive into old age like me, we have a certain something inside of us. A true monster."

"You could never be a monster."

"I can. And I am. I am like a soldier. You understand?"

"Of course."

"But I am a very seasoned veteran of countless skirmishes. I have this thing in me. I truly believe I am invincible. I cannot be killed when I fight. That is my belief. But it's more than that. I lose myself completely. I become war itself. I become death. I destroy, and I think and feel nothing of it when I am consumed by bloodlust. I kill because they would kill me otherwise, and I will not let that happen."

"That so doesn't sound like you at all. Dad, you're scaring me."

"And that's the last thing I ever want to do. Just know that I would never, ever hurt you or your mother. But those who would do me, and especially you or Phage harm, I will obliterate them. Completely. Know that about me, Jen. Know it always. I will defend you both with my dying breath. I am not afraid to die. I am afraid of losing the two women I love most in the world. That's who I am. All you need to know about me. I am your father and I will protect you. You can always count on me. You can always ask me for help. You can rely on me. Understand?"

"I love you, Dad." Jen was crying so bad I was dying inside, but I kept hold of her shaking hands as they trembled and told her, "I love you too. I know this is a terrible, and almost impossibly hard thing to accept. But it happens, and your mother and I do these terrible things. Does it make us bad people? Yes, and no. Killing is wrong. But we are not normal people. We are like Wonjin. We are something other. We are different. We have a terrible burden but we have a life like no other. It is the price we pay. Now, do you think you can accept that? Accept who I am, what I am, and find a way to deal with it?"

"I... I think so. I think I already have. I try to laugh it off as some terrible joke, as it can't be true. It just can't. But I think deep down I do know, and I do accept it. Somehow, it's like I've always known." Jen leaned close to me and said, "Sometimes I just know things. It's like voices in my head, but not actual voices. Just a kind of knowledge. Does that make sense? It makes me sound crazy."

"We've told you about that already, but maybe you were too young to remember. It's because of the kind of Necro you are. It's the sisters, they call them. At least Phage and Peth do. It's the memory of your lineage on the female side. All the witches, or whatever they want to call themselves. You're tapping into it subconsciously."

"That's what Grandma said. She told me I was special and not many can hear them at my age. Most not ever. So it's a bunch of dead old women talking in my head?"

"No, that would be mad. Think of it more like a big book of knowledge that you can't quite understand yet. Like a book partly in a foreign language but close to English and most of the pages are stuck together. As you get older, and if you want to learn more, then the pages will become unglued and you will learn the language of how to read it. But know this, young Jen. There are things you might not want to discover. Dangerous things. Before you delve too deeply, do your research and ask lots of questions. You need to understand what you might uncover before you go delving in. Some things are best left unknown. Am I making sense?"

"Sure. Thanks, this has helped a lot." Jen dried her eyes then sheepishly pulled out a card from her back pocket. "Sorry, it's a bit crumpled. I felt silly and didn't know if I should give it to you or not." She handed it over and I took it with a smile and a nod.

I broke the seal and laughed at a picture of Woofer with a red ball in his mouth. I read what it said inside. "Play ball with Woofer? Lots of love, Jen and Woofer. Kiss, kiss, kiss." I laughed as Jen squirmed in her seat.

"Sorry, it's lame."

"No, it's perfect. Thank you." I got up and put the card on the kitchen counter. This was turning out to be one of the best birthdays ever.

"Sorry about all this," said Jen.

"You have nothing to apologize for. Look, you sure you don't want to do anything for your birthday? You had the week off school and you haven't seen your friends or had a party or anything. That's not like you."

"I just wanted it to be us this year. No friends, just us. This year is different. I wanted to get my head around it all. That okay?"

"Of course. I know this is tough for you, but next year will be different."

"Maybe. We'll see." Jen gave a half smile then presumably left to go clean her face up.

I sat there alone for a while, wondering how much we'd damaged our child. One thing was for certain, she wasn't as broken as either Phage or I had been at her age.

For that, I would be eternally grateful.

When I entered the living room, I found Phage, Jen, and Woofer all curled up on the sofa. They were all reading books, apart from Woofer who was playing a game on his tablet. Or maybe he was just snoring and chasing his ball as he dreamed. It's so hard to keep up with the kids these days.

"How about we finish off the day with a birthday drink?" I asked.

"What, am I old enough to have wine now?" asked Jen excitedly.

"No, you are not. I meant a beer in the pub. You can have a lemonade."

"I'm not going in there! He's there. Ugh." Jen shivered at the thought of the resident in the Necropub.

"I could drink a beer," said Phage. "Jen, you should come. It'll be fun. And he might not come out. He usually doesn't."

"I know. But whenever I go in there, Brewer is always there, right behind me. He makes me jump."

"I don't think the Brewer does it on purpose. It's just his way," I told her.

"Why do you always say *the* Brewer? Not Brewer?" asked Jen. "It sounds weird."

"Because we had a really, and I mean *really*, long conversation about it with him. I insisted his name was Brewer so we should just treat it like that, his name. He insisted he was *the* Brewer. Then we got into capitalization, but again, he insisted that The was the, but that he was still the Brewer. Like, his name is Brewer and he is the one and only. So he's the Brewer. Like the Queen. You don't capitalize The Queen. You don't capitalize The Brewer."

"I'm just gonna call him Brewer because that is so complicated and it doesn't make any sense."

"Makes sense to me," I said.

"It doesn't to me," said Phage. "But if that's what he wants that's fine. Come on, Jen, it'll be fun. Then we can come back and watch a movie."

"No TV remember?"

"We've got loads on the hard drive. Loads of discs too," I reminded her.

"Fine, but if he does that thing with his ear again I'm so outta there." Jen shuddered again.

Woofer refused to leave the sofa, so the three of us headed down the garden and to the Necropub.

After winter wet, cold, and snow, then a humid and steamy spring, and now just the heat, the Necropub's exterior was looking a little the worse for wear. Where once I had believed it was stylishly shabby and weather worn, it now merely seemed tired, and rotten. Maybe that made it more apt, a closer reflection of the owner. A job for another day. Maybe another year.

I opened the door, or rather, I yanked it until it became unstuck, then stepped aside as the protesting stale beer molecules performed their usual dastardly assault on the senses.

Jen got hit full-force, the amateur, as Phage and I hid behind the door.

"Yuck. So gross. It stinks in there. How can you drink that stuff?"

"We like to live dangerously," I told her. And it was true. The last proper session had been in the throes of winter with Peth, and I'd ended up spending a fortune on takeaway. There was a thing about lemons that I could never quite recall, too. I'd visited regularly since, of course, as who wouldn't, but the Brewer was under strict instruction not to make anything too potent. He'd completely ignored me, but I'd only been caught out once so it was all good.

We stepped inside the humid interior and I flicked the light switch.

It was obvious immediately that something wasn't right.

The normally gleaming beer taps were dull, the mirror behind the bar was cloudy and streaked, there were dirty glasses on the bar top which was filmed in a layer of dust with long finger lines running through it, and the brass rails were turning green.

"What's been going on here?" asked Phage. "When did you last come?"

"Last week, I think. I saw the man himself and he was same as usual. It looks like the place hasn't been touched in years." I skirted around the bar and tried the three taps in turn. Each spluttered. Nothing but air and foam. The infinite well of beer-induced possibilities was dry.

"Maybe he's ill?" suggested Jen.

"He doesn't get ill. He can't really get ill because he's, you know..."

"He's what?" Jen dragged her finger through the dust then sniffed it. "Ugh, smells funky."

"I wouldn't do that if I were you," I told her. "You don't know what's in that."

"It's just dust."

"Yes, but dust of the Brewer," Phage told her. "He's, er, not like us. Like other people."

"Oh, really? And there was me thinking he was a regular guy who just happened to live in the cellar of a made-up pub and spent all his time making weird drinks and freaking everyone out."

"No need to be sarcastic," I told her.

"So, what do you mean he isn't like us?"

"Later, okay? Let's see if he's in." I indicated the trap door set into the floor behind the bar.

"I am absolutely not going down there," insisted Jen. "Have you never seen a horror movie? If we all go down there, then it will slam shut, the lights will go off, and we'll get eaten. Or worse."

"Okay, suit yourself," I said. "But if you're such a horror buff, and you shouldn't have seen any at your age, then you know that the one who stays behind to 'keep watch' is always the one who gets taken first. It's only after that happens that the trap door slams shut. Take your pick." I grinned, but neither of my ladies seemed to see the funny side.

"Soph, don't be so mean."

"Just trying to lighten the mood. Come on, let's see if he's in. He might just be having a few days off. A vacation kind of thing."

"Has he ever had a vacation?" asked Jen.

"Not in all the time I've known him."

I reluctantly pulled on the huge iron ring set into the slab in the floor and heaved back until it hinged up. It slammed open and kicked up a cloud of dust. We peered down into the darkness.

"Hello. Anyone there?" I called.

Nothing but a bad smell.

With little option, I nervously descended the steps carved into the bedrock beneath the Necropub. It was one of the reasons why he'd come here. Said that he liked a solid room underground, nothing man made, and usually he ended up just getting muddy and wet. Here was different. A spot where he could be sure his home wouldn't cave in on him. It also meant the Necropub didn't sink into the hole he'd dug.

Jen and Phage followed me down. We huddled close in the cramped room, not that we had a choice.

Jen asked, "Where's the rest of it?"

"This is it. The Brewer's home."

"Shut up. Haha." She looked from me to Phage. "Seriously?"

"Yes." It had been a long time since I'd come down, for understandable reasons, but nothing had changed. The entire space was nine feet long, with a single bed tight up against one corner, giving you enough room to walk down the steps and stand at the foot of the bed. To the left was a gap of three feet, containing three barrels taking up most of the free space. Hoses snaked their way up to the taps. Beside the bed, a niche had been carved into the rock. It held a candle, a pair of reading glasses, and a single book.

On the bed was a neatly made, rough-hewn hessian blanket. No pillow. There was a stain where he rested his head against the wall to read. There was no electric light, no clothes, no nothing. And there never had been.

This was the Brewer's entire life. He loved it. In his own unique way. What he got up to when he wasn't sleeping or making his mysterious brews was anyone's guess, and nobody's business but his.

"Well, he sure isn't here," I said.

"Why is this so small? Where's his stuff? How can he live like this?" Jen chewed at her lip nervously as she searched our faces for answers.

"It's what he wants. How he lives. His choice," I told her. "Come on, let's go."

"What about under the bed?" Jen asked. She pointed at it, in case I somehow missed it.

"He won't be under there. He's claustrophobic."

Jen's mouth opened and closed wordlessly.

"Gotcha." I shooed them out of the way, then bent down to take a look. Nothing but dust and a pair of slippers. He might have been monastic, but he hated cold feet.

"Anything?" asked Phage.

"Nope." I struggled to my feet then followed them both back upstairs and closed the trap door.

"Where can he be?" mused Phage.

"I honestly don't know. He's never done this before. Although, yes, maybe he has. There was that weekend when we couldn't get the pumps to work and he wasn't in his room, but that was years ago. Remember?"

"Vaguely."

"How can you let him live like that?" demanded Jen. "It's cruel. Barbaric."

"No, it isn't," Phage told her. "The Brewer is a, um, very special kind of person. He likes to lead a very simple life. He has dedicated himself to his art, and that is his passion. Think of him as a monk. No distractions. He wants it that way. He doesn't like to be disturbed very often, or spoken to much, and he likes to keep focused. He's almost a hermit."

"But monks don't live in pubs. Dad pubs especially. And even they have proper sheets."

"Lots of monks live like him," I told Jen. "It's a way to stay close to the divine. To remove yourself from the trappings of the material world and be at one with the cosmos. That's the Brewer. Monks invented beer and all kinds of alcohol back in the day. It's not so different."

"And how long has he been here?"

"Gosh. Years and years. Since the beginning. Before that he was at the old place, and before that he was at the older place, and—"

"So a while then?" laughed Jen.

"Yes. A while."

"And, um, you know, what is he?"

"He's the guy who makes the beer. Come on, let's get back into the house. Wine it is, I'm afraid."

"Yippee."

"I meant for the adults. You're still on lemonade."

"Aw, no fair."

"What can I tell you? Life's a bitch."

"Dad!"

"Sorry. But it's still no to the wine."

I closed the Necropub and followed my two girls back up to the house. Where was the Brewer? I hoped he was alright. I hadn't been strictly honest with Jen about when he'd disappeared, or why, but there were some things she didn't need to know. Surely he wouldn't have gone there. I was being silly. No way. He'd kept to the promise he made to me and himself for over a century. Sure, he'd gone missing quite a few times since then, but he'd never gone where he promised he would never set a misshapen foot again.

But I still worried for him.

Morning Farewells

I was not hungover, which was a shame. But sometimes sobriety is forced upon you. Instead, I felt invigorated after my daily morning exercise ritual and a nice hot shower.

My gear was packed and ready, so I just had to sort out a few odds and ends. One of those odds was Tyr, one of those ends, a bellend, was Bernard.

I chose Bernard first.

"Hey everyone, how we all doing?" I asked the family of unicorns as I opened up the stable door.

"Cold, and hungry," moaned Bernard. He glanced outside then whinnied, by actually saying, "Whinny." Then he added, "Actually, I'm hot and hungry. Oh, why is it so hot?"

"That'll be the sun. And you aren't fooling anyone. How is Betty this fine morning?" I asked.

"Very well, thank you, Soph. I had the most wonderful sleep."

"Great. That's great. Kayin, how about you? Are your parents looking after you?"

"I guess," she shrugged. "But how would I know? I don't have anything to compare it to. They might be terrible parents and I'd never know."

"Trust me, they are the best. At least, your mum is." I winked at Betty. She bared her pearly whites and snorted with amusement. I liked her.

"Can we come out now? Or do we have to stay cooped up in here all day?" asked Kayin.

"Sure, you can come out. You okay there, buddy?"

"Yes, I suppose. Just a bit bored."

I stepped aside as they filed out of their stable and I led them down to the paddock where they spent a lot of their time now. Things were different since the neighbors had been outed. Shae knew all about what went on here, so there was no need to pretend, or hide any animals away.

As Kayin and Betty wandered into the paddock, I stopped Bernard and whispered, "What's up with Kayin? She's been pretty down lately."

Bernard turned his head, nearly impaling me, but I jumped back in a very practiced manner as he said, "She's been getting worse ever since that fight in the garden last year. Now it's warm and nice out, she's been talking about adventure more and more. Itching to have some action, unfortunately. Don't know why. It's so dangerous, and so gory. Ugh. But she really wants to do something. Something exciting."

"I see. Sorry, I know that's a worry for you. But remember when Jen named her? That we all knew then the kind of unicorn she'd be. I know it's hard, and I wish it were different for both of them. But we have to accept what they are. Kayin isn't like you or Betty. She's a warrior."

"I've done my fair share!"

"You've done more than that. You have saved my life, you have looked after us all. But it was different. You hated the excitement. Kayin craves it. I know there's a lot you've done with Phage that neither of you have told me, and I thank you for protecting her, but yes, she is not like you."

"I guess I need to accept that, don't I?" Bernard said, utterly miserable. "But don't take her with you!" he added.

"I have no intention of doing any such thing. If I need a ride it's you and me. Kayin will not be taken with me. She is Jen's aide, her companion, and it won't be until she is of age that they go out on a dangerous mission. Okay?"

"Okay." Bernard moped off down to the others. Poor guy, I knew exactly how he felt. Damn, he really was worried. He didn't even complain much.

"Okay. Next stop, Tyr."

I couldn't find him, and decided not to call out to him. He'd appear soon enough, or I could call him once on the road. It wasn't like he had to pack or anything.

I discovered a few other things to occupy my time, then reluctantly found myself outside the house standing next to the car. It wasn't much, but it was ours, and it didn't stand out from anyone else's. Living amongst regular people, seeing them for parties or the occasional excruciating barbecue and whatnot, meant we always did our best to seem like everyone else. We definitely had the car to prove it.

It sat in the garage at the side of the property, moping and lamenting its prison. Poor thing hardly ever went anywhere. Maybe an occasional trip to the shops if we had stockpiled fuel, but mostly it sat idle, waiting impatiently for me to start it up once a month for a few minutes to keep it ticking over. Electric vehicles had come and gone. They were still in the majority, but the problems associated with actually charging them meant that those who still had the gas guzzlers held on to them and were glad they did.

We'd gone through so many iterations of what was best to drive that nobody knew what to do. Fuel had obvious drawbacks, and there had been minimal rations for years now as we were all basically banned from driving any vehicle, but for a while when electric was hyped, it's what everyone bought. And then within a few years the ban came into place and people were stuck with an expensive, unusable vehicle that needed regular charging to maintain the battery health but not enough of an electric quota to be able to run their homes, let alone a car they weren't allowed to drive.

So Francis the Ford hunkered down in the dusty garage and waited for the day his freedom would return.

Today was that day. He was old, but solid. A boring dark blue, but he had leather interior, air con, and I'd polished him especially.

Time to get rolling.

"Here, and don't eat them before lunch." Phage handed me a stack of containers with all manner of goodies inside. I eyed them greedily.

"I won't."

"Promise?" she asked, eyes twinkling.

"No way! I'll see you soon, okay? Be back in no time." I pulled her close, took in her scent, then kissed her.

"Be careful," croaked Jen, welling up and shaking a little.

"I absolutely will. Don't worry about me. I'm tough as old boots and twice as wrinkly. Be back soon. Look after your mother, and see if you can cheer Kayin up. She needs a good long ride. Tire her out, burn off some of that energy. Maybe go for a ride with Phage and Bernard, too. And Woofer would enjoy a run. Stay safe, and don't forget, it's school on Monday."

"Ugh, I like being at home."

"Me too. But school is important. Well, better get going." I kissed the top of Jen's head, loaded the containers onto the passenger seat, just in case I got peckish, and with a cheesy grin to Jen, plus a nod to Phage, I got in and started up Francis.

He spluttered into life, then purred like a kitten. With no reason apart from every reason ever to remain at home, I drove off with a wave and a smile when all I wanted to do was cry.

By the time I was on the outskirts of Shrewsbury, my sadness was forgotten and I was in game mode. Soph the Necro, the man who destroyed, was in control now, and he needed a goddamn smoke.

Huh?

"Pam, what the fuck is that?"

"The raven-haired, busty beauty leaned forward, revealing a little too much cleavage, and flicked a glossy braid over her slender, sexy, exposed shoulder. Sighing demurely, she glanced up from the counter where she was scribbling furiously, and raised a perfect, arched eyebrow. She smiled ever-so-sweetly at the scruffy hunk of man-meat who stormed into her place of business, frowning as usual."

I stopped just inside the door of Necrosmoke and frowned. Damn! Was I that predictable? "What are you talking about? What's happening? Why are you talking like that? And you didn't smile sweetly, you sneered. Plus, I didn't notice your bust. Have you even got one? And who's scruffy? I've got a clean shirt and jeans on. I ran my fingers through my hair earlier, and my beard hasn't answered back in weeks."

"The dark, mysterious lady put down her pen and wondered if she could reach the man and take his knife before he had time to react. Maybe she would shift. Maybe she could distract him by bending forward more. She decided to lick her lips." Pam licked her lips. I felt suddenly hot. "It worked, and before the man knew what was happening, she launched over the counter and was beside him, her breath hot on his neck as she released the popper on his knife and—"

"I may be dumb, but I'm not that dumb," I growled, grabbing her hand as she tried to take my knife.

"I knew it! You men are all the same. Damn, even you, Soph. You know I don't swing that way, but you are still helpless when confronted by a woman. Even though I was telling you what I was doing, you still let me do it! Unbelievable!" Pam pecked me on the cheek then sashayed over to the counter, leaving a trail of sweet horse smell in her wake.

I shuddered, shook my head to clear the musk, then eased into the room carefully, wondering what mind tricks she was playing and what whispers she had somehow learned. Pam wasn't into any of that stuff, but she had certainly done something to fog my mind.

"Um, where were we?" I asked, as I stepped up to the counter and Pam took her place behind it. "What was all that? You been taking lessons from the witches?"

"No, don't be silly. I told you, I'm writing a novel. Or trying to. I've been testing out various scenarios on the customers. You know, to see what's believable. And I have come to the conclusion that anything is believable if it involves either sex, a promise of sex, a hint of sex, or even a faint whisper of a promise of sex. Especially if it's men. Basically, tits."

"You mean, men, or those?" I pointed at the entirely dangerous articles.

"Both."

"Yep," I agreed. "Tits will do it every time."

"He fell for her cunning trap!"

"Aha, so you have been learning how to whisper?"

"No, just how to bedazzle."

"More like bejazzle." There was a very awkward silence. Pam cocked her head and stared at me quizzically. "Um, sorry, I only said that because it rhymed. I don't even know what bejazzle is. Is it something to do with your lady parts?"

"You are such a prude. Look at you, squirming."

"I am a man of a certain age, from another time, and although I pride myself on always keeping up with the current lingo, I still have the outlook of someone from a very different era."

"Fair enough. And bejazzle is when you—"

"Hey, so you're writing a book?" I asked hurriedly. "And what, you're trying out scenes to see if they would work in your novel? Sounds cool."

"Did you just change the subject? And repeat what I just told you?"

"What subject? If there was one, I didn't change it. Now, can we please stop talking about whatever it was we weren't talking about?" I grinned at Pam, one of my oldest friends because I didn't really have any others, and she laughed. "Good, great. So, what's new?"

"Nothing much. Apart from the bloody till not working and I can't take any payments anyway, so it's all fucked. Nobody has actual cash money as nobody can keep up with all the changes and we haven't used any for years. If you can't use your card or phone or whatever, then you can't pay. And there's no internet so nothing works. Damn, I didn't realize how much was run via the bloody web. The cameras are down all over the country. There's no surveillance. Did you notice there are no drones? Even half the bloody lights are via wi-fi and nobody can make a phone call or anything. That's why I'm using a pen and paper instead of my computer."

"You can still type without the internet."

"Aha, but there's no backup. Plus, I kind of, um... Yeah, I forgot, okay? I was thinking without the internet then my computer wouldn't work."

"What? That makes no sense. You must have turned it on and used it to find out there was no connection."

"Just shut up, alright? Stop trying to confuse me."

"You're the one confusing me. But it is weird, isn't it? No phone, no internet, and no surveillance. It's going to be a shit storm. You hear anything?"

"I've heard plenty. Business has been great since yesterday. If any of them ever pay. Everyone's out and about. Just look at the number of cars."

I followed Pam's gaze out of the window and stared at the traffic. But I'd already experienced it driving over, and it had been weird.

"It's not busy or anything out there, but there are a lot more cars. Hell, any cars is more than usual. Guess everyone's risking it as there are no cameras working and the police don't seem bothered at all."

"I bet they just know it's not worth the hassle," said Pam. "I wonder if their radios even work. They certainly can't use their tablets or phones. And how did you get here?"

"I drove." I grinned excitedly; it had felt awesome. "I got a surprise pass in the mail. And a can of fuel. Ever heard of that happening before?"

"No, but how come?"

"I assume because 'they' knew this was coming and it meant I could drive without any hassle. Dunno."

Pam mulled it over for a moment then told me, "That makes no sense. If they gave you a pass you could have driven anytime. They never do stuff like that. What difference does it make that the internet's gone down?"

"Um, I hadn't thought about it like that. Anyway, I'm past caring. It's been so long since I got to have it easy on a job, so I'll take it."

"Be careful. This doesn't sound right at all. Why would they suddenly give you special treatment? I mean, we all get a pass to allow us to travel without a problem, but never to use a car. They don't want it to be easy for us."

"True. And it never is easy. Damn, now you have me worried. What do you think it means?"

Pam shrugged. "No idea. Just watch your back. And hey, maybe it is because the cameras are down. I guess in the past anyone driving was seen as suspicious even with permission to travel. It would draw attention to you wherever you went. But with no cameras there will be lots more vehicles, so you won't stand out."

"That's probably it," I agreed, now very unsure about the whole thing. But we had all assumed this was why we didn't get to use cars in the past, so we would blend in. Maybe this was the new way to be incognito? It didn't quite sit right, but I had more important things to worry abut. Like smoking.

"So, you gonna hook a guy up?"

"Of course. And at least I don't have to get annoyed about having to take an IOU because my promise for free tobacco stands."

"You truly are an angel."

Pam flicked a braid and said, "Don't you ever forget it." She winked, then sorted me out a nice fat pack of tobacco.

With a ring of the bell, I exited Necrosmoke then swore when I couldn't find my bike. Then I laughed as I remembered I was traveling in luxury this time.

Sweet.

Buying Peaches

A very annoying electronic buzzer tried to burst my eardrum as I pushed open a spotless glass door, careful to use the handle as it would be a shame to put a smudge on it. I could smell the cleaning solution—lemon. It was so fresh and inviting I could already tell this was a small business owner who took immense pride in his establishment.

As the door closed behind me with another irritating buzz, I stopped just inside the entrance and looked around the corner shop. It brought back a dizzying number of memories through the ages. Of small shops when I was young that stocked little in the way of provisions, before canning and packaging was even a thing, to the heyday of the corner shop and small local businesses selling anything and everything, competing with so many others that the daily shop was often a fun time where you got to gossip with the owner and catch up on things with the locals.

Then places such as this all but disappeared as the supermarkets took over, only to reemerge revitalized and utterly necessary when travel became a hassle and everything switched back to being local once more. Funny how so much had come full circle. I wondered what was next? Probably tiny pills that contained all your daily calories and food becoming a thing of the past. Could that happen? I hoped not.

The dark tiled floor was spotless. I sniffed, taking in the scent of more cleaning fluids, but it wasn't overpowering. Just a background aroma that told you this was a clean place, that there was pride and hard work contained within the fresh white walls.

Neatly stacked shelves showcased all manner of seasonal fruit and veg. Early raspberries, strawberries, plenty of new potatoes, and other things we'd grown accustomed to eating rather than anything exotic. A huge basket of shiny green cucumbers promised a refreshing crunch on a blistering hot day.

Opposite me on the far wall was one of the large, energy-hungry machines for dispensing milk, and next to it loomed a dark beast of a soft drinks dispenser. You saw them everywhere now. Businesses got better energy quotas so they could offer such services, and it made sense rather than throwing away a container every time you wanted milk, but I couldn't ignore the utter lack of choice nowadays. It really was like stepping back into the past, except you could still buy things that weren't very good for your health.

The deli counter was rammed with numerous local cheeses and cooked meats, there was a micro-bakery with still-warm loaves steaming up the glass, and as I got close the smell was divine. The meat section contained various cuts along with sausages and bacon, and on the top of the deli counter piles of Scotch eggs and pork pies shone under the warm light from a single luxurious wall light.

I breathed deeply as I stepped up to the bread and picked up a dark, crusty, nutty loaf then lifted it to my face until the crust scratched my nose. I sucked in the yeasty tang—nothing like fresh bread you know was made that morning by a true artisan.

A basket containing ripe peaches caught my eye. I dared not touch in case I bruised their perfect, blushed skin. Delicate as a newborn's bottom and just as glowing with health and vitality.

"Ah, hello my friend," said a portly guy as he pushed through a bead curtain from the back. His ruddy cheeks fattened as he smiled warmly, and he followed my gaze to the peaches then laughed when I sniffed the bread again.

"Hi. Everything looks great."

"Thank you. I am the baker, the cleaner, the butcher, the owner, and the entertainment," he said with a chuckle.

"Then you're doing a fine job. You've got a great place here. And I am definitely having the bread. Can you sort me out with a few slices of the ham? And what's the damage for the peaches? Don't go trying to steal my shirt," I warned with a friendly wink.

"Aha, a true connoisseur. And truly, my prices are reasonable. I make a pittance, but I enjoy my work. I get to hear all the gossip," he said with a mock whisper and a glance around the cramped room. "And today there is much to talk about, is there not?"

"Oh, bugger, yeah, I totally forgot. Um, how can I pay? I'm assuming your internet is down?"

"Of course it is! The card reader won't work, and nobody has cash any longer. With so many changes to the currency, how could anyone possibly keep up?"

"Bet that's a nightmare for pricing. Having to change it and work out the new numbers?"

"A true headache," he agreed. "But I don't think they'll change it again. And besides, it keeps my brain active. But no internet means no ability to read cards, no way to scan a phone or a watch or any of these new ways people can pay."

"So what, you can't sell anything?"

"I could barter. Do you have much to trade?"

"Not really." I tried to think what he might want, but there was nothing I was willing to give up for food, and what I would wasn't worth enough.

"As I thought. Then we will have to continue with trust, my friend. I shall take your details and process the transaction when the services return. You can give me your card number and I will charge you when all is well."

I tried to think of a reason not to, but back in the day, not so many years ago, you would always give your card number and the code on the back to buy stuff. Either over the phone or online. This was no different, was it? "Okay, you have a deal. So, give me some numbers. And how much for the peaches?"

"Ah, you truly do have fine taste. The peaches were grown by these very hands." He showed me his pink, meaty hands. Spotless, of course. "I have a fine garden with all manner of produce, and the peaches are so juicy. But the day is wearing on, custom is slow because of the outage, so I will do you a deal if you take the rest. I normally have a customer for these peaches, but he hasn't come today and I don't want them to go to waste. I will sell you them all for a great price."

"That's a lot of peaches."

"But for a great price." He nodded his head, keen to get them gone so they wouldn't spoil.

"Okay, hit me."

He gave me the price, and it was fair and not too extortionate, so I agreed. He packaged everything up expertly then took my details. Poor guy was probably having a nightmare without being able to take payment, and my guess was it would be the same everywhere. Everyone would just hunker down at home unless they were desperate, and wait this out.

I nodded my thanks and made to leave.

"My friend, do you think things will ever return to how they were?"

"Honestly? No, I don't. I think long term, they will be better, but also worse. We don't have our freedom. I don't know that we ever will like we used to. But maybe the cost is worth paying if it means we tread a little lighter."

"Yes, maybe. Well, enjoy the peaches." He waved me off and I got assaulted by the buzzer as I left.

Right, what was the plan? It was strange having the option of driving. I decided to keep going for a while until I found a nice spot, sleep out for the night, then get my note completed the following day. I knew better than to try to rush it.

I had to get my head in the right place, which meant sleeping rough and getting back to basics with a nice fire, a long smoke, and some crap wine. It was what I'd done for centuries, and so far it had worked, so I saw no need to make a change now. And besides, apart from the knot in my stomach, I enjoyed this time alone.

The chance to reflect and have no responsibilities, to be free of all I held dear because it made me value it so much more. This quiet time made me enter the right headspace to ensure I would do whatever it took to return home.

I smiled as I sat in the car, wondering what my two special ladies were doing. I hoped they missed me as much as I missed them. They did, and I would see them soon. I promised myself that. I'd make it home, and nothing could stop me.

With my food taunting me from the passenger seat, and the sweet smell of peaches filling the interior, I started the car but just sat there, as if waiting for something. I felt isolated, cocooned in my cool shell, distant from the sounds and smells of the world. I wasn't sure I liked it one little bit. Too much comfort wasn't good for my head. I needed struggle. To get dirty, down in the fields, wading sickly streams, not lording it up in this bubble. I laughed. What was wrong with me? I should go with it. This wouldn't last, so I should make the most of it.

As I pulled away, a car tore up the street. The driver skidded to a halt then was out the door of his snazzy Tesla almost before it stopped moving. He ran to the shop and entered, slamming the door open, putting his hands all over the glass. Guess the dick really needed milk, or maybe toilet paper.

I pulled off and headed onto the open road.

There wasn't another car in sight. I passed a few trucks, and once onto the A5 I took a steady sixty-five and cruised past several of the giant, multi-trailered behemoths delivering to the ubermarkets. I wondered how the systems were coping without any means of keeping track of stock levels and how they were handling payment. Best steer clear of those places until this all got sorted out.

Soon, I settled into a dreamy state where the world whizzed by and I drove without conscious effort, just letting my mind drift whilst maintaining my speed and not having to focus too much on it. It was almost a meditation.

The car juddered and I was snapped back to the present. I glanced in the rearview as the car shunted forward, only to find a car flashing its lights and honking as it revved up and slammed into the rear again. I gripped the steering wheel tight and eased up on the accelerator as I fought to maintain control. What the fuck was this prick playing at? I glanced back again and recognized the car. The man from the shop. The one in a hurry.

He came at me again, so I swerved over to the other lane, hoping he'd got whatever this was out of his system and he'd pass me by. He didn't. He slowed, then changed lanes and sped up, coming straight at me again.

Confused as hell, as who does this, I switched lanes again then slowed right down so he was far ahead. Should I stop? Did he want to fight me? I didn't know the guy, but that didn't mean he wasn't someone from my past. Another Necro maybe? Just in a bad mood?

Several other cars shot past, blaring at me for driving so slowly. I sped up a little, my head spinning, freaked out at such antics on the road. Didn't this person know it was insanity to be acting like this?

He'd get us both killed.

Nice Car

This bastard would not leave me alone. What was with him? Could I not just have this thing? Be left alone to have a nice, quiet drive before I bloodied my hands once more? Why was it always like this?

No, it wasn't always like this, I had to remind myself. I'd driven for years without ever having a problem. Had been on the road when roads were first a thing. Even now, I could recall the massive undertaking across the country as roads slowly morphed from dirt tracks. They'd been quagmires of treacherous muddy messes where the wheels of your cart could snap, you got bogged down in the mud, and hardly a soul traveled further than their local village as why would you?

Gradually, it evolved. Tarmac became a thing, and concrete was the norm, so real roads for the first cars crept across the landscape. Then that changed. Cars got better, there were bridges and motorways and you could sail along, hardly another vehicle on the road, waving and smiling at each other as you sped along the country at speeds seemingly impossible unless you happened to own a unicorn.

And then the madness hit and everything became challenging. Sitting in traffic for hours, breathing the noxious fumes, stress levels rising. It felt like the minute that started, life changed once again. The strict rules on travel, then the outright ban, then the myriad complexities nobody could keep up with until we found ourselves where we currently were.

Travel was so tightly regulated that it was next to impossible to obtain a permit. Strictly for the transport industry, the politicians, and the big, important businessmen. Everyone else had to suck it up and go buy a horse.

And yet here I was, cocooned in a metal box, nary another soul on the road, the smell of polish, leather, and peaches a delight. And this fucker had to go and ruin it all.

What was wrong with him?

I slammed my foot onto the accelerator, visions swimming of me tearing off, leaving him for dust. The car spluttered and maybe picked up several more miles per hour, but it was hardly impressive.

The Tesla tore past me then swerved into my lane and the guy's brake lights blinked a warning as he slowed dangerously. I bounced into his rear, was rocked forward until my seatbelt snapped tight, my neck whipped with an audible click, and I almost lost control as I eased on the brake so I didn't lose it completely.

He tore off while I picked up speed again, aware there was nowhere to go, no point trying to turn around. Knowing my luck, one of the behemoths trailing multiple containers would be coming up behind me and I'd be toast. Squishy toast. And I like my toast like I like my bones. Hard, and in one piece.

I rubbed the Christmas tree air freshener with my fingers then put them to my nose and sniffed. The unmistakable scent of chemical pine was like a hit of smelling salts and it snapped me back to the reality of the situation. That being, I was going to crash unless I did something to deal with this guy.

But what?

He had a better car, was undoubtedly a better driver, and seemed to have it in for me personally.

Me? My car was a bit crap, I could never seem to get the hang of any fancy moves, and I couldn't care less about this man.

I did the only thing I could, and kept on driving. I would wing it. My best plans were always when I had no plan at all. That way, nothing could go wrong.

He was dawdling up ahead, waiting for me to catch up, so I eased alongside him. We sped along the road, just us, two men in their cars, seemingly rivals because one of us had an as-yet-unknown issue with the other. I pressed the button and the passenger window lowered. I pointed for him to do the same. His window came down and I shouted, "What's your problem?"

He cupped his hand to his ear and shook his head.

"Pull over," I mouthed, and pointed to the emergency lane.

The grinning idiot shook his head and mouthed back, "I'm gonna fuck you up," then laughed as his widow closed and he tore off. See, the problem with these electric vehicles was there was no impressive cloud of noxious fumes. He was just gone. Silent, no drama.

I closed my window and shrugged. Guess this would play out one of two ways. Either he'd get cocky and crash, or I'd just crash. I trundled along at fifty; no point risking anything at this point and it would conserve fuel, anyway. Gotta think of the environmental impact.

It was at about this time I realized I hated cars and wished I had my bike. Hell, I'd even swap the car for Bernard. It felt wrong, too much of a disconnect. I wasn't out there, part of the world. I was passing it by, not immersed in the reality of existence.

But the air con was nice. Shame there was no up-to-date sat nav. It would have been nice to discover where the roadblocks were. At least the old maps were stored on it, although I didn't know when it had last been updated.

I drove on, ever mindful that I was playing a game of cat-and-mouse with a stranger when I had much more important things to be doing. Like having an afternoon nap, or smoking my pipe. Could I smoke in the car? Was there a way to get my pipe going whilst driving? I figured it best not to find out. Now wasn't the time for puffing. Now was the time for huffing.

For several miles there was no sign of the car, and I wondered if he'd turned off at a slip road. No such luck. There he was up ahead, driving like a responsible citizen. Had he got it out of his system? No, of course he hadn't. I came up alongside him and glanced over. The slack-jawed fool smirked, then spun his wheel hard left and caught the driver's side door. The impact was astonishingly loud. What were these things made of, tin?

I began to skid, and knew I could flip, so wrestled with the steering wheel, easing off the accelerator but not punching the brake as I knew enough to know that could spell disaster. I bumped onto the hard shoulder and halfway into the verge before I managed to regain control and righted the car then got back on the road, sticking to the hard shoulder as he was right there beside me. Again, he swerved and slammed into me, battering the back door this time.

The rear tires locked out and I began to skid again, but righted fast and pressed hard on the accelerator. Once past him, I might have panicked a little, and out of instinct I slammed on the brakes. He rammed into me from behind, locking the seatbelt. I jolted forward before flooring it then braking again, hoping to force him off the road, hopefully crash and explode in a massive fireball.

He simply swerved around me and raced off, horn blaring with glee. Fucking Teslas. How was I meant to compete with a Model S? It might have been old, but it ran like it was just out of the factory. I'd heard they could do zero to sixty in under two seconds. I couldn't even change gear that fast.

I checked the map on the sat nav, then moved over and took the upcoming turn that wound around the slip road and followed the signs for a service station. The car park was empty, not a soul in sight. The place was closed and had been for years. No point staying open when there's nothing but the occasional horse and unicorn to cater for.

My heart beat fast despite having been in much worse situations countless times. It was the lack of control that was doing for me. I needed to be hands-on with my fights, not hurtling along a road in a steel coffin. Stressed, and more shaken than I'd expected to be, I unbuckled my seatbelt and got out. My legs were shaking as I slammed the door shut and leaned back against the car, breathing deeply to calm myself down.

The heat hit like a bucket of warm water. Humidity was high, the sun at its zenith. Talk about a scorcher. I liked it. For once, I welcomed the ridiculous anti-British sun as it beat down mercilessly on my ancient locks. My body felt alive, my head cleared, and a calmness settled as the sun baked away the stress bubbling inside.

The Tesla pulled up silently in the car park. The door opened and out stepped a big, solid guy wearing a cut-off t-shirt, jeans, and cowboy boots. I think his jeans were meant to be a loose fit, but on him they hugged his muscular thighs tight. He grinned moronically at me as he squeezed out then closed the door with a nice soft clunk. His car was battered, but nothing compared to mine. I just knew it wasn't his. He'd nicked it, for sure. Not that it was an uncommon crime, as nobody would do anything about it.

The peace I'd felt deepened. Here it was, the calm before the storm. I lowered my hand and undid the popper that kept my blade secure in its sheath. The driver followed my hand with his eyes then locked on mine and said, "What, you too much of a coward to fight me with your hands?"

"I'm not afraid, but I want to win." I shrugged.

"Coward. You're a fucking pussy."

"Nope, you got that wrong, buddy. But like I said, I win my fights."

"Chickenshit," he laughed. "You took my peaches."

I stared at him, nonplussed. "Huh?" was the only smart thing I managed.

"My peaches. Your type are all take. You grab what you want, don't share. Don't think about the next person. It's people like you that mean there's not enough to go round. Always stockpiling. Greedy fucks, the lot of you."

"Look, I have absolutely no idea what you're talking about."

"You took my fucking peaches!" he screamed, then wiped the spittle.

"Your head looks like a ripe peach," I told him calmly. "Why aren't you wearing a hat? You'll get burned. It only takes a few minutes. Have you got sunscreen? Did you get your quota?"

"What?" he snapped. "What business is it of yours?" Unconsciously, he rubbed at his glowing bald head then glowered. "You people are all the same."

"What are you going on..." Then I understood. "You mean in the shop, don't you? That shop at the last village? Um, I bought some stuff, yes. The owner said he had peaches from his orchard, so I bought them. They were a good price. He was nice. Is this what you're talking about?"

"Like you didn't know. I came in right after you and I always buy peaches from there. And what do I find? Some greedy fuck bought the lot. No consideration for others."

"If you want the peaches, you can have the peaches. I didn't even consider I was being greedy. The owner said he was worried they'd go to waste, seemed keen to sell the ones I bought. I thought I was helping him out."

"Bastard."

"Hey, I said you can have them. You try to kill me over peaches and I let that slide, even offer them to you, and you call me names? What gives?"

"What gives? What gives?" he roared. "Everything, that's what. It's all so fucked-up. There's no phone, or internet, or anything now. Did you know that?"

"Yeah, I know."

"And what, you happy about that are you? One of these nutjobs who thinks we should go back to living in caves and wear fucking sandals and eat lettuce every day? Is that it?"

"Sandals keep your feet cool in summer." I stared down at my own boots and then his even more inappropriate ones.

"You taking the piss?"

"Just trying to lighten the mood. I know it's rough at the moment, but we just have to stick with it, see it through."

"I'm sick of doing that. Not allowed to go anywhere, do anything. Can't visit my parents, can't go to work as they decided they only need half the people and we can all work from home. They keep changing the money. I don't know what the fuck it is at the moment. And you gotta have a fucking recycling bottle to buy milk. Where's the bloody snacks? That's what I want to know. No choice, no nice things. And there's no cheese. Cheese! Where's the cheese at? I need cheese!"

"My wife was saying the same thing. There is definitely a cheese conspiracy going on. I mean, if there's milk, there's cheese, right?" I winked, which looking back on it maybe I shouldn't have.

"Are you trying to fuck with me? What's your problem, pal? You are so going to get your ass kicked."

"Hey, come on, I was just trying to make a joke. Why are we fighting? What, would you try to kill someone over peaches? Have them. I told you. I don't want to fight you."

"You ain't got a choice. I am sick of this crap. I want electric and I want to watch the TV and go to the cinema and have a pint down the pub and just be normal."

"It's not normal to run people off the road in a stolen car then threaten them because they bought peaches," I told him.

"No, I guess not. But then, these aren't normal times, are they?" He sneered, then flexed his muscles.

"I get it. You're pissed off, want things to go back to how they were, and you're beyond frustrated. I understand all of that. But why take it out on me? I'm asking you nicely, can we just forget about this?"

"No, we can't. Now, drop the knife and let's have us a good old fist fight." He grinned, then cracked his knuckles and stormed forward.

I fondled the hilt of my knife. It brought comfort. It was warm and fit my hand perfectly. It would be so easy to stab him in the eye and leave him for dead. I could drag him into the bushes and let him rot away. But we would have been watched on the motorway. I was surprised there were no drones here already. Surely the police should be out? Then I realized that no, nobody would have seen. That was why he was acting like this. Because he could. Because nobody was watching. He wouldn't be in trouble because nobody saw.

But if that was the case, I could always...

I sucked it up and morphed. The pain hit before the morph by a millisecond, then I was screaming in and out of the void as I appeared beside the dude's car. I whistled, and as he turned, bewildered and wide-eyed, I scraped the point of my knife across the side of the car in a pointless act of vandalism I regretted instantly for its moronic nature and because I'd blunt my knife.

"What the...? How did you...?"

"I'm your worst nightmare. You want to take out your frustrations on someone? Pick someone your size. You're a bully. I gave you countless chances to leave this alone. You already nearly killed me, and I get that you're angry with the weather, with the stupid laws, the whole thing, but you have to be honest with yourself and admit it for what it is."

"You vanished! How did you do that?"

"I am not like you. I'm different. To be honest, that was a stupid thing to do. But nobody is watching, are they? That's why you did this to me. Because you can. I get it now. You just needed an excuse to do something violent. And not being seen was that excuse. Not the fucking peaches. Which, by the way, were delicious." I licked my lips and smiled at the confused man.

Looking at it from his point of view, it was understandable how shell-shocked he was. After all, people do not simply vanish and appear behind you. It doesn't compute for regular folk. Their brain can't handle it and it crosses their wires, utterly disturbs what they think is true and what's magic.

That's what was going through his head right now. How had I performed this trick? How was it done? What trickery was this.

I didn't give him time to think. As he walked back towards me, I morphed again, opened my car door, and pulled out the bag of peaches.

"Here," I told him. "I honestly don't want to fight. I have killed more people than you could possibly imagine or believe. I have done it to protect my family. Or killed because people attacked me. Have even killed because they threatened to hurt my dog. And I have killed because it is them or me. But I only do it as a last resort. If there is no other option. There's an option. So take the damn peaches and go home. But promise me one thing?"

"What?" he asked in a daze.

"Don't let it change you. All this that's happening, the way the world is now. It's never going to return to how it was. I don't know what's coming, but everything has changed so much already. You can bet it will change again. Trust me, it always does. So go with it. Try to find peace somewhere. And enjoy the peaches."

I threw the bag at him. Surprisingly, he caught it. I reached back into the car and ripped the loaf in half. "And a bonus for you." I chucked the loaf which he caught one-handed.

He stared at the bag then pulled out a perfect, rose-tinted peach.

"Go on, take a bite," I encouraged.

He bit into it. Juice dribbled down his beard. He locked eyes on me and said, "Sorry."

I nodded, then got in my car and drove away.

"Guy sure did like his peaches," I told myself as I rejoined the A5 and continued on my way to destroy the life of a stranger.

Then I changed my mind and turned around.

Tough Decisions

I pulled up beside the battered Tesla where the fruit lover was standing and eating the peaches greedily. The stones were discarded at his feet. The paper bag was on the ground too. So was the half loaf of bread I'd given him. It was squashed. He'd stuck his boot on it.

"It's me again," I told him as I exited the car.

He wiped his mouth as he glanced down at the mess at his feet then up at me. This blight on the earth, this maggot, glared, trying to act the hard man. "You forget something?" he asked gruffly.

"Kind of. I think I made a mistake. I was trying to be nice. I'm not even sure why. Maybe because I'm sick of the killing. Sick of bad things happening. Bad people." I locked my eyes on his and refused to look away even as he glanced sideways.

"Yeah, well, these are tough times and people do desperate things."

"Right?" I agreed. "And that's why I was so calm when we just spoke. Even though you tried to kill me because you wanted peaches. I decided to give you a chance, was going to give you a chance. I gave you my bread." I made it a point to stare at the mushy loaf.

"Sorry, dropped it. It's just bread." He shrugged.

"No, it isn't just fucking bread," I hissed. "It's everything. Those peaches you're stuffing into your face then dropping on the ground, that bag there, and especially the bread I shared with you, it's everything."

"What are you talking about?" He tensed up and changed his stance from casual to ready to fight. He had no idea.

"I'm talking about what's wrong with the world. I'm talking about me trying to be nice and not hurt anyone. For a change, I wanted to be the good guy. Even though you are clearly psychotic and tried to ram me off the road, I still gave you the benefit of the doubt. I wanted to believe you were just having a rough time and that the way things are right now was just too much for you. And I nearly convinced myself. But you aren't good. You aren't nice. You're mean, don't give a shit about anyone else, are so consumed with how unfair the world is for you. Just you. You're a bully. That's what you are. And I despise bullies."

His face reddened as he threw the peaches to the ground and snarled, "You'd best get back in your car and get the fuck out of here before I do something you'll regret. You don't get to talk to me like that. Nobody talks to me like that."

"What, you just take what you want and backhand anyone that argues, is that it?"

"I stand up for myself."

"No, I stand up for myself. You're a bully. There's a big difference. So, I want my peaches back." I stared at the pulpy mess, the litter, and just sighed. "You're a litter lout too. Pick it up. All of it. And maybe I won't poke your eyes out."

"You're crazy, you know that? I'll destroy you. I don't take shit from anyone. Especially not some wimp who thinks he can bluff it out."

He stepped forward; I caught the smell of his body odor. Stale, but with a sickly sweet aroma of peaches. He pulled a fake punch and said, "Boo!" expecting me to jump back and he'd have a good laugh about it, but I didn't move a muscle. I could read him; I'd had years of practice. He frowned, then rubbed at the sweat on his forehead. Then he grinned. "Guess you and me are going to have to sort this out like men then. None of your magic tricks," he warned.

"Guess so." I unfastened my knife again and gripped the ebony handle. It felt like coming home.

"Hey, what the fuck do you think you're doing?" he blurted, eyes wide.

"I'm going to kill you," I told him.

"Very funny. Come on, fight me like a man. Put your hands up and let's have at it."

I frowned, making a show of it, exaggerating my movements. "Why would I do that? I have a knife. I told you, I'm going to kill you. After what you did, the fact you could have killed not only me but others on the road, I think that's fair, don't you?"

"Are you bloody serious?" he asked, still unsure if I was joking or not.

"Let's find out." I shifted left, and as he moved to follow, not even considering it was a feint, I turned sharply to my right, ducked, swung at my waist so my right arm could get in low and fast at his side, and embedded the knife into his kidney. I yanked out hard, skipped lightly behind him, then reached around and slit his throat before he had the chance to do anything but scream. It cut off fast as blood bubbled from his gaping neck wound.

I jumped back as he toppled over; his head smashed into the curb and cracked his skull. Blood seeped from the fracture. The pool spread, mingling with the peaches, and soaked into the bread and bag.

I walked to my car, grabbed a bag, and scooped everything up then wondered what I should do with it. Find a bin, I supposed, but nobody came here, no bins would be emptied, so I'd take it with me then burn it later.

What about this guy?

I looked skyward, but of course there were no drones, no cameras here either, but had we been seen on the road? Would someone remember me if the body was found here? Would there be a search for a missing person and could it lead to me eventually?

Maybe I was over thinking things. But it always paid to be careful and ensure your tracks were covered. I went through the whole scenario. Cars had passed us. What had they seen? Nothing. We were alone on the road when he'd rammed me. What could link me to him then? The damn peaches, that was what. He'd come after me, and if anyone inquired at the shop about him, my name would come up, and my details thanks to the bank card. Damn. This wasn't good.

What to do?

"Where are you, my friend?" I called to Tyr.

"Tyr is here," he replied. I scoured the sky and he suddenly appeared, a glowing fireball as the sun reflected off his immortal hide. Tyr spiraled down then landed silently on the grass beside the man.

"Soph killed man?"

"Yes, I did."

Tyr stared at me for a while, seeing all, knowing all. It was almost disturbing, but I had nothing to hide from my friend. He did not judge me; he wasn't wired that way. The world was a different place for a creature like Tyr. He was a true hunter, an immortal of the Necroverse, and under my care. He trusted me implicitly and knew me so well.

Tyr was now fully in control of his newfound abilities to see beyond the everyday and read mannerisms, but more than that. He had the abilities of a seer, could see the many possible futures, wind back the present to witness the past, and above all else he simply did not care about the man before us.

"Can you get rid of him for me, please?" I asked.

"Tyr can dissolve man no problem." Without any further communication, he simply craned his head forward and vomited the acid juices, a byproduct of the fires that burned within, and spewed over the man from head to toe. Not wasting an opportunity, I threw the bag onto the man's fast-dissolving stomach and everything slowly dissolved. First the skin bubbled, then the meat, then even the bones liquefied under the power of Tyr's acid.

The skull split open as the acid ate through the fracture first. Brain popped and spat then that too was gone as the head sank into the slushy pile.

Tyr watched it without emotion then opened his jaws wide and belched fire over the entire area, washing it clean and destroying any shred of evidence, until nothing was left but a patch of chewed tarmac.

He glanced over to me, watching me without moving, then asked, "Soph is happy?"

"I've been in better moods, my friend, but thank you for the help. What have you been up to? Having fun?"

He nodded his noble head. "Tyr has been hunting on the wing, catching birds for practice. Not many drones, only Necrodrones. Tyr likes it when they are quiet."

As if on cue, a solitary Necrodrone buzzed overhead then descended and spun around Tyr once. It darted over to me at head height and held still for a moment before lazily rising then shooting up. The damn thing might have been out of my sight, but I got the feeling it could see us in minute detail even from up high.

"I think it's time to leave," I told him.

"Tyr will follow Soph. Watch over him."

"Thank you, my friend. We will rest together this evening, if that sounds okay."

"Would like that. Be with Soph now Tyr is grown and big as the bus. Have large fire?"

"Um, it's a bit hot for a big one, but we'll have a fire for sure."

Tyr vanished. I heard the beating of his wings as he flew off, felt hot air waft my face. I could smell him. An unmistakable scent of dragon. Fiery, sharp, like a crisp fire. Yet he was invisible, and you would never know he was there unless you knew what the signs were.

I stared at the still-hissing ground. It was hard to believe a man had been lying there moments ago.

And the peaches. Those fucking peaches.

Getting on With It

I ummed and aahed about what to do regards the car. At some point, and it could be within hours, the internet would be back on, someone would report this guy as missing, and the search might begin. It was doubtful it could be traced back to me, but there was always a risk. There was no body now, so it would be impossible to prove I'd done anything, but I hated crap like this. Last thing I wanted was the police snooping around. We had enough hassle in our life as it was.

Could the cameras monitoring the roads still be recording without internet to relay the information? I wished I could look it up to check. I decided that no, they were as good as dead. Nothing to worry about. But I should ditch the car anyway, as then I could easily deny all knowledge and there was no way to prove a damn thing. At times like this I missed having a companion, but I would hate for it to be Phage, and there was nobody else I would be able to endure at such a time.

Could I get Tyr to drive? He could become a man, and had some crazy powers now. Maybe he could drive the car out of here and push it off a cliff? No, that was stupid. He'd never manage it. Maybe I should just set fire to it? Burn it out. But what was the point? It would still be recognizable as a Tesla, and could be linked to the missing man. They would know it was his. But that wasn't right either, because he'd admitted it was stolen. I decided to just say screw it and leave it exactly where it was without touching it. Main thing was I couldn't be linked to him.

How many cameras were there on the roads? I figured a lot, but couldn't be sure, and I genuinely had no idea how they worked. Surely they would have computers inside that kept records even if they couldn't send the signals to a remote monitoring station. Were they even monitored? I tried to pull up old information I hadn't really taken in very well, and believed it was all handled via computers theses days. Automatic speeding fines, automatic license plate recognition, but how many of them still worked? After all, there weren't enough vehicles to worry about such things.

But I wasn't taking any chances.

"Tyr, I need you again. I need you to go back to the shop and destroy any cameras in the area. I know it makes you feel funny, but you just need to fly close to them and they'll malfunction. Can you do that?"

"What they look like?"

I sent several mental images to him and I sensed him nod. Communication with Tyr was so different now. He used less words, but understood so much more.

While I checked the area to ensure I was in the clear, and I knew I was overthinking this, he updated me on his findings.

"Big yellow boxes not working. No computers. Big dark ones same. No strange things inside. Cameras on streets made Tyr's head go funny, but Tyr flew past and now not work."

"Great. That's great. Thank you."

I felt Tyr's hot breath on my neck. I turned and stared into his large eyes. He snorted; the scent of sulfur and death soothed me. "Soph happy now?"

"Yes, very. Sorry to be a pain."

"Tyr always help Soph. Are best friends. Like Jen."

"Yes, we are. Right, wow, glad that's over with. Okay, that's it until later. Keep an eye on me. We'll find a place to camp for the night later on."

Tyr nodded then was gone again.

It wasn't difficult to understand why so many cameras were now defunct. Why bother? The checkpoints were how they controlled everyone's movements. That, and the drones which had improved coverage and were much better tech than many of the antiquated fixed cameras. My guess was that over the years many had been decommissioned, leaving just a few on the main roads but relying more on the drones and an actual police presence to deter people. It was one thing thinking you might be spotted via a camera, quite another to have an armed policeman telling you to go home or you'd be arrested.

I was in a catch-22. With the kill switch in full action, people were already acting wild, but if everything had been working then all of that would have been recorded yet probably never have happened.

What I really wanted was for it to be a hundred or maybe two-hundred years ago where none of this would have been a concern. I'd also have been able to keep the peaches.

Finally, I was satisfied, or satisfied enough that I could never be found guilty. Even if I got a visit, I could act dumb. Deny everything apart from having a ding with the guy then going on my way. I got back into the car and headed off.

It wasn't until I got several miles down the road that the obvious hit me. What the fuck had I been worried about? Every single year Phage and I headed out into this world full of drones and cameras and spies on every corner. The Necroverse always protected us. I made it a thing to ensure I never killed with a regular drone or camera watching, and always got rid of the body if I could, but I had never been visited by the law because I'd been tracked on camera. Our progress was always kept secret, or at least the important parts.

Maybe I didn't need to worry, or maybe now the kill switch was in operation I needed to worry more. The more I thought about it, the more I believed our unseen masters would take care of things. After all, they wanted the action to take place when the notes were fulfilled. They wanted us obeying their rules, not anyone else's. They needed the spectacle, the drama, the misery, and the blood. Always the blood.

Pain and heartache was their goal, their intent. Not some local policeman getting overly keen and taking you in for questioning.

Maybe I had nothing to worry about at all.

Maybe I had everything to worry about.

Drunken Musings

After more mind-numbing miles than I cared to count, I was thoroughly bored.

No Tyr to talk to, no chance encounters with other creatures, no mishaps, trips, punctures, or moaning about the heat. I was trapped in a cool box while the world whizzed by without me being a part of it.

Traffic was sparse verging on comic. It was only when driving that you got the true picture of how much the world had reverted. The massive three, sometimes four-lane roads cutting deep swathes of death across the countryside, where nothing grew, were still a blight. More so than ever now they served such little purpose.

Had it really been so choked with traffic that even in the middle of nowhere we had to cater for so many vehicles? It had. It wasn't just cities that were rammed with vehicles, it was the whole country. Where had everyone been going? What were we all doing? It was understandable that delivery vehicles and certain trips were necessary, but what had everyone else been doing?

I had no idea. But they had been busy. You never got far without a traffic jam, a series of roadworks, or an accident of some description stopping you dead and leaving you trapped in your vehicle, frustrated, your temper rising.

I was alone.

Cut off from what made me whole. What made me feel like I belonged. Time outside was so important to me. I got antsy, grumpy, and depressed if I didn't get daylight, didn't surround myself with nature and get stuck in to the gardening.

One day it simply clicked. Do the things that lift your spirits. Watch your mind, see how it reacts to different tasks. Then do those tasks on a daily basis if possible to keep yourself in a positive frame of mind. It's why I exercised every morning. Why I dug holes, repaired posts, tended the garden, and kept the animals in as much comfort as our budget would allow. All of those things kept my brain in check, gave me the positive vibes I needed to face another day.

But I was on a road to perform another kind of dirty task, where my hands would be bloodied and my mind twisted just that tiny bit more. Even more reason to ensure I felt a part of this world, part of nature, as I'd have to dig a fuck ton of holes to feel better after what I was about to do.

I knew what I needed, so I decided this was enough for the day. After checking the route, I made a decision, and slipped off the road at the next junction and crossed into quieter country, weaving my way across Wales until I was on lanes surrounded by fields. I pulled over in a lay-by to check the map as the sat nav was hopelessly out of date, and searched for blue lines indicating streams. Five minutes later, I was parked up at an old car park for walkers at the edge of a large deciduous forest.

The moment I stepped out of the car I felt better. I breathed deeply of the smell of nature in all its glory. The shade and the peaty soil in this area meant the ground under the dense canopy was still damp despite the crazy heat. The humidity was high, but so was the water level in the numerous steams that criss-crossed the forest right by the car park. Keen to enter, I grabbed my gear and hiked along a wide path that sank down into the woods.

Huge ancient trees loomed either side of the path. Down a steep drop off on the left, spindly young saplings grew high and straight, reaching for the light, fed by meager streams almost hidden by ferns and rhododendrons. The blooms were over, but their glossy leaves dazzled when dappled sunlight hit. It was glorious.

I stopped just to take it all in, and breathed deeply, washing away the tang of car fumes, replacing it with nature's majesty. I followed the path then took a turn on a narrow mossy track that climbed up high into the woods. The low light and the springy ground eased my throbbing back and left me relaxed, almost hypnotized.

Not a soul around, not even the shout of a distant walker calling their dog. Just me and the trees.

Perfect.

After ten minutes, I reached the summit of a modest hill and found myself staring at the beautiful countryside in a panoramic three-sixty view. Rolling hills, dry stone walls, stock proof fencing, small thickets. It was wondrous. Houses dotted the vista like sheep in the distance. Farms and villages large and small nestled in the creases of hills or hunkered down in valleys, where drying rivers crawled sluggishly through the landscape. The best of the British countryside in all its majesty.

I admired the view for several minutes then had to escape the sun so moved into the woods beside the tiniest of streams, little more than a trickle. But the ground was soft and green with numerous moss species, the water made a relaxing gurgle as it tickled the boulders, and I found a deep pool where I set a sneaky bottle, okay two, of nasty wine and willed it to cool as fast as possible.

While I waited, I set up camp. I gathered plenty of dry firewood by snapping off low hanging dead branches, collected larger logs and plenty of kindling from the open at the edge of the forest where it was baked dry by the heat of years, then returned several times until I had enough to last the night.

Once the fire was roaring, I pulled out my sleeping bag and placed a blanket underneath on a dry patch of earth beside the fire. A tree offered welcome support for my aching back. I wasn't used to sitting in a car, so my hips were tight and my shoulders knotted. I spent ten minutes just sitting there, letting each muscle relax until I felt better than I had since this all began.

I focused on the fire, listened to the crackle and pop of the wood, enjoying the silence. I didn't need the heat, but a fire offers more than that. It provides a sense of place, a focus. I was famished, too, so cooking up a treat sent my mouth to watering as I considered my options.

There was chicken or there were sausages, bacon, and eggs. Being wise, I chose chicken, plus bacon and eggs. And sausages. I was alone, so nobody could comment on them not going together, and if a man can't cook his dinner however he wants when alone, when can he?

I laid everything out, careful to set the compact pan right on the edge of the coals, and let it cook slowly while I just messed about with the fire, removed my boots, and generally just prodded stuff until it looked ready.

When it was nearly done, I retrieved a bottle from the pool, poured myself a hearty mug of nasty British wine, then set the bottle back in the water and sat by the fire, eating, drinking, and listening to the coals crackle and the birds sing.

What a treat to return to my usual habits when on my yearly expedition. Why didn't I do this more often, rather than just once a year? It would be so much better without the stress of having to kill looming over me. Rather than this kind of trip being forever associated with bad things, I could turn it around and make it purely for fun.

I knew I wouldn't. I was no man out for answers on an expedition through life. My summit had been reached and I wanted nothing more than to stay at the dizzying heights of home and family. That was truly my place.

But how enjoyable this was. Being alone, no immediate worries, plenty of food, cheap booze, a nice fire, and no tech.

When would the kill switch be flicked back on? Would it ever be? Or was this our reality now? A true severing of humanity's technological progress, and a return to simpler times? Part of me wished for that, another not. And I knew it wouldn't last. That one way or another all that was lost would return.

I could only laugh when I thought about the uproar around the world that would currently be in progress. Governments would be going all out to uncover the reason for the blackout, tech companies verging on meltdown. There would be untold disasters and endless problems because of this, so it would undoubtedly all be turned back on soon enough.

Unless, and this was the chilling thought, it was done with complete cooperation of the world's rulers. Maybe now we'd truly see who ran our countries, our world. Would we finally uncover the truth that it wasn't our leaders in government who were in charge, but an as yet unknown secret organization? A massive tech company, or a pharmaceutical giant that actually called the shots?

Or maybe I was just a conspiracy theory junkie, and what we saw was truly what we got. A bunch of people ruling us so out of touch with the reality of existence down here in the mire that it may as well have been a troop of monkeys in charge. They'd probably make better decisions and at least there'd be bananas.

But I had to remind myself that I wasn't exactly a regular guy, and had no real clue how "normal" people went about their lives. Sure, I got an inkling, maybe even a sour taster of it, but my life was not theirs, and theirs was not mine. What the fuck did I know? Less than nothing, probably.

So I comforted myself with wine, and a lot of charred protein, and all was well in the world for a while.

Late into the night, brooding on the death I'd felt compelled to dole out earlier that day, and the haunted faces of the hundreds of men I'd killed floating above the fire with their silent screams, I stumbled into the woods for a steaming pee. The wine had got to me, but I already had the beginnings of a hangover so I knew there was only a single recourse. After I'd zipped up, I fished out the other bottle and slumped back against the tree and stared into the flames.

Where was Tyr? I was about to reach out to him when I decided to leave him be. He was more independent now, didn't need me badgering him and checking up all the time. Much like Jen, scarily so in fact, he was beginning to find his own place in the world, and I should let him have this time alone if that was what he desired. Instead, I swigged wine from the bottle, no longer bothering with the tin mug, and watched the flames dance.

There were no sprites this fine evening, just me and the fire and the moon. It was almost full, but not quite. A cold, strong light that lit up the forest in monochrome, affording me brief glimpses of deer, rabbits, and other creatures taking advantage of the warm evening and the chance to forage or hunt in their own piece of paradise.

Would the promises of those in charge ever come to pass, and our country once again return to the rich, diverse ecosystem it once had? Would new trees in their millions be planted, the grip of monoculture finally eradicated, the forests expanded, wild boar re-introduced? Was that even the right thing to do? We had to feed people, we had to look after each other, but we had to ensure the country wasn't bulldozed over and every spare piece of land built on.

Again, no answers from me. I just thanked my lucky stars I wasn't the one making these kinds of decisions.

Every new idea to save our planet was met with equal measure of enthusiasm and backlash. Things had definitely changed for the better, but there was no permanent solution to the energy crisis. Plans had been implemented to cover huge swathes of the Sahara and other desert lands with endless rows of solar panels, enough to light up the entire world. It had seemed great.

But the first trials uncovered insurmountable problems. We'd simply generate too much heat, the panels would warm the world more than it had already done, the volume of water needed to run such undertakings made it impossible to be viable, and the cost of producing, then replacing, the panels and the damage that caused meant it was dead in the water before it even got properly started. Not to mention the issue of actually storing such a volume of energy until it was needed, and the incredible losses when electricity was sent through cables over long distances.

Who was right? Nobody knew.

Countless other ideas had begun then halted. There were breakthroughs, setbacks, and complications I could never understand. The only overriding thing anyone could agree on was that if everyone turned the lights off and nobody drove, then that would definitely work. But everyone sensed the unease. It had to end soon or there'd be serious repercussions. Humanity was coming to the end of its tether, and this kill switch business might be the straw that finally broke the camel's back.

Or we'd all get along and decide that yes, it's awesome without the internet or communication or driving or going to shops or having any nice cheese, so let's all buy a horse and begin a new hobby. That'll teach the bastards.

Maybe that would happen. But I had my doubts.

I laughed out loud at my own idiocy. Here I was, half pissed, trying to figure out world problems the greatest minds of our time couldn't even agree on at a basic level. Hell, nobody could even decide what constituted family any longer. But I knew.

It was the ones you loved and wanted to spend time with. End of. Not blood relations, not just a sense of duty, but people you genuinely loved and cared for. That was family in my eyes. Just a shame all of mine apart from two wondrous ladies were fucking mental. But that's what made life fun and interesting, at least for this pissed Necro alone in the woods talking to the fire because it was the only time he was allowed to spew his crap without getting a serious tongue-lashing.

Damn, I need another pee. I grabbed the tree for support, heaved up, and stumbled off.

When I returned, and stared back into camp, I suddenly became very sober, very fast.

Old Not Friends

My gear was strewn around camp, everything in total disarray. The remaining food was gone, the bones and all, and I had myself to blame for that. The fire roared, casting a strong orange glow on the pitiful creature prowling around the clearing at a safe distance then darting forward to snatch at things, sniff, then discard if it wasn't edible. It was doing a good job; I think he'd got everything already.

Too late to shimmy up a tree, the creature's head snapped around and unsettling green eyes locked on mine. The man-wolf snarled, baring sharp teeth that would make short work of me. I inched my hand down to my side, hoping to grab my knife, but there was intelligence behind those eyes and he snarled louder as he shook his wild, patchy mane from side to side in warning.

I nodded my understanding, and instead moved my hands in front of me then clasped them together, hoping he'd realize I meant no harm.

On all fours, the poor beast continued his search, taking his eyes off me only for a brief moment at a time, flashing his teeth repeatedly in warning. I got the message loud and clear.

But something wasn't quite right with this werewolf— although the term wasn't very common amongst Necros, as it conjured up too many images of bad movies and misinformation. He was a simple shifter, an animorph. But somewhere in his genetic history something had gone screwy, so rather than having the ability to shift into the shape of a wolf, things got confused and he ended up being neither fully one thing nor the other.

The few stories of lycanthropes I knew of, and could be at least partly relied upon, told that much of the time they were like others who could morph. They could choose the time and place, and it certainly helped them fulfill their notes if they could keep their minds focused enough and not lose themselves to the animal. According to Phage, something commonplace amongst their kind.

But when the moon was powerful, close to full, and especially when full, then they had little choice in what happened. They could fight it all they wanted, but change they would, so extreme caution had to be taken. Theirs was a life no other Necro envied. They were prisoners of their own powers.

Most died young, either unable to live with themselves and the things they did when a wild animal, or killed by other Necros when the yearly notes rolled around because they were a danger to our kind, to innocents, as it was all too easy for them to let themselves be seen and risk exposure. That was not something many Necros wished for.

Sure, a few thought we should rise up, take control. But truth be told, we were few and far between in a world of regular people. Uprising led to nowhere but more trouble than we all already had.

This poor soul was clearly struggling. I guess the pull of the moon wasn't quite strong enough to force him to change fully, but he couldn't draw back enough to become human. He was stuck in a terrible limbo where every thought would be like a scream, every movement confusing to a human body, and every forced human movement bewildering to the animal within.

I was stunned he'd lasted for so long. Well into adulthood and beyond. And I recognized him. I'd seen him before, when I had the blessing of foresight and was up a tree. That was several years ago now, but the markings were unmistakable. Guess this guy was either lucky or seriously hardcore.

The thick white patch of fur beneath his chin was dirty white, longer than the rest of his brown fur and hair combo. It was hard to tell which was which as either this was a naturally hairy dude or he simply grew it all when he changed. I'd met bald men who were shaggy dogs, and shaggy men who were bald cats, so you could never tell.

His face was just as unfortunate as the rest of him. The eyes were wolf-like but unmistakably human—aside from the bright green. His snout was stretched out but the nose was that of a man. His ears ended in blunt points but he still wore an earring, and although the eyebrows were bushy, it was nothing a quick trim wouldn't sort out. He moved mostly on all fours, but would stop and squat then bounce forward in a crouched position only to use his long fingers to scramble about with great dexterity. The legs and arms themselves were definitely human, but his ribcage and chest were as you'd expect from a wolf, and the long tail certainly made the overall effect very canine.

Seemingly finished with his rounds, he squatted with his back to the fire and watched me.

"Hey," I called quietly, "you still hungry? Can you understand me?" I reached out mentally to him as I had once before, but unlike last time I didn't have to retreat instantly. His head was a mess of warring thoughts and emotions, but there was more man than wolf there and he was regaining control fast.

He never spoke, but I "heard" the silent hunger within, so I tried speaking directly to him, more imagery than words, in the hope it would get through easier. I pictured myself searching in my pack and pulling out bread, slices of meat, and several apples, then tried to conjure the emotion of us happily sitting under the tree and biting into the apples, him less wolf, more man than currently.

He didn't speak out loud or even silently, not in words, but I felt the longing for company, to be a man again, and the incessant hunger. Yes, it was mostly for raw, fresh meat, but beggars can't be choosers. He would settle.

We snapped out of the connection the moment I moved guardedly towards my pack. With a growl, the beast shuffled forward, ready to pounce, but I kept going and soon I had the food. I sighed as I wondered what the hell I was playing at, and understood that maybe I was lonely. That I needed company tonight, and hardly ever spent time with other men, even very hairy ones. Was that it? Did I just want a pal?

I honestly didn't miss other people's company, but maybe tonight was different. Maybe I needed something to stop the nightmares, the dreams of killing over and over. Not that the killing was the nightmare, it was my lack of guilt at what I did that always got me. I should feel worse, yet although I hated killing, I lamented being unable to feel true sorrow and regret for taking the lives, just an overall ennui for having to kill at all.

Maybe it was a defense mechanism. I certainly knew what I did was wrong, and I was broken on too many levels for me to ever understand, so I did what I could and just felt sorry for myself. But maybe tonight there would be a reprieve.

I placed the food on the ground after taking an apple for myself, then sat there, meeting the poor thing's eyes, and took a bite.

Crunch.

Crisp, fresh, and delicious. At the sound, his ears pricked up. He sniffed the air then came within reach and snatched the apple. He tore it in half with a twist of a hand, which was impressive, then stuffed the piece into his mouth and chewed loudly. Juice ran into the fur, and as he began on the second half so his body began to relax. With relaxation came a slow, painful change.

There was nothing I could do to help. All I could do was watch and sympathize. At least he was changing, so I wasn't about to be the main course.

The hair receded first, then his torso shortened with loud cracks as ribs rearranged, and then his face gradually returned to that of a man. It took several minutes in total, rather than the usual few seconds for other shifts I'd witnessed.

When it was over, he lay on the ground, naked and panting, until the pain receded and he regained his focus.

"How you doing?" I asked when he moved to a sitting position.

"Been better. Been worse," he said gruffly, his voice deep and sour.

"I bet."

"What would you know about it?" he snapped, locking still-green eyes on me.

"I've been around. Seen a lot, done a lot. But I don't shift."

"There you go then, you don't know. Even the other shifters think they know, but they don't. It's fucking miserable. I hate that side of me. It's not even me, just a dumb animal I'm trapped inside. Don't remember it most of the time, and that's better. It's the remembering that gets me." He hung his head, long brown straight hair with a little silver covered his face and sat lank on his shoulders. His beard was thick and full with the same off-white patch on his chin. It looked cool.

"Sometimes it's better not to know," I agreed.

"Yeah, maybe. But it's a lot to live with. I've done some crazy shit, and that's just what I remember. Sometimes I get flashbacks days or weeks after and it scares the shit out of me. Know what I mean?"

"I know."

"Can I?" He indicated the bread and meat. I nodded for him to go ahead. He jumped at the chance and grabbed it then ate greedily, decimating the half loaf and getting it covered in grime.

When he was finished, he looked down at the remains and said, "Sorry. Excuse my manners. I'm not normally like this. It's the animal, it's still inside. Be better in the morning."

"Don't worry about it. I offered. I'm Soph, by the way."

"Shit, sorry man. Where are my manners? I'm Shiun. But call me Shi. And thanks."

"For what?"

"For not freaking out and trying to kill me. That's always a bonus."

"I wouldn't do that."

"No, but you'd hide up a tree, right?" He winked at me and smiled. "I remember you, from years back. I could sniff you out a mile away. Maybe I did this time. I'm a bit outside my usual haunt, but I go where the wolf goes, so what you gonna do, eh?"

"Guess you have to tag along," I chortled.

"Yeah. Fuck, man, this is so weird. I haven't sat down and spoken to another guy for like, ages. Keep to myself, if you know what I mean?"

"Me too. Less hassle, and I like a quiet life."

"Me too," he agreed, nodding vigorously. "Not that I ever get it. Between this animorph life and the fucking notes there isn't a lot of peace. I mean, it's once a year, right, but it haunts me and seems to take forever. Always recovering, then it's time to go again. Bastard notes, I hate them. What about you? You like some of the others and get a kick out of it? Think it's cool and gives you special rights?"

"No way! I hate it too. If there was one thing I could change, it would be the notes. But I can't."

"Amen, brother. Soph, where do I know that name from? I'm sure I've heard it before."

"No idea. I keep a low profile, but my name gets about. Not out of choice," I grumbled.

"Oh, shit! Of course. You're *the* Soph, right? The one every Necro of a certain age knows about. Shit, man, it's an honor."

"Trust me, it isn't. And you aren't serious, are you? I understand some know my name, but not many, right?"

"Mate, like everyone knows about you. You're a legend. You're what, over three hundred? Aren't many of that age still going."

"I know a few."

"Yeah, sure, but not on your level. Everyone else gets to wind down, but word is you get harder jobs than any other. And you get to see stuff, is that right?"

"Who told you that?" I didn't like where this was going. How would anyone know what happened to me? Then I realized that of course they didn't, it was the usual Necro gossip many loved to get involved in. Especially Necros who hung out together, thinking they were special when they were anything but.

"Dunno, just people. Nothing specific, mind you, just the usual drunken crap I suppose. Anyway, I'm kinda out of the loop, so to speak, so don't listen to me. Don't sweat it. They'll be jabbering about another guy soon enough. You know what they're like."

"Thanks, I appreciate that," I told him, even though we both knew he was just being kind and trying to stop me stressing out.

"No problem. And look, don't suppose you got any spare clothes knocking about, do you? I'm not cold, but I bet you don't want to be staring at my shriveled dick all night."

It took every ounce of willpower I had not to look, and after an awkward silence we both burst out laughing.

"Sorry, now it's all you can think of, right? Sorry."

"It's okay, but let me see what I have. By the way, you have a lot of scars, almost as many as me." I nodded at his chest and the large slash right across his firm pecs.

"Yeah, comes with the territory, right? But I'm not even a hundred yet, still just a kid, so give it time."

"I hear that." I rummaged around and passed him a pair of jeans and a t-shirt as I didn't want to lose one of my valuable shirts. He slipped them on. They were a little baggy for his more wiry frame, but he didn't look half bad.

"What do you think?" he asked, spinning.

"Looking fine," I told him. "You want a drink? I was half pissed but you sobered me up, but now I could do with one."

"Oh, man, seriously? You bet. What you got?"

I held up the bottle and shook it. "Um, a small mouthful of warm wine each. Okay wait here, I'll be back." I headed down the trail and grabbed two bottles from the car then hiked back up. It took half an hour, but it allowed me to get to grips with having a guest, and offered him some privacy to get his head straight too.

I put a bottle in the pool and poured out a generous mug of the other bottle for each of us.

"Cheers," we said, as we clicked metal mugs.

Shi spluttered as he took a big mouthful. "Damn, that is fucking vile. This bloody wine issue is becoming serious."

"Tell me about it. I should have brought my own. I have some seriously vintage homemade brews in my basement. Don't know what I was thinking."

"You should taste my beer. It'll blow your socks off. Mind you, it tastes worse than this shit. Anyway, here's to shit wine and good company."

"Shit wine and good company."

We chatted late into the night about not much at all. Just general banter about life and the Necroverse, without going too deep or depressing each other. We kept it light and funny, and the more wine we drank the lighter we got. He was a good guy, and I was impressed how together he was. It was a rare thing for his kind, and I hoped he'd make it another century. If he'd made it this far, then luck was on his side, so maybe he would.

When I opened a bleary eye in the morning, he was gone. The fire burned brightly, there was a stack of neatly aligned wood, and laid out atop the pile was a skinned rabbit.

I liked him.

Revolution!

The easy roads morphed into smaller typical Welsh ones once I got closer to my destination. I was taking a slight detour to Barmouth, a familiar coastal town on the west coast of Wales. Once a popular place with the tourists because of the massive beaches and awesome ice-cream. I'd always enjoyed the atmosphere, so figured the few extra miles were worth it.

What bugged me most about this trip was that by the looks of it I was heading towards a lighthouse on somewhere called Bardsey Island, which meant it wasn't attached to the mainland. That was a problem. A big one. Boats were not my friend. They liked to rock side to side, but my stomach liked to not be rocked side to side. It enjoyed knowing which way was up and down, and to remain settled exactly where it was, thank you very much.

It was almost like this had been done on purpose.

I tried to put the complication out of my mind. After all, if I'd been sent this way then there was clearly a way to get across to the island. I didn't doubt it would suck, but didn't it always?

The road cutting through the middle of Wales was quiet, verging on empty, as I began the second leg of my journey. A familiar route I'd traveled many times over the years. Not as far north as a few years previously when I'd encountered that bastard Eleron, and he'd had his fun with me, but Wales wasn't exactly a large place so it still brought him to mind, probably because of the boat thing.

It still rankled. Being sent all that way just to mess about with an elf, with no chance of killing him. I was nothing but the warning shot, sent to remind him he wasn't welcome here. Problem being, the bastard had come on purpose just to get into a fight and have a little fun. And then I'd had to jump out of a boat and swim for my life, and had enjoyed neither activity.

Now here I was again, heading towards the sea, except this time I was driving rather than cycling.

Slowly, I got into that mindless state again. Just driving, my mind empty, everything working on autopilot. I just drove, eased around the light traffic, and kept on going.

I don't know when things changed, but I gradually came back to myself and realized that the traffic was actually starting to build up.

No longer was it just the occasional delivery vehicle or monster truck, there were cars and motorbikes, even several coaches with people waving out of the window at me, clearly excited to be out for a trip.

What was going on? Had everyone got a pass like me? These couldn't all be Necros. Could they? I shook my head and laughed at the thought. Of course not. It was because of the kill switch. The world had gone dark and people had finally realized they could do what the fuck they wanted.

The beginning of the end, maybe? Revolution?

No. It seemed more likely that everyone was just out on a jolly to the beach.

I eased up on the speed and took proper notice of the world outside the window. Last thing I wanted was to stand out now. Cars zoomed past, motorbikes roared ahead, the drivers probably feeling free for the first time in years, if they ever had. Some of the younger ones would never have experienced such release, and it showed by the dodgy driving. There were bound to be accidents.

Several miles later, the strangest thing happened. I was in a traffic jam. I slowed, then stopped, and immediately began to tap the steering wheel impatiently. What the fuck?

I couldn't even recall the last time I'd been forced to stop in traffic. Hell, I hadn't driven more than a few miles in so long that I didn't even recall when it was. We didn't do traffic jams these days. It went against all the rules. Everything those lucky enough to drive had come to expect.

I inched forward in first gear, then managed to get up into second only to have to drop back down immediately, and then we came to a dead stop. Ten minutes later, I was edgy and bored so turned off the engine, pocketed the keys, and got out to stretch my legs and check things out.

The driver behind beeped his horn and shouted through his open window for me to stay in my car in case the traffic moved. I glared at him. He wound his window up.

Moving over to the verge, I got a proper look at what the problem was. Seemed like there was a checkpoint, so I headed that way and I wasn't the only one. Most drivers up front were out of their vehicles too, impatient to get wherever it was they were going. Everyone was converging on the problem, which would only make it worse, but I was so intrigued I just had to go see for myself.

It was an utter confusion of stupid people and even more stupid government policy as far as I could gather.

Across the road in both directions, a series of movable barriers were manned by a massive police presence. They were constantly talking into walkie talkies and they didn't look happy about any of it. At least one question of mine had been answered. The police communication channels were open at least to a degree, and their walkie talkies didn't rely on any kind of internet connection. It would severely limit what powers they had, and any information input onto computers wouldn't be connected to their databases, but they were still up and running by the seems of it. I bet it was a nightmare for them, trying to keep control when they were basically working blind.

Not everyone held the same opinion. At the barriers, people were shouting and swearing and generally harassing the poor souls tasked with keeping them safe without receiving any thanks for the hard work.

"Seems like everyone wants to get to the beach," I noted to a young lad standing next to me, wearing a pair of bright swimming shorts, even brighter flip flops, and nothing else apart from a wide-brimmed hat.

"It's revolution at last," he said, clearly very happy about it.

"Or people going to the beach," I told him.

"This is the beginning. We're sick of being held hostage in our homes. We want freedom, and we wanna do what we wanna do. We want to have a good time and we—"

"Isn't that a song?" I asked him.

"Huh? Oh, yeah, old timer, one of the best. You know it?"

"Know it? I was around when it first came out."

The young man studied me, then cracked a wide smile and laughed. "Good one. You nearly got me there. You aren't that old, mate, nobody is."

"Just messing with you. But what's the deal? Why's everyone giving them so much grief?"

"Because we're sick of being trapped. What right do they have to keep us locked up? We want to travel, we want to go party. We want to surf." He indicated a VW camper with several surfboards strapped to the roof. "It's our time now. Time for revolution!" He fist-pumped the air and grinned at me, hyped and eager for action.

"I get that. But what about the rules? You don't care?"

"Why should I? I'm young and I want to have fun. You know," he whispered, moving close to me until I could smell his strange aftershave, clearly a homemade concoction that maybe was what all the youngsters wore these days, "I've never been more than ten miles from my home until now. It's ridiculous. I read all the time, and this ain't right. In my folks' time, and yours I guess, I heard you could drive anywhere, take a flight abroad whenever you wanted, go visit any part of the country just because you felt like it. Even use as much power as you wanted. People used to go surfing every single day. Can you imagine it? Course you can. Bet you got some stories to tell, am I right?"

"I've got a few," I conceded. If only he knew.

"Damn straight. And now I want cool stories of my own. I want adventure. Me and my mates," he indicated three young guys hanging out at the front of the VW, "are done with this shit."

"What about saving the planet? What about keeping the air clean and not using what little fossil fuels are left? Look at all these fumes. Can't you taste it? Can't you smell it?"

"It's the taste of freedom," he laughed. "It's time to shove it to the man. The world has gone dark, the coppers can't possibly process all of us without their computers. I heard the prisons are falling apart, that people are escaping left, right, and center because everything is connected to the web these days. Same for everything. It's meltdown, and we're taking back what's ours."

"But what about the planet?" I asked again, interested to discover how this generation saw things, and what they thought about the life they'd grown up believing was the norm.

"Planet's healed, my friend. They're keeping us in the dark about it all. It's been long enough. The air is clean, the world has changed. We have more than enough power now from wind and solar, and those bloody monstrosities out at sea harnessing the waves. They just don't want us to have it. They want us locked up and under control so they can..."

"Can what?"

He shrugged his shoulders. "Dunno man. But that's the fucking problem, eh? What are these fuckers really up to? Revolution." He ran forward, his mates tagging along, and soon they were lost to the crowd as they joined the chorus of shouts for revolution and general uproar.

I stepped back and onto the verge again, and watched as the crowd turned violent as I knew they would. The police resorted to truncheons and shields to batter them back. It was clear it wouldn't hold, and that this time the police orders were different from before, where the odd shooting had been common for anyone who stepped out of line. The crowd jeered as the police got back into cars and vans, and within several minutes they were simply gone.

The crowd shifted the barriers aside before everyone slowly returned to their vehicles, patting each other on the back and talking excitedly about a new beginning and how they were never going to go back to how things were.

I returned to my own car, and wondered if maybe this was the start of a revolution. Or would everyone fall back in line and do as they were told the moment the kill switch was flipped back on? And what choice would they have? It was all well and good, everyone taking advantage like this with the fuel they had stored, or the bootleg stuff they got, or they'd used a massive amount of their electric quota to charge their vehicle, but give it a day or two when all that was used up and then what? No, we weren't free. We were just blowing off some steam while we had the chance, then we'd be right back where we started.

Or would we?

It was all more than I could understand. All I knew was I had a guy to kill and these bastards were in my way. But I sat in my car, and tapped my foot and slapped the steering wheel until finally the line began to move. Within ten minutes, the vehicles were spread out enough to make it feel like life was how it had been for years, but with a few more cars on the road.

The rest of the journey to the coast was entirely uneventful. More traffic, but nothing major. Nothing like it used to be when anyone could take a trip whenever they felt like it, and fuel was in ready supply. It was more like a very quiet day in the middle of winter, when nobody felt like venturing out. But it wasn't winter, it was the height of summer, and as I hit the narrow road mere feet from a sheer drop to the estuary, I recalled having been stuck in traffic here more times than I cared to remember.

Partly the sheer volume of tourists, but the Welsh seemed to have this uncanny knack of performing all major roadworks during tourist season. At least, they put out the temporary traffic lights to cause problems, although I never actually saw anyone digging up the roads.

Driving under the cover of trees as I skirted the coast, my spirits lifted when I caught sight of the single track rail line running along the bridge that connected Fairmouth to Barmouth. I drove past almost empty car parks right next to the beach at Barmouth, which was a surprise, and watched small groups of people carry gear down the long stretch of sand.

I caught a glimpse of the surfer dude and his buddies running eagerly towards the waves far away. The tide was out and it was quite a ways, but I wished them well and hoped they enjoyed learning to surf. Could they even swim? Did kids learn to swim these days? Jen could, but only because we took her to rivers. There were no open swimming pools any more. Chlorine, and too much energy needed to heat the water, apparently.

Maybe the kid was right, and this was time for revolution. It was easy to forget how simple things like being able to teach your kid to swim in a heated pool had become the stuff of dreams, rather than something you could take for granted.

In just two minutes I was past Barmouth and heading up the coast again. I passed Harlech castle, then on to Portmeirion. A very cool place filled with architectural salvage from across the globe, arranged in a valley where houses were built into the rock and the sprawling gardens and forest were a shady delight on a hot summer's day. But I had no time, or inclination, for sightseeing. I was on a mission, and wanted nothing but to be done with it and back home where I belonged.

Past Portmeirion, I turned west once more along the meandering coast road, heading to the very tip of the county of Gwynedd where the Llŷn Peninsula jutted into the sea. Then I guessed I'd see what the deal was with this fucking island.

The road was good for a while, but soon turned into a royal shitshow of potholes and general neglect. It was passable, though, so I kept on keeping on until I reached the peninsula's end. Steep cliffs and rugged landscape greeted me, but I wasn't quite in the mood for contemplating my crossing just yet so I headed back to a place that looked more inviting, and pulled up in a deserted car park at a place named Aberdaron. Guess the tourists hadn't made it this far.

A long, sandy beach greeted me, and it was just what I needed to clear my head and get some focus. My hips were also killing me, so it would be nice to shake out the stiffness and let the water ease my sweaty feet. The moment I opened the door, I craved the freshness of the water. It was fucking blistering out here.

A faded sign at the end of the car park told me about the local area, but more importantly about the island I'd somehow have to get to if I was to finish this thing. Bardsey Island was just a few miles off the coast, apparently the fourth largest island in Wales, although it wasn't exactly well-known as I'd never heard of it. Apparently, the only way to get there was by boat, obviously, and that there was only a single man who ran trips there. He even had a website. Not that it would do me much good as this was all from years ago, and the tourists weren't exactly flocking here any more. He would have packed it in and moved on to other things.

I figured it would still be worth a trip to Porth Meudwy to check on the off chance I could get a boat somehow. Maybe I'd strike it lucky and find someone willing to take me. That, or just borrow one while I did what I had to do then returned sick as a dog.

The faded board went on to extol the many great things about the lighthouse itself. It was over ninety-eight feet high, which went to show the age of the sign as we'd been metric for so long now, built in 1821, and very unusual in that it was built upon a square design rather than round as was the norm. It was painted in red and white stripes over the bare ashlar limestone and had been converted to solar late in the last century.

Sounded special. If I was here for different reasons, it would have been a cool place to visit and maybe have a picnic. No pleasant family outings today, though. No inclination to marvel at the feats of those long dead, wonder how many lives the lighthouse had saved over the years, because I was here to take one off that number. A destroyer rather than a vanguard of hope.

First things first. It was time to dip my toes in the cool Welsh waters. I knew better than to just get about my business unprepared, as one thing this Necro life had taught me was the one time you aren't ready, the bastards will try to get you, so I spent a while sorting through my gear, tidying everything in the car so it was easily accessible, and cursing the relentless goddamn sun intent on frying a poor, lonely Necro to a frazzled crisp.

Once I'd loaded my pack with essentials only, and felt ready to confront whatever awaited me, I decided to first take advantage of the shade offered by an old toilet block and headed over to the crumbling edifice. I sat under the shade of the nautically themed roof and ate the rest of the rabbit I'd cooked that morning, then finished off the pasta dish Phage had prepared for me. Washed down with some water and a crisp apple, I felt rejuvenated, and if not ready, then at least reluctantly willing to face my immediate future.

Time to get it on.

But first, I got it off. Boots and socks, that is.

The baked car park was so hot my feet began to blister almost immediately, so I had no choice but to put it all back on again and wait until I was closer to the water.

With a groan of self-pity, I made my way down to the beach and hoped I'd be alone. I wasn't in the mood for chit-chat with would-be revolutionaries or anyone else. I liked some alone time before the shit hit the proverbial sharp-edged fan of destruction.

On The Beach

The sun's ferocity stepped up several gears as I ambled along the shore. The damp sand felt joyous beneath my feet. It rasped as I dug my toes in, alternating with pressing my heels deep and watching as the indents filled with water.

A warm breeze brought tantalizing promises of adventure, and misadventure, from the west. Salt caught in my hair. I tried to untangle it with calloused and torn fingers, then gave it up as a lost cause. Tyr, who'd appeared from nowhere and without warning, or even a word to me yet, followed my progress from the bottom of the sand dunes, almost purring with contentment as his thick pads sank into the bone-dry sand. It was too hot for me to walk on, but for him it was like being in paradise.

There wasn't a soul in sight. After all, what idiot, even an Englishman, would be out walking on the beach at midday on such a blisteringly hot day? Only one with a Necronote to fulfill, or fluff, that's who.

I imagined I spied the unusual lighthouse in the far distance, little but a red and white finger pointing to the sky, as if asking for redemption from the big guy. Beckoning. Calling. Pleading. But I couldn't see it from here. I would need to get onto the island for that.

There was no redemption. There was nothing but hurt. Pain upon pain. Compounded until I just wanted to scream. To tear everything apart, rip it away and reveal something fresh and pristine beneath. Like the tide going out, leaving nothing but smooth, untainted sand behind. But I knew however many layers I peeled back, there would always be more corruption. More foulness. Always more mess than it was possible to scour. I could never scrub clean so much filth. Much of it my own doing.

A sharp gust tugged at my hat and I almost lost it, so I folded it up and pocketed it, then rubbed my meager allowance of lemon-scented, sour sunscreen over my face again. It irritated my skin as I smeared sand and salt into my cheeks. The protective balm mingled with sweat immediately.

The unique air of the coast, the salty tang on my tongue, the wind and wildness was something I'd always enjoyed, but the water made me nervous. The sea brought back too many memories, and I hated it for what it had done, for what it had made me.

I stopped dead in my tracks at the thought. It was the hat, wasn't it? Brought back the memories of what happened all because of a stupid hat. I turned to face this cruel, violent mistress, and I roared, "I forgive you. Is that what you wanted? I forgive you." I shook my fist and raged at the endless blue. Drool slid into my stubble and I wiped it away, the abrasive rawness a welcome distraction. It returned me to the visceral, to the now. I had to be present, not get lost in the mire of a past I was helpless to alter.

I failed utterly at that too. Like so much else.

So sad. My heart broke yet again for the loss of my boy. I would never get over it. I could never see the water and fail to wonder what might have been. The depth of my heartache was almost too much to bear. My anguish deeper than the deepest ocean. Why was life so cruel? So devoid of mercy? It just hurt so bad I wanted to cry and cry and spend a lifetime thinking on what my son would have been like, the fine man he would have undoubtedly become.

There had been others, many children lost before him, but none after. But not since my youth had I lost a child through accident. The others, and it pained me to think how many, had passed the way they should. Of old age, of disease, none of them Necro. I was so thankful for that, but also hated that they had missed out on a long life. But this extended existence came with such a high cost. They had escaped that misery, that total loss of all innocence, and they were better off for it. Dead. That's what they all were. Dead.

But not Jen. Not my girl. Jen was alive, and would follow me down the ages.

If she survived.

She had to. I wouldn't lose her. I simply wouldn't.

I turned away from the sea and continued along the beach, just clearing my head a little, no destination in mind. I splashed in the water like a child, forcing the darkness away as best I could. The freshness was a delight, cooling my entire body as my toes turned red and the wind and salt bit at my face.

Off in the distance, like a mirage, I began to make out a figure walking towards me. He was nothing but a blur, wobbling in the heat-haze, but he was definitely coming my way.

My mark? Someone out for a stroll? A dog walker? I saw no dog, though. Another Necro trying to eradicate his sins? Good luck, buddy. Been there, tried that. Failed miserably.

Or was it simply my imagination? Was it just a large piece of driftwood? I stopped and squinted, but it was too far away to be certain.

"Tyr, can you go check on that?" I asked, pointing. "And hello, nice of you to make it."

"Can see from here. Is man. No, is not man. Is like one, but not. And Soph does sarcasm. Is sarcasm?"

"What do you mean? A woman? A different creature? And yes, well done. You're learning fast."

"Tyr is very smart," he said proudly. "And is man but not man like before. Like when Soph go on boat. What call it? Elf? Yes, is elf. Is same elf. Want Tyr to burn?"

"I wish you could," I groaned, about as in the mood for a second encounter with that bastard Eleron as I was for a ride on a rocking boat then a swim in the murderous depths. What was with this guy? Did he have a thing about the water? About boats? Maybe he was a lighthouse geek?

"Tyr try?" he asked hopefully.

"Let's just see what he wants first. Then if I say so, you can have a go. Okay? But you can't kill elves. Trust me, I tried my hardest. You can damage them, but they will recover."

"Tyr use elf as practice, then. Will be good to learn what elf can do."

"Just hold back. Make yourself scarce, please. Only come when I call. And Tyr, you must obey. Don't try to fight him unless I say so. I don't want him doing anything to you."

"Tyr never be killed."

"That might be true, but I don't know if that applies to elves. They aren't like humans, or dragons. They have different powers and can do different things."

"Like what?"

"That's the problem. I don't know. I don't think anyone does."

"Tyr not scared." Tyr watched me intently. Serious, stoic, confident.

"Have you ever been scared? In your whole life?"

"Scared once." His tail twitched as he held my gaze.

"Oh yes. When was that?"

"Soph told Tyr would be banished if disobeyed. Tyr was scared would do wrong and never see Soph or Phage or best friend in world, Jen, ever again. So scared then. Is bad feeling in stomach? Knots and heart hurts? Thought heart might burst. So sad." His head hung low, but only for a moment. Then he raised it up and returned to watching with his steely gaze. Waiting for me to react.

"I understand. You know why I said that to you, don't you?"

"Tyr knows. Not scared now, though. Knows is family. Family more than good or bad. Family is love. Can do wrong thing and still be together. But Tyr never scare Soph again. Never attack or hurt. Is promise," he hissed.

Even with the distance between us, the strong tang of sulfur from his hot breath caught in my throat, drying my mouth. I coughed and swallowed then said, "I know you wouldn't. You were young, consumed by bloodlust, couldn't stop yourself acting in time, but still you didn't hurt me. And yes, you are right. Family is a very strong bond. You can do wrong and still be loved."

"Like Pethach?"

"You learn fast, young dragon. Very fast."

"Am still very young? Not feel it. Feel old and smart."

"And so do all young adults and growing children. Tyr, never forget, you are still developing. You think you know things, but you aren't always right. Your brain has a lot of maturing to do, same as your body. When you look back on how you are now in a thousand years' time, you won't even recognize yourself."

Tyr nodded, then turned away to follow the progress of the elf sauntering along the beach. I followed his gaze. I should have been worried, but I wasn't. This was not my time to die. I was the calm before the storm. A tsunami that would wash over all in its path and leave desolation and destruction in its uncaring, impassive wake. A force of nature not to be fucked with. I might not have defeated him before, but that didn't mean I couldn't scare him off again.

The only problem was, I knew this wasn't my mark. Not why I was here. Something told me he was merely here to have some fun. This was not who I had come to kill.

Whoever that was, still waited in the lighthouse.

I fucking hated the beach.

Elven Antics

With no choice, I was drawn strictly into the present as the distance between us closed. I reached out mentally to the myriad unseen creatures that made the sand and shallows of the sea their home, and called them forth. Let their mindless bodies almost become a part of my own. My head was crowded with a blanket of white noise that cut right to the primal parts of my brain, filling it fit to bursting with a sense of these thoughtless creatures.

There was a peace within this gaping maw of otherworldliness, a silence. They neither loved nor hated. Desired or loathed. They merely went about the business their biology dictated. Eat, excrete, sleep, wake. Live. And die. Always death. Utterly unavoidable.

I pushed out with a single mental image once their essence became almost overwhelming. As Eleron and I closed the gap, so the sand and the shadows came alive. I might not be able to kill him here, but I could make his life fucking miserable for a while. Although, thinking back on our last encounter, I recalled he seemed to get off on the pain. The thrill of encountering something new.

What choice did I have? He wasn't here to chat about the weather and offer me a fish supper.

Wanker.

Lugworms, sand fleas, tiny crabs, even some poor, unfortunate fish, wriggled, crawled, scuttled, flopped, or ran across the sand, emerged from holes, and even launched at the sauntering elf as he strode through the shallows, splashing the water in a carefree manner like we was having the best day at the seaside ever.

I stopped and waited for him to approach. His short, shining tunic danced and dazzled, almost blue with the reflected light bouncing off the water. He slowed as his body became covered in the creatures of the coast. Worms latched onto his exposed arms. Crabs clung to his smart trousers, tearing micro-holes in the fabric that seemed to repair as they scuttled up his body.

Eleron brushed them aside like they were dust, a smug, self-satisfied smile stuck onto his punchable, handsome face. His fine hair blew in the wind like he was about to do a photo shoot for *Twatty Elves of the Necroverse*. I hated him more than I had before; the smarminess almost oozed out of him. His power and knowledge, the deep-seated belief that he was my superior, better in every way, dripped from every alien pore like my sweat. Sweat he didn't have. He was cool and calm, even as he was consumed by the critters.

His pace slowed as I redoubled my efforts to at least cause him discomfort, the weight of my tiny helpers slowing his limbs, hindering his progress. But still he came, locking his eyes on mine, boring into my head like the worms that were now slithering up his slender neck and sliding into his ears. Crabs snapped at his exposed flesh, blood flowed freely, but he either just brushed them off or ignored them completely.

What was with this guy? He truly must have been getting off on it.

He stopped ten feet away, a walking embodiment of all the bounties of the shore. He was unrecognizable now. His entire head and body was covered in a writhing mass of worms and crabs as they squirmed and wriggled over each other, obeying my instructions to inflict as much damage as possible. The head was twice the regular size, thick with sucking worms gripping onto his once flawless flesh. They squeezed up his nose, nipped at his eyes, tore his eyelids, entered his ears, and covered his mouth. Could I stop him from breathing? Would this work?

Just as I knew would happen, he shook his body madly, waving his arms and legs, stomping his feet, flinging creatures across the sand. He rubbed his head, dislodging the majority, then cleared his nostrils. The tattered lids snapped open to reveal clear, cold blue eyes that held no emotion save amusement.

This guy was starting to piss me off big time.

With our gaze locked, Eleron reached languidly to his nose and pulled a long lugworm from his nostril. He put his index finger over the cleared one and snorted out several smaller worms from the other. Then he bent forward and hawked roughly. A wedge of curled up worms plopped to the sand with a squelch.

Eleron shook his head until it was a blur; insects scattered to the wind.

And then there he stood, clothes repairing, skin healing, his face bloodied but the wounds not enough to cause him more than minor discomfort.

I hadn't attempted to kill him yet, just a taster to warn him I wasn't in the mood for this shit.

"What gives you the right?"

"And nice to see you again, too," he said with a thin-lipped, callous smile. "It's been so long." Eleron flicked a large crab from his leg then looked up, an eyebrow raised. "Is that it? Oh my, how disappointing."

"Sorry I couldn't be more entertaining. What do you want? I'm busy."

"I know. And you've had a marvelous adventure already. Rather a lot of adventures since we last met, in fact. And what fun it is. You are quite the hero."

"I'm not a hero. I'm just a man who wants to be left alone. So, fuck off, there's a good elf." I pointed back the way he'd come. I wished with all my being it would be that easy. I knew it wouldn't be.

"Don't you want to play first?" he whispered right in my ear, his morph so good there'd been zero warning sign.

I was gone in a moment, our positions reversed, and I clamped down on the pain as I hissed, "I'd rather not."

"Oh, I'd forgotten just how amusing you are. Dear, poor Necrosoph. So confused by the world. So befuddled. Yet so robust. Tell me, how are you able to continue after all that's befallen you? I'm genuinely interested. Everyone is."

"Everyone?"

"Yes, everyone. Come, let's not play these games of stupidity any more. You do know you are being watched, don't you?"

"Of course. By the drones, and whoever's behind them. But that's not what you're talking about, is it?"

"My, you really are as dumb as you look. You humans, it's a miracle you've survived this long. I mean, honestly? You genuinely don't know?"

"Know what? Look, can you please just piss off? What do you want here? I know it isn't just to have a fight. Or maybe you're just as foolish as me?"

Eleron snarled, his eyes flashing with anger at the insult. At being likened to something like me, a creature he saw as little but an animal, here for his amusement.

This time I caught the telltale signs, and as he morphed so I made calculations out of instinct rather than true thought, and when he appeared beside where I'd been I came up right behind him and slid my knife into his kidney with satisfying ease.

"Damn, you smell nice," I whispered to him, as I pulled out the blade and came back to the world up on the parched sand beside Tyr.

Eleron whipped around and grunted with pain, anger, and humiliation. He wasn't smiling now. "And you stink like a farm animal. You make me retch. After our last encounter, I couldn't get the foulness off me for days. I burned my clothes and bathed for hours just to feel clean again. How can you stand it?"

"It's the smell of truth," I told him. "Of being something real. Something honest. Something flawed. See, this is your problem," I shouted, the sweat pouring off me as the hot sand radiated heat and Tyr's body acted like the mother of all heaters, "but you don't see it. You think you're this higher being, perfect in every way. But you're more flawed than any human. Because you're blinded by your own sense of superiority. You aren't better, you just have nicer hair and better shampoo. Okay, and the ears," I admitted. "There's definitely something about the ears."

"What about my sword?" he snapped, as he morphed right in front of me, the blade already arcing to spill my guts onto the sand where they'd sizzle and bake like sausages.

I jumped back and parried with my knife, the edge catching on the guard. The power he had was unmistakable as the strength of the swing reverberated up my arm.

As our eyes met, I jabbed at his nose and felt the familiar crunch, then shoved him hard enough to topple any man. He hardly budged. I jabbed again, but he ducked, then kicked out fast with his right leg, the timing and aim perfect. I was swept off my feet and landed with a thud in the scorching sand. He gripped his shortsword in both hands and thrust down, seemingly intent on putting an end to me, but I rolled, got a faceful of sand, then threw a handful up into the looming face of the smiling elf.

He coughed as he brushed away the sand and stabbed, half-blind. He took a nick from my waist then punched out fast with the shortsword and removed a good slice from my side.

I morphed to a standing position back beside Tyr, who had behaved perfectly and hardly moved a muscle. Wasting no time, and with Eleron not quite battle ready, which is how I prefer my opponents, I bent and charged, careening into his hard midsection with enough force to lift him off his feet and slam him into the ground on his back.

The work I had been performing in the background ever since he'd arrived came into play now. The moment he hit the sand, in the exact spot I'd been waiting for, he sank. The untold millions, trillions, of creatures all along the beach had converged and created an endless series of tiny tunnels beneath the sand with just enough remaining for it to appear stable.

Eleron descended into the six-foot hole instantly. The creatures beneath continued to burrow, the ones either side of this coffin-sized hole pushed the sand over him. As he disappeared under the onslaught, I jumped in right onto his head and stomped hard on his arm before it was buried too deep. With a satisfying crack my reward, I bounced up and down repeatedly on his head and chest, then stabbed wildly, over and over as he sank.

Sweat oozed from my face, my shirt stuck to my back, my jeans were soaked through, and I smelled riper than a draw full of Shey Redgold's socks. Exhausted, I clambered out of the depression as the sand poured in all around me.

I turned to Tyr and said, "Well done. Thank you for staying still. Now, can you burn the sand? Melt it, turn it into glass if you can. Trap him there and make him suffer. Sear his insides, overheat his organs, anything you can do to get rid of this fucker once and for all."

"Tyr will burn," he hissed, eyes dancing with anticipation. His long tail thumped the ground once, then he simply jumped over beside me and drew back his head on thick neck muscles, ready to let rip.

I stumbled away, connected with the underground creatures, and checked they were clear. Most were, some were not, but there was no time to wait. And then Tyr did what he did best.

With an almighty roar, a great geyser of intense orange burst from his mouth and instantly super-heated the sand. Flames bounced off the surface high into the air, the temperature incredibly fierce even from a distance. I scampered back, eyes still locked on the burial site, but it was too bright, and I had to shield my eyes. Again, and again, Tyr belched impressive streams of fire. Orange, red, yellow, then deepest blue. The conflagration oxidized and blackened the sand which then turned to white. A wide area shifted, a glassy slick on the surface that I knew was getting deeper and deeper as the sand broke down and became glass.

Tyr paused, inhaled a mighty breath, puffed out his chest, then released a blaze so dark it was almost black. The air was super-charged, the heat so dangerous I had to run away as I feared I would be boiled alive. And then, just like that, all was silent.

I returned cautiously, but had to stop before I got anywhere near him because the ground was emanating so much heat I couldn't stand it. Tyr turned to me, and as his eyes faded from deep red to their usual strange mixture of purple and orange, he asked, "Tyr did good?"

"You did great! What a team. Thanks. My friend, my true friend."

Tyr's body rippled with satisfaction and pleasure at being able to help his family, then he walked away slowly, gasping for breath, somewhat unsteady on his feet.

"You okay?" I asked, concerned.

"Tired. Hungry. But okay. Practice lots. Can do this now without using all power."

"Great. But go feed. Do it quick, before the adrenaline wears off. Hunt and come straight back."

Tyr nodded. He carefully unfurled his wings, shook them slightly, ran forward, then soared low over the beach and across the water. Almost as fast as he could morph, Tyr dove beneath the still waters. He emerged with several flapping fish in his jaws, swallowed them whole, then dove again. He repeated this a handful of times in a matter of seconds, then surfaced with what appeared to be a bluefin tuna. It was as big as me, and five times fatter, but he clamped down tight, flapped his wings hard, clearly having made his mind up to do battle with this beast of the depths, and turned sharply to return to shore. He dumped the flapping creature on the dry sand beside me and immediately severed the head to end its life.

"Better?" I asked, gobsmacked by the power Tyr now had and the downright wonder and beauty of the unfortunate tuna bleeding out on the sand.

"Better." Tyr focused on his feeding and placed a huge foot on the fish, hooked it with his claws, and tore at it eagerly with deadly teeth.

I turned my attention back to the spot where Eleron was now cocooned beneath the glassy surface. Was he dead? Was he broken beyond his ability to repair? Would he remain there for days, maybe years? Centuries?

A drone buzzed excitedly high in the sky, then descended to hover over the sandy grave. It turned it's beady red eye on me then zoomed in close, spun around once, and shot up, taking in the scene below. Of me, red-faced, overheating, and soaked in sweat, and Tyr devouring his reward for a job very well done.

What would they make of this? And was it not only the Necromasters watching, but the elves too? That's what Eleron had said, wasn't it? That they were privy to our ordeals? I looked up at the drone and gave it and anyone else watching the finger. Fuck them all.

My feet felt like they were actually melting, and I dreaded to look. I'd done the hard man act when up by the dunes, but the pain was excruciating. I dashed down the beach, sighed as I hit the cool, wet sand, and I swear my soles sizzled.

Keen to cool down further, I dropped my pack and ran straight into the water, letting the shock bring me back to myself, to wash away the sweat and the stench of Eleron and to overcome my downright fear of the water. As I submerged, I finally forgave the sea for taking my boy, and although I could never truly forgive myself, I at least felt the load lighten. I surfaced, then waded to the shore, dripping away the shame and guilt and slowly letting the anguish slide a little.

It would never be gone; I wasn't sure I wanted it gone. But I felt baptized. Not washed clean of my sins, but of the blame. I had tried, and failed, to save him. That was the truth of it all. I had failed, yet I'd never been able to accept that. Maybe I finally had. That I wasn't destined to always be the victor.

As I returned to Tyr and the buried elf, I knew better than to think life would forever be dandy, but I felt in a better position to face the future.

The sun had other ideas.

It beat down with renewed ferocity, probably because the coolness I'd experienced vanished in an instant as my clothes dried and stuck to me and my skin was no longer covered in sunscreen. I used a tiny amount of what was left to cover my face, aware how ridiculous it was to be applying sunscreen when my life was very much still in danger. I understood that I had not killed Eleron, that it was not possible here, but I hoped I had at least got rid of the problem for now and he'd simply gone home.

Had he? Could he? Would he?

The glassy surface erupted in a shower of shards as one very mangled, very bloodied, very pissed-off elf crawled from the grave then stood, shaking, before me.

Guess that was a no then.

Fun and Games

"You don't look so good," I told him as I shouldered my pack and rested my hand on my knife handle. Call it a comforter for weary Necros. I licked my lips, the salty tang making my stomach rumble as it reminded me of eating fish and chips whilst sat watching the placid waves caress harbor walls.

"You buried me!" he gasped, aghast at such effrontery,

"Sure did," I smirked, then nodded to his arm. "Bet that smarts. Looks broken to me. And your nose is kinda squished. Your hair's a mess too. I think it might still be covered in glass. Ugh, nasty! Oh, and I wouldn't plan on a date night any time soon, not with your chest caved in like that. And look at your clothes. Tsk, what a tragedy." I gave him an especially wide grin. Partly to piss him off, but partly because I really was enjoying myself. At least, enjoying his obvious discomfort.

"How dare you speak to me in such a manner? Don't you know who I am? What I am? I could destroy you in a heartbeat. I could grind you to dust."

"No, you couldn't. If you could, my guess is that you'd be doing that right now. But you can't, because we got the better of you." I looked to the drone, right into the red eye, and said, "You hear that? I got the better of him. Leave me alone. Leave us all alone. This isn't your business." I turned back to Eleron. "That goes double for you. This isn't a game. It's my life. Why are you doing this?"

"If you recall," he said, pausing to spit out thick blood, "I didn't start this. You did. You attacked first."

"Spare me the obvious bullshit. You came here to engage me, that's clear as the fucking sky. So save the crap for your own kind. Now, you ready to bugger off?"

Slowly, a smile spread across Eleron's bloodied face. As it widened, so he began to repair his broken body. His aquiline nose straightened and clicked back into place, the bruising on his cheeks receded, the numerous cuts and abrasions over his exposed skin vanished, and his ruined clothes repaired as the dirt shed to the sand. I could make a fortune if I could get the secret sauce for that.

"Burn the fucker again, Tyr," I told the watching dragon. "He seems to enjoy it."

I morphed a safe distance and Eleron had the presence of mind to do the same. But Tyr was smart now, had the power of the seer, and read his move easily. As the smug elf appeared down the beach, so Tyr was already belching flame at him as he thundered towards the shocked elf and increased the ferocity of the blast.

Eleron flailed in a panic, then got his act together and focused on protecting himself with what seemed like a second skin. The blaze bounced off the silver shroud encompassing him, but it was clearly far from infallible. Clothes burst into flame and his hair caught alight. He stumbled back in a panic while Tyr redoubled his efforts. We both advanced towards the elf as he retreated backwards towards the water.

His feet hit the gentle waves licking at the shore. He looked down in shock, then clearly had an idea. He turned, then ran into the water. The shimmering light that surrounded him extinguished as the flames died. Eleron dove under and was gone for a moment, before resurfacing and standing thigh high in the water, looking like the half-drowned rat he undoubtedly was.

"What, didn't it go according to plan?" I called.

"Of course it did!" Eleron slapped his palms against the water, splashing like a carefree kid. "I do so love our little get-togethers. You make me feel alive. Truly alive. How jealous they will be," he said, lifting his chin to stare at the group of drones that appeared from nowhere.

"Tyr, I know you hate them, but fancy a drive-by?" I asked, as he lifted his head and swallowed a chunky lump of tuna.

"Make Tyr's head go funny," he complained.

"I know, but it'll piss them off." I directed my words to the drones and said, "This is for the elves, not you," hoping it was enough to stop any repercussion for such an act of hostility.

Tyr circled me several times then darted at the drones. They scattered and sped up, but Tyr was in hunt mode now and raced after one. He banked hard, dove at the drone, but as he got closer it winked out of existence only to reappear well behind him, it's beady eye trained not on the dragon but on me.

"Okay, fine, I get it," I admitted. "Bad idea."

Tyr got the message too and came down to earth way too fast. He landed badly, his usual elegance gone, and skidded to a stop leaving deep gouges in the sand behind him.

"Tyr's head hurt. Not like drones. Worse than others. Something wrong inside them."

"I'm sorry. I shouldn't have asked. You okay?"

"Am okay. Not ask again."

"I won't. Now, what shall we do with this fucking elf?"

"Burn again?" he asked hopefully, his ears pricking up, his body suddenly animated.

"I don't think that's going to work." I moved right up to Tyr until I could smell his breath. Fish and sulfur, a strange combination. I cupped my hands around my mouth and whispered, "Watch this."

We turned to the pompous elf as I let my conversation with the king of the sea fill my mind. In seconds, the agreement had been made, and we watched the water ripple behind the splashing, grinning Eleron as huge jaws erupted from the water and snapped down with incredible force on his left arm.

The small blue shark, not exactly a monster but large enough to do you serious damage, dragged Eleron off his feet and under the water as he lifted his shortsword. Panicked, I reached out to the shark and asked after it, but it wasn't a Necro, just a regular creature, so the conversation was almost non-existent. Just mental images of its will to hunt, its desire to kill.

Eleron surfaced, gasping, and raised his weapon.

I couldn't let the innocent creature die like this, so I morphed the short distance, and as I mentally pushed the shark away and it sped off, I slapped out at Eleron's already damaged left hand, slicing through tendons and coming up hard against radius and ulna. He cried and turned, aware of me for the first time, so I grinned, then head butted him and waded to shore as fast as I could.

On the sand, I watched Eleron emerge from the water, leaving a bloody trail behind him. He stood there with small waves lapping against his boots as blood dripped from his fingertips onto the sand. Shockingly, and leaving me in no doubt he was utterly insane, he laughed for all he was worth as the wound once again healed and the wind tousled his hair in an infuriatingly majestic way.

"I love it!" he hollered. "You are a worthy adversary, Necrosoph. Deserving of your victories. I look forward to battling you again when the time comes. What a treat that will be. Oh, and as for you," he said, glaring at Tyr, "next time we meet, I will skin you alive and use your hide to make a fine belt. Be warned, dragon, you will not be forgiven for this. Until next time." With a salute, he walked forward several paces then a rend in the fabric of our world opened... Cheeky fucker!

Meet the Elves

The eye into the faery realm wobbled. Eleron stumbled forward then regained his composure and shifted his shoulders back. As he stepped through, he turned and grinned at me, the bastard.

I put my hand onto Tyr's flank as I gasped for breath, feeling nothing but pain and an anger like I'd never felt before.

"What gives you the right? What makes you think you can play with us like this? I'll fucking kill you. You hear me? I'll find a way, then tear you to pieces."

"I am an elf," he laughed, as he carefully brushed a lock of golden hair from his cold, hard eyes. "You cannot harm me. Look what you did to me, but I am already mended. I do so enjoy our little fights, Necrosoph. What a treat. And they all enjoy the spectacle. I'm quite the celebrity nowadays." Eleron turned sideways and lifted his already repaired arm to indicate I look. I caught a quick glimpse of untold thousands of elves seated in rows, then my elven nemesis turned back to me and blocked the view. The air shimmered around him, making it impossible to focus on what was behind.

"I don't know what you're talking about, and I don't care. Just know I keep my promises," I growled, then bent forward, coughing. I spat; it was bloody. Was I done for? Internal bleeding? I felt awful, beyond battered, but I didn't think so. When had he even got to me? Something was missing, some part of the fight I couldn't recall. Bloody elves and their twisted magic.

"I look forward to the next time. And I can't wait until your offspring are older. Now, that will be some real fun. Girls are always so hilarious when they know they're about to die." Eleron turned his back to me and waved over his shoulder. His hair shone brightly in the beautiful light from his home world.

"Elf threaten Tyr. Threaten Soph. But also Jen. Jen is Tyr's best friend. Tyr will destroy elf." His jaw snapped shut and he snorted loudly, angrier than I think I had ever seen him. Maybe even angrier than me. Tyr didn't usually get cross, he merely acted in a way he believed was right. But this was different. This was personal. "Will burn," he hissed. His eyes darkened, his body tensed as long teeth dripped thick saliva. It hissed as it hit the ground, burning tiny holes through the sand.

"Good luck with that," I mumbled.

"Thank you," he growled.

Somehow, I was off my feet and moving back. It took me a moment to realize Tyr had physically lifted me in his jaws. Before I had a chance to complain, he flung me onto his back between the ridges. I landed straddling him right on the saddle that was now a permanent part of his hide in anticipation of Jen riding him when older. My clothes smoldered where the slightly acidic saliva burned the cotton. Note to self. Don't let this happen again.

"Hey, what are you doing?" I shouted, as Tyr began to move.

"Burn," he hissed, the emanations coming from him leaving me in no doubt that he was deep into the bloodlust now. He thundered forward, pounding the ground, picking up speed incredibly fast. I tensed my thighs to hold tight then gripped the blunted, spread spines in front that acted like handles as Tyr pelted towards the eye and Eleron.

"Tyr kill evil elf. Tyr buuuuuurn," he hissed as his wings angled and we were airborne. Tyr flew low to the ground, his belly almost scraping the sand, then tucked in his wings. With his head low, he darted forward and slammed into the back of the receding figure of Eleron, sending him sprawling forward.

My brain felt swollen as if it would burst from my skull, the pressure unbelievable, and my nerves lit up like the nastiest morph I'd ever performed, as we passed from our realm into somewhere I'd believed it was impossible to venture.

As I screamed in agony and my guts threatened to burst from my anus and my eyes bulged dangerously, temporarily blinding me, Tyr sailed past the prone elf and then it was as though the brakes had been slammed on. We stopped dead, all our mighty momentum suddenly gone, and Tyr dropped like a boulder. I tumbled from his back and rolled over and over on ground that smelled so sweet I wanted more than anything to just cease moving so I could lick it and dream delicious dreams.

With a mouthful of sweet-tasting dust, I finally stopped tumbling and jumped to my feet then turned in time to see the eye revealing where we had been a moment before. The air sparkled around the tear in reality and my insides twisted as I expected it to snap closed, marooning us here for a brief moment until we exploded, turned to ash, burst into flames, or something even more horrific. But it remained open. A giant eye in the sky that Tyr and I had just flown through. Into, and I couldn't believe I was thinking this, the land of the elves.

I spun at the sound of thunderous applause, and found myself standing in the middle of a meadow full of flowers that put Job's summer display to absolute shame. Curved around it in a semi-circle were tier upon tier of bright green grassy banks that rose up and up. Standing on the tiers, applauding loudly, were tens of thousands of elves in clothes of every hue. The air shimmered with magic around each and every one of their smiling faces as they clapped their slender hands together, seemingly staring right at me.

I turned, not quite believing what I was seeing, the amphitheater too large to truly appreciate, and was confronted with an astonishingly vast curved screen. Bigger than anything I had ever seen or envisioned. It must have been longer than a street and easily forty, maybe fifty meters high. The resolution was incredible. Better than real life. Was this how the elves saw things? There were details in the details, bringing reality truly into another dimension. It felt more three dimensional than the world around me. And guess who had the honor of being featured in all his gnarly, bloodied, unkempt, and disheveled glory? Did I really look like that? I guessed so.

Perfectly circular glowing silver orbs danced around me erratically, reflecting pale light from a sun high in the sky. Cameras, I assumed. Drones of the elves. Overwhelmed, I was glued to the screen. The images displayed switched seamlessly every few seconds in perfect cuts from close-ups of me to wide angles encompassing both myself and the joyous crowd. They erupted with deafening cheers every time they were featured.

Suddenly, the image switched to Tyr's face. Silence fell like a hammer blow. I could practically taste the anticipation, the weight of it almost physical on my mind. The drone hovered in front of Tyr and then on the screen his impossibly large eye opened. Purple iris, orange sclera in incredible detail stared out at us all. The scene zoomed out to show both eyes and part of his head. The scales shimmered myriad colors as Tyr's confusion revealed itself.

The spectators erupted into a frenzy of applause and shouts as the angle changed then faded into a full-body shot of Tyr as he stood and whipped his head around, baring his teeth and snorting through his nose as his spines bristled and he spread his leathery wings wide.

A quick zoom in on the eye once again, timed perfectly to capture the bloodlust return and his orbs slide to deadly dark red. Full of murderous intent.

He belched a geyser of flame that scorched the flowers, turning them to ash in an instant. The elves went utterly wild with cheers, then a chant began.

"Tyr. Tyr. Tyr."

Utterly bewildered, unsure if I was dreaming or not, and feeling sick to the pit of my stomach, with a headache akin to the worst hangover in history times a thousand, I staggered almost blind over to his side once the flame dispersed and rapidly swung myself onto the saddle despite my protesting joints.

Instantly, the fog cleared, my stomach settled, my muscles were my own once again, and the heaviness in my limbs dispersed, leaving them light and seemingly brimming with energy. It was the connection to Tyr that would save me from this place. I had to stay close if I was to remain in control. Otherwise, the sheer otherworldliness of this taboo land would destroy me. The saddle was a tight fit. He wasn't really large enough yet to accommodate me, but there was no choice. It was a sore bottom or die. I knew which one I'd prefer.

"Get us the fuck out of here, Tyr, before this shit gets really weird. If that's even possible."

"Tyr sorry. Not know would be so many."

"Yeah, I think even you might have a hard time burning this many elves. Come on, let's go," I whispered into his ear.

But my whisper was a boom as the screen relayed every sound we made.

The masses continued to chant as Tyr stretched out his neck and turned to face the eye.

Eleron stood in front of it, grinning like the twatface he was, and I told Tyr, "Just forget about him. We need to get home."

"Tyr must kill elf for threat."

"Kill. Kill. Kill," roared the audience.

"My, now that was unexpected. But they came for a show," he indicated the crowd, "so let's give them one. This will go down in history. The first human to ever pass through, and all because of me! You truly honor us this day. And you brought your pet. How wonderful." Eleron ran fast and agile from the eye and stood in the middle of the field, his hair blowing on a warm, gentle breeze; he grinned as he beckoned us with his hand.

"No, Tyr. We must leave. Ignore him."

"Elf challenges Tyr. Cannot fight it. Must engage."

"Okay," I acceded. I knew he had to do this, that it was a matter not of pride so much as honor and duty. Not only had he been threatened by Eleron, but so had Jen. She was his ward, he hers, true friends with deep love for each other, and he would not, could not, let the threat pass without action.

"Tyr can fight?"

"Like I have any choice," I laughed. "Just make it quick. But you can't kill him. You can't kill elves. But do what you must to satisfy your honor then take us fucking home. I can't stay here, it hurts too much. And stay close. Without you, this will destroy me in seconds. Understand?"

"Tyr understand." He nodded once then stampeded. The ground shook then we were flying, surging towards the elf in a battle televised in definition higher than reality itself.

Tyr stretched out his thick neck and I felt his chest rattle as he drew in a sharp, deep breath. His insides rumbled loudly as the fires within were stoked by the oxygen. I clung on for dear life, about as used to riding dragons as I was hedgehogs.

Tyr roared.

A wide torrent of flame shot forward as I hunkered low to avoid the backdraft as best I could, but there was no avoiding the heat as we sped directly through the air Tyr had basically incinerated. I wasn't sure you could actually burn air, basically give it the finger and tell it to fuck right off, but it sure felt like it.

Tyr turned sharply, ready for another fly by. Eleron was gone. Could Tyr have cremated him? Could you even do that to an elf? I turned to check behind us as Tyr banked for his second pass, and saw Eleron jumping to his feet from his prone position amongst the flowers. The throng cheered for him, but then began to chant Tyr's name, and mine, as we headed straight back for more.

My dear companion expunged a line of flame at the ground that chased after Eleron as he danced forward. Just as we passed overhead, he skipped aside easily, outmaneuvering Tyr. We both roared in frustration, but Tyr was no dumb creature, and he swiped out with a forequarter claw and snagged Eleron under the arm, dragging him off his feet.

I grinned at the stunned elf, but felt sick at the sight of the ground racing by.

The crowd gasped as Tyr lifted the elf higher, ready to chomp down on his head and finish this, but the fabric tore and Tyr lost his grip on him.

Eleron bounced hard on the flowers and was still for a moment. Tyr circled once then swooped, ready to burn again, but our quarry was up and smiling for the drones, his stupid, perfect face impossibly large on the screen.

All of this had happened so fast since we came into this place that I was still bewildered and trying to play catch up. I had never been to another realm. Even Pethach, who had traveled extensively into dangerous places, had never been here. To the best of my knowledge, nobody had.

You couldn't even know the name of this world, and the elves themselves were unable to speak of it, even think much of their world when in ours because, just like the goblins and other Necro creatures not of the earth, it hurt so much.

What chance did we have?

Every chance. I refused to even consider losing. That was not who I was. Not here. Not anywhere. Not with a crowd or working alone. Losing without giving my all was not in my blood. I focused on Eleron and nothing else, knowing this was a battle same as all the others. And I always, always emerged the victor, no matter the cost. Fuck the spectators. I had to ignore them, not feel the pressure. They could watch one of their own die if they wanted, but that was on them, not me. I hadn't asked for this. If some bloody elf wanted to play stupid games, then he picked the wrong fucking guy to party with.

Distracted, I almost got myself burned as Tyr spat fire. I flattened against his hide just in time and watched as Tyr hit his mark. Eleron burst into glorious flame. His entire body was engulfed as the torrent raged around him and danced high into the perfect air.

Tyr landed gracefully. About as cool as cool can be. I jumped down and stood beside him. Watching. Waiting.

I turned to the screen and sneered. A drone zoomed in for a closeup and my grin grew wider as it was broadcast to the masses. Were others watching too? Were there millions of elves sat crowded around screens at home, or glued to strange devices I couldn't even imagine?

As the crowd was silenced by Eleron's excellent impersonation of a burning effigy, the screen simply blinked out of existence. There was nothing there. Just a simple pole either end of where the picture had been. A view opened up to a magical vista I had no time to admire.

There was uproar. They booed and hissed and I could see that untold thousands looked down at devices they held, only to chatter amongst themselves as a murmur of discontent blossomed.

Then the screen flipped back on, seemingly from nowhere, to reveal thousands of images of endless battles to the death. Men and women, old and young, punching, kicking, biting, clawing, stabbing, shooting, rolling, and gouging whilst screaming in victory or begging for mercy. The primal brutality of it all shook me to my core. The Necroverse worldwide in action as we watched.

I understood then exactly what this place was and what was happening. I was merely their daily, or hourly, entertainment. As soon as I had fought, had killed or been killed, no matter how popular I currently was with the elves, there was another to take my place.

Maybe we all had our fans. Maybe those assembled were mine. But I assumed that for every poor soul not on the screen, each still had their own supporters who dipped in and out of their lives when they saw fit. Probably just when the battles were close. But who knew? Maybe there were countless millions watching the everyday crap we all did.

But how?

A link via the Necrodrones, or another way? They probably had their own ways of viewing, something like the eye maybe, or maybe not. The details weren't important. What I knew was that I was correct. I was just part of the feed, one amongst countless. Their entertainment. Their addiction.

And then the screen flickered again as the fights cut out one by one. Left to right in lines across the monstrous projection. Slowly at first, second by second, then the remaining thousands simply vanished.

I knew instantly what it was.

"Ha," I shouted, although I doubted they could hear. I was wrong though, as a drone zoomed close and my voice was magnified. "Guess your internet's down too. Fucking kill switch, bitches. Come here, you." I beckoned to the drone with a crook of my finger, careful to keep my other hand on Tyr's flank to ground myself. It approached cautiously, then suddenly dropped at my feet. The other drones did likewise, and somehow I knew for a fact deep down inside that whatever their version of the internet and mass communication was, it too had been severed.

Elven kill switch in action.

"Soph be careful," warned Tyr.

I turned as Eleron charged forward, naked and regal, beyond beautiful with black steaming rags trailing in his murderous wake. Blisters covered his body and his hair was full of soot, but even as he covered the short distance his skin shone and regained its vitality. His hair was once more an annoying lovely blond.

Tyr smashed him aside with a whip of his head, and Eleron was flung backwards with a force that would have crushed anyone else's ribcage and ended their life. He merely laughed, then clambered to his feet, certainly bruised and dazed, but far from out of the fight.

"Get us out of this madness," I told Tyr.

"Tyr must kill elf. Will hurt everyone otherwise."

"What if we get trapped?" I eyed the portal, gap, whatever it was, warily, but it seemed stable. For how long, though? Was it because we were here when we shouldn't be? Would it remain open until we went back through?

"Will burn again."

"It didn't work. Try something else."

"What Tyr try?"

"Damn, I don't know. Look out, here he comes." I jumped up into the saddle, knowing Tyr was antsy and could take off at any moment.

Eleron ran at us, seemingly unconcerned by either of us, or what might happen to him. I recalled the fight we'd had years ago and the bugs I'd summoned to destroy him. I thought I'd had him then but no such luck. What could I do this time?

I hugged Tyr's neck as he spat fire, forcing Eleron back by the sheer pressure. The damage it caused clearly took it out of the elf, as the more Tyr burned him the more he retreated, but he would never be destroyed. He began to recover from his blistered flesh the moment Tyr stopped his assault. Maybe it would have worked in our world, but here, where he truly was immortal and beyond powerful, it was not going to be enough.

"Let me down," I told Tyr.

Tyr lowered himself by squatting. I flipped my leg over the side of the saddle then slid down his flank and landed on the sweet-smelling flowers, what weren't already trampled. I almost vomited as I swayed from side to side. The sensation was like being on a boat. Guess my dragon riding days were over before they'd even begun.

Unable to hold it, I puked onto sizzling earth as I wobbled. I felt green with sickness from being in the air, and my insides didn't know which way was up or down. My head spun. I was blind again for a moment as everything slowly balanced out. How did birds and dragons handle this? Guess they were born for it, unlike me.

The crowd were still loud with their murmurs as the screen flickered from black to white and buzzed incessantly, but their viewing pleasure was ruined and long may it last.

Eleron stood, regal and naked, skin black but healing as easily as ever. His eyes bored into me, deep and angry. Gone was the smug smile, replaced with a snarl of anger for denying him a stupendous, televised victory. I think he was more put out about this not being on the big screen than anything else.

He sauntered forward, cocky and aggressive, yet relaxed; like an animal stalking its prey. It was bloody off-putting, but I was approaching the zone now.

The sound of the crowd lessened until it wasn't even a background murmur. I had hearing only for Eleron. Saw only him. I could hear his breathing, sense his heart beating fast, see the twitch of his neck and the way his left earlobe pulsed. His quadriceps quivered like the muscle was knotted; I glimpsed a flash of annoyance at the cramp.

Eleron paused, then ran swiftly to the ash pile that was once his clothes and pulled out his shortsword. He held it aloft, gleaming in the elven sunlight. I glanced up. The sky was perfect. Rich and deep blue. Birds circled high overhead. Maybe that was how they watched us in our world?

The crowd roared as he thrust his sword into the ground then retreated several paces. Then I zoned out from their participation and I focused purely on this ridiculous, pompous, arrogant creature standing before me.

I flicked the popper on my sheath and wrapped my hand around the ebony handle of my knife. My heartbeat slowed, my breathing even. With the connection to my weapon, my mind snapped into sharp focus, awareness expanded, and I saw Eleron like I had once before when we fought on a boat of all things.

"Must not think of boats. Must not think of boats," I said as my mantra, while my stomach gurgled.

Eleron, skin still dark and somewhat blistered, with his face smeared with dirt, and his hair like he'd just had it shampooed, walked backwards several more steps from his weapon then bent and picked a delicate, pale-yellow flower. He sniffed it and sighed with delight then threw it over his shoulder and ran forward, snatching up his shortsword as he pelted after me.

I held my ground, didn't budge as he closed. I caught the look of concern as he expected me to at least change my stance, but I was as still as Wonjin in the depths of winter.

Cool, still, hard as stone. Mind empty.

Take That

Eleron was almost upon me. He'd believed he had it all figured out. But even as he readied to deliver his death blow, his eyes gave away the uncertainty he felt. Why hadn't I moved yet? Why was I not indicating what defensive move I'd make? This wasn't how it worked. I should be twitching at the very least.

But his decision had been made, his body instructed, and there was no turning away from what he'd set his mind to do.

As he sprang forward, shortsword arcing back just enough to swipe in the next half second, I still remained motionless and utterly unready to stop his attack in any way.

When he was a hair's breadth from slicing through my neck, I smiled at him as I morphed a matter of inches. As I reappeared just behind him, and we're talking as close as he'd got to decapitating me, so the plan truly came into its own.

Tyr morphed the same instant as me, so we basically swapped places. Rather than Eleron opening up my neck, his weapon clanged against Tyr's indestructible head, stopping his arm dead. Tyr snapped into Eleron's midsection as I thrust out my knife and pierced his torso from behind.

Eleron slammed his head back, smashing my face, and thrust his blade at me repeatedly. I dared not move, or this was over. As the shortsword tore at me repeatedly, and the wounds bled profusely, yet I felt nothing, I remind steadfast.

I knew from past experience that simply stabbing would do nothing and he'd be right as rain in minutes, but this time we had a plan. I kept the knife in deep and used all my strength to slice up, down, left, right, until I found a sweet spot where the blade slid easily through the weakened flesh. It still wasn't fatal, but it served its purpose to act as a distraction to the true star of the show.

But the bastard refused to give in, and he smacked his head back repeatedly into my face whilst elbowing me wherever he could. His sharp edge almost removed my manhood as it cut across my hips and he managed a deep thrust into my thigh before we finally got the better of him.

Tyr tore a mouthful of meat from Eleron's belly as I freed my knife then kicked the back of his left leg, forcing him to his knees. I plunged the blade into the base of his neck until the tip exited through his Adam's apple. Quick as a flash, I yanked the steel free as Tyr clamped down on Eleron's skull then ripped up with the strength of the dragon.

I waited with growing anticipation for Eleron's head to pop off, but it didn't happen. Tyr strained, veins pulsed beneath the skin of his extended neck, but the head refused to be parted from the body. Eleron actually laughed, the bastard, as Tyr redoubled his efforts, using his forelimbs for purchase as he tugged and tugged upward to no avail.

Using both hands, I sliced the back of the neck until fresh flesh was exposed. Again and again, each cut a little deeper, as Tyr continued his tugging. It was as though our nemesis was rooted to the ground. By rights, he should have been lifted into the air like a rag doll with the pressure Tyr was exerting, but he was still on his knees.

But he wasn't laughing any longer.

The bloodlust consumed us both. We had ears and eyes only for the kill. I slashed repeatedly, deeper and deeper, until I was almost through the cartilage between bone, and I shouted, "Now," as I cut as hard as I could. Something gave beneath the knife.

With a mighty yank, Tyr ripped Eleron's head almost clean from his shoulders. As Tyr stretched his neck up high and straightened his bent limbs, so the entire body was finally freed from whatever magic had kept Eleron tied to the earth. The torso hung by sinewy strands from the head, and then, finally, the last few threads of gore snapped. Eleron fell in a crumpled heap at our feet.

Tyr's eyes were nothing but glowing red orbs. He shook the head like a prize, then stood tall and proud. Slowly, knowing exactly what he was doing, he turned in a circle, ensuring every single one of the elves witnessed the fate of their latest star.

Sickening by the second, almost ready to collapse, I took several shaky steps to Tyr then clambered into the saddle gratefully. My companion spoke to me silently and I nodded my agreement, as why not give them what they wanted?

He flung the mess of flesh and bone up over his body as I raised my knife until my arm was straight. My blade pierced the head like a kebab as it fell.

Still not finished, I flicked my arm. The twisted features of Eleron arced through the air and rolled across the trampled flowers, coming to rest amidst a beautiful group of blood-red poppies.

Tyr lumbered over, then jumped high and came down with several tons of force right onto the top of the skull with his right forelimb. The bone split open, and although I couldn't see it, I heard the pop then the squelch as he jumped again and turned the head of Eleron into nothing but mush.

Enraged, he sucked in until his chest was ready to burst, then spewed a monstrous blaze at the mess on the ground until he'd completely run out of puff. For good measure, he spat a bucketful of acid over what was left.

I jumped down and rested my left hand against the super-heated flank of my friend. The head was gone. Severed from Eleron's body, I guess it had lost whatever elven voodoo made them immortal. Ha, so much for that! All that remained was a charred fragment of bone and a black, sizzling hole.

As the bloodlust receded, I gradually became aware of the absolute silence in the arena. You could literally hear a pin drop. Tyr's breathing and my own raggedy breaths were the only sound.

And then the crowd erupted in monstrous, sick applause. Every single elf got to their feet amongst the bright grass and the joyous flowers and applauded the murder of one of their own. I mean, damn, it wasn't even as though they'd hated the guy. They'd all fucking come here to watch him play with the human, although it was clear Tyr and I had our fans.

Done with this shit, I moved to mount Tyr when a voice called out from the other end of the field.

"Stop!"

The crowd was silent once more as I stood there, full of disdain, a bloody sneer on my smashed face. I loathed every single one of them. Not for what they were, but for what they'd clearly become. I didn't blame them or dislike them because they were cold and heartless, I detested them for their attitude. Their sense of superiority, the intelligence and resourcefulness that they abused, and for the things they understood yet ignored.

A wild animal knows nothing of the pain and suffering it causes to the creatures it hunts to survive. It's instinct, nothing more. The elves understood the pain they inflicted and plain didn't care. But could I blame them for their lack of empathy? Surely they were wired that way? Just like little children, they simply didn't seem to understand that other beings had feelings like them. But that wasn't justification for this. For how they acted.

Maybe the truth was they were too close to us humans. After all, hadn't we reveled in death and murder in the Roman arenas not so long ago? Where noble creatures such as elephants and even fucking giraffes were killed for sport and entertainment? Surely those who watched had laughed and joked, hollered and screamed, and loved every minute of it? Maybe that's why I despised them. They were what was worst about humanity. They should know better, was what it came down to. They did know better, but they chose to refute it and revel in barbarism for its own sake.

They got off on it, and that was unacceptable,

So I sneered at the bastards, my distaste evident, as an elderly elf walked across the empty battlefield then stopped in front of me. He held up a hand for silence, not that he needed to, and then he cast his steely eyes upon me like I was somehow finally worthy of his attention.

Screw him.

I met his gaze without flinching as I breathed raggedly and my chest rattled. Sharp pains stabbed inside; maybe my ribs were bust. My face ached, my sides killed from the puncture wounds, but I squared my shoulders and showed no emotion as he continued to watch me without a word.

The silence stretched out as he took me in, studied me from head to toe like a prize specimen, and then he pulled out a beautiful knife tucked into a nice leather belt and thrust it skyward.

A massive cheer went up from the assembled throng. I didn't know whether to pull my own blade or sink to my knees and let him put an end to this.

But I did know. Even now I would not kowtow, would not be beaten. I'd carry on fighting right to the bitter end, and who knew, maybe with Tyr's help I'd even beat this fucker too.

He had a different idea entirely.

The man, looking like a very fit sixty-year-old, with pale golden hair and a regal stature, bent at the knee and stretched out his hands, holding the knife across both palms as an offering.

"Take it. It is your prize."

"I don't want a prize. I don't want anything. Not from you, not from any of you," I shouted.

"As expected. Nevertheless, you have done the impossible and defeated Eleron. His games went too far and now he has paid the price. It will be many moons before he recovers from such ignominy, and he will henceforth be forbidden from ever leaving our lands. You can rest assured you will never meet again."

"Seriously, you mean he isn't fucking dead?"

The elderly elf stared at me, clearly confused. "Of course he's dead. Your dragon destroyed his head. A head that is no longer attached to his body."

"Yeah, that's what I thought. Come on, enough with the cryptic crap. How will he come back?"

"I am not here to answer your questions about things you have no right to know and never will," he snapped. So much for the nice guy act. "You have won the right to this knife, never before given to another race, only ever offered to our best, most skilled fighters. You have surpassed them all, you and your dragon, and this is your reward. Come, let me show you why it has earned the name it has. This blade is indestructible, forged from ore retrieved deep in the elven mines. It is over thirty thousand years old and not a blemish. Passed down from one worthy to the next, it has not been offered in over a millennium. Now it is yours." He stood and walked over to Eleron's corpse. He beckoned me to step away from Tyr so I did, but it would have to be quick.

My head swam instantly and the sickness threatened to overwhelm me, but he intrigued me as he lifted up the mangled arm of the dead elf and handed me the knife, hilt first. I took it and instantly the sickness eased, as though this was a key to unlocking the ability to remain here. A warmth and a power soaked into my fingers and up my arm. My strength returned, and I felt truly powerful in a way I never had before.

"Come, a simple slice to show you the power of the weapon you have earned. Cut through the arm with a single blow." He nodded.

Halfheartedly, I swung down across the upper arm. The blade severed the limb without me feeling little more than slight resistance. It was truly like cutting through paper.

The regal elf held the arm of Eleron aloft and once more the throng cheered. This time they didn't let up. They shouted and screamed our names, hollered with joy and triumph. Caught up in the madness, I thrust the knife into the air, nodded to the elf, then retreated to Tyr's warmth.

"Bone Slicer is the name of the weapon you may call your own for as long as you live," shouted the elder above the raucous din. "A true one of a kind. The elven runes along its blade will ensure it never dulls, never tarnishes, will give the bearer power, and can never be yielded by another. You cannot lose it. If you ever do, call its name and it shall return to you."

I nodded, unsure whether I wanted such a thing or not. I hated all the magic mumbo-jumbo back home, and had refused more magical artifacts than I cared to recall over the centuries, but damn, this would come in handy. Maybe I should take it. After all, I deserved it after all this crap the elves had put me through.

I mounted Tyr and said, "Let's go home, my friend. Thank you, Tyr, you saved us both."

"Tyr not like elf. Soph is good fighter. We are a team."

"We sure are."

Tyr walked proudly towards the static eye. A glimpse of the beach appeared through the blackness before we were airborne, then he sailed through the rend in the fabric of our worlds and we emerged into blistering heat on the shore. Tyr landed gracefully and I hopped down, already feeling sick from the short flight, and turned to watch the eye shrink, then pop silently out of existence.

I looked down at the knife still in my hand, half expecting it to have been a dream. It wasn't. I turned it so I could see the runes. They meant nothing to me, but the blade shone bright and true in the harsh glare of our sun. The strength in my arm remained.

"I fucking hate elves," I groaned, as the true reality of my broken body began to seep into my consciousness now the bloodlust had receded. I sank to the scorching sand and knelt there, exhausted, sick, but not beaten. Never beaten.

"Tyr hungry."

"Me too," I croaked, my throat suddenly raw.

He struck out alone, and all I could do was watch him as he flew out to the water then dove down expertly. He emerged with something large flapping in his mighty jaws. Jaws that had removed the head of an elf.

It was only then that I realized he hadn't tried to feed on Eleron. The bloodlust hadn't taken him over and forced him to suck the elf dry. Maybe dragons couldn't feed on elves, or maybe Tyr's standards wouldn't allow him to even consider such a truly corrupted soul.

"So, that went well," I muttered. "And you," I said, staring at the knife, "Bone Slicer, is it?"

I swear it vibrated in my hand, as if sentient.

It Ain't Over Yet

As I sat panting in the sand, sweat stinging my eyes, my body feeling like absolute shit, but with enough residual adrenaline still pumping to mask the true horror of my condition, I realized that I hadn't even done what I came here for.

I was yet to fulfill my note.

Last time I'd encountered Eleron, he was the mark, but that wasn't the case this time. The Necronotes were never wrong. If it said the lighthouse was my destination, then the lighthouse it was. I had to go there and decide whether to kill the person inside or leave them be. My choice, same as always. Get it wrong and it meant my certain death.

It was enough to make a grown man cry. Almost enough to make me curl up and let my mind unravel. How were any of us supposed to cope with this level of madness? How was I?

Because if I wanted to go home, I had to. No choice.

What had my plan been? Drive down to the location I'd seen on the map at the car park and see if I could find someone to take me across to the island.

Guess I still had some work to do. I'd better make it quick, or I wouldn't be able to do this. But how? I could hardly feel my body. Everything was numb, yet weird and tingly at the same time, and I was sure that wasn't good. But I had my new knife, Bone Slicer, and I hadn't died yet, so I knew I had to muster the will and the energy from somewhere and get going.

This was an emergency, so I searched through my pack then found the container with the dried power pellets, basically dry shit. Reluctantly, I tipped out a generous portion into my palm, then threw it into my mouth and washed it down with several swigs of warm, stale water.

I decided to switch out my regular knife for Bone Slicer, but I felt disloyal. My old blade had served me so well for so long that it had become part of who I currently was. Maybe that wasn't a good thing. Maybe there should be more of a disconnect, a strangeness, so I decided to give it a go.

I wasn't at all surprised to find it fit into the sheath perfectly. As I slid it into the leather, it stretched a little to accommodate this foreign blade, as if one was talking to the other. The two weapons were almost the same size, but a different weight and a very different sensation when I tested it out by opening the popper and gripping Bone Slicer.

The security of the ebony handle had been a real boon in times of stress, but this new blade was something altogether different. It was truly like coming home. A sense of familiarity and rightness I had never known by touch alone. It belonged. Did I want an elven knife, though? Hadn't I just assured myself it was better for a weapon to be less comforting, not more? I gripped the warm wood tight and accepted that, yes, I wanted this. Because it felt like an extension of my arm, and could cut through bone. Plus, I'd never have to sharpen it, which was a real bonus.

While the power of the dragon slowly kicked in, and my aches and pains subsided, at least temporarily, I took the time to study my "prize" properly.

It was simple, but deceptively so. The overall feel was solid but light, but somehow the balance was perfect and the weight just so. The blade comprised a flat spine as thick as my pinkie, but the cheek tapered almost imperceptibly to a ferocious grind that cut me no sooner than I looked at it. Almost as though the edge was ground out further than I could physically see.

The point was the same. I checked it against my thigh; it pierced the denim before I could see it touch. The convex tip curved back gracefully to the spine and the whole blade was about a hand and a half long. The steel had been blackened; the damascus seemed to suck the light in and keep it there. Did that make it carbon steel? Wouldn't it rust then? Guess the elves knew something we didn't.

A delicate choil before the ricasso was a cool little feature, but most likely there to protect the guard when the blade had been sharpened for the first, and maybe only time. The cheek may have been black, but the entire edge was as shiny as Bernard's horn. Down the entire length of the visible side of the cheek, right up to the plunge line, were a series of etched elven runes as bright as the edge itself. They shimmered as if alive.

The guard was a simple affair, nothing ostentatious, but still beautiful nonetheless. The handle was of a warm, pale wood akin to blond oak, but presumably another species entirely. The knife was full tang, so the handle was split into two sides, but clearly from a single piece of wood. Each fixed to the steel by three rivets. The pommel ended in a blunt curve shaped to fit my hand perfectly. The more I held it, the more comfortable it became, almost as though it was making subtle alterations. My guess was that was exactly what was happening.

I held it up and turned it this way and that, admiring its understated beauty. If I could say nothing else nice about the elves, then they sure made cool as fuck knives.

Feeling better now the magic meds had kicked in, I secured Bone Slicer into my sheath, stashed my old knife in my pack after wrapping it up in layers for safety—always safety first—and tested my mobility. My legs were stiff, and my stab wounds weren't pretty, but I'd live. I'd be ill, for sure, and was probably already infected, but I'd had worse and struggled on.

I shook out my arms and cricked my neck, and once the blood was flowing properly through my system I knew I could do this. Just. But my energy was dangerously low even after the boost, and I certainly wasn't about to morph any time soon.

I called out to Tyr and told him I was heading to the car, then down to where the boats supposedly were. He grunted in response. Guess he'd had enough excitement for one day. Hadn't we all?

The comedown from such a weird experience was the harshest I'd ever experienced, but I was currently still in denial about the whole thing. Maybe he was too. It was as though my mind had put up a barrier to the whole experience, and although it was letting some of it filter through, the monumental weirdness of it was being held back so it didn't overwhelm me.

Had we really fought Eleron on his home turf in front of tens of thousands of elves? Had I actually been somewhere no other human had gone before? Maybe others had. I wasn't exactly up-to-date, or even interested, in such knowledge.

If I dwelled on this now, I knew I would be good for nothing. The smells, the sounds, the utter otherness of it was too much for me to process, so for now, I'd let my mind run the show, and keep the experience locked away until I had the time and right frame of mind to process it at my leisure.

The soft sand made the going tough, but I made it to the car, stowed my pack, then drove the short distance down to another small car park. From there, I had to walk for ten painful minutes to where the boat usually took people across the water.

"Bloody hell. No boat." I clambered down to the water's edge and scoured the coast, but there wasn't a single boat in sight and I had no idea where to go looking for one unless I traveled back up the coast a fair way. That wasn't going to work. I couldn't be out at sea on my lonesome. I knew as much about controlling a boat as I did a submarine, and that was if I could even get the damn thing started.

There was only one option, and it wasn't swimming.

"Tyr, buddy, fancy giving me a ride?" I asked, cursing under my breath for what was to come.

I waited for the reply, then almost jumped out of my skin when his hot breath was on my neck and he said, "Yesssss. Tyr fly Soph to island."

"Hell, you scared the life out of me. How'd you get here without me seeing?"

Tyr considered me with his head cocked to the side. "Tyr can morph. Remember? Very good now. Hardly hurt at all. Soon never hurt. We go?"

"Yes, let's go." I clambered on, and the moment I was settled Tyr ran forward then we were on our way. The sickness began immediately. I was not cut out for this. It was like the worst fairground ride in history.

But even as I thought it, Tyr was landing at the western end of Bardsey Island. There before us was the lighthouse.

As expected, there was nobody here, just sheep. A lot of sheep. They ignored us, which was weird, as how many dragons had they seen before? I didn't dwell on it; I had more important things to be concerned with. I slid off Tyr then said my thanks and he was gone, as I asked. It was for the best, as I didn't want to make more of a drama out of this than was absolutely necessary. There was something else too, and I hated myself for even feeling it.

My pride. My stupid pride. I wanted to do this on my own. There'd been a lot of help from Tyr over recent years, and somehow it didn't feel quite right. Like I wasn't taking on enough of the burden for the yearly Necronote. Enough responsibility. Even Bernard had helped save me. I knew it was stupid, that I had more than enough on my plate, and certainly hadn't watched from the sidelines, but this was me being truthful.

Undoubtedly, you took whatever advantage you could, and it was those with such help that survived, but I still felt like I had to do this solo. Just to prove something ridiculous to myself. Even in my current state. Prove to myself I was still up to the challenge, maybe? That there would be countless times ahead when I would have to face things alone, and I'd better ensure I was up to the task. I wasn't quite sure. But nevertheless, I would do this alone, or die trying.

Or, and I grinned at the thought, call Tyr at the last minute to come save me. I might have been a bit dumb at times, but I wasn't that daft.

There had been no time to check out the island on the trip over, mainly because I had my eyes closed, so now I was alone I decided to take a quick look so I knew the lay of the land in case anything went wrong.

Tyr had dropped me close to the lighthouse. It was off in the distance, just far enough away to give me some breathing room and to not make my appearance too obvious. Not exactly ninja style, though, what with the huge dragon and the island being bloody tiny. I could see it all from where I was standing. What had the sign said? A few miles long at most and half a mile wide.

There were sheep, and fences, and the lighthouse with several houses around it, and not a lot of anything else apart from grass that looked sicker than I felt. The sheep must have really struggled here. Someone must come to feed them, as no way could they survive on such meager rations. Maybe someone lived in the lighthouse full-time to tend them. A mystery never to be solved, as I wasn't about to go knocking on doors back on the mainland to find out.

Speaking of knocking on doors.

I trudged over the rough, windswept terrain towards the lighthouse, a strange sight on this bleak island. It truly was an anomaly, and was indeed painted in red and white stripes.

The surrounding buildings had seen better days. It was highly unlikely anyone lived in them, considering the state of repair and the detritus littering the surrounding land, but I'd been known to be wrong in the past so I'd just have to wait and see. As I approached, so the lighthouse came into its own. The few I'd visited over the years always impressed me with their size and the sheer determination to build such beacons of hope in such inhospitable places. The work involved, the sheer, bloody-minded determination, was certainly inspiring.

But today there was one life the salvation of many a sailor wasn't going to rescue. I had come to kill, and kill I would. Then I could finally go home and try to put this fuck-up of a birthday far behind me.

Closing in, my thoughts turned to Woofer. I wondered how he was doing now he was quasi-immortal. I smiled at the prospect of him giving Jen and Phage the runaround. A Woofer with bundles of energy really didn't bear thinking about.

I was happy for him, and more relieved that he'd come through the ordeal than I'd anticipated. It wasn't like he was the first dog I'd lived with. There had been so many, and I missed every single one of them dearly, but unfortunately it was the deal when you had animals. Chances were high they would pass long before you, so had to savor every moment and accept the inevitable. But when I'd feared I would lose Woofer it was different. Deeper.

Why had I risked his life like that? What if it had failed? Maybe it was because in his own daft way he was a smart boy, and it definitely was what he'd wanted. But had he truly understood the risks? Maybe he had and that was what had concerned me so much. That more than anything in the whole world, all Woofer wanted, even more than sausages or to play ball, was to be with us. His family.

"Ugh, get it together, Soph. Why are you thinking about this now?" I mumbled to myself as I paused behind one of the buildings and tried to clear my head.

Now was not the time for sentimentality, or reminiscing. I was here to kill someone. I knew I was. This wasn't a voyage of discovery to see if this person should live, this was purely a Necrohit. I was a hitman and I needed to just do this and get the fuck home to my family. And that included Woofer.

Then it clicked why I was thinking of the daft guy. He was innocence personified. Full of love and hope and looking to the future. Not a bad bone in his body. He just wanted his family and to spend eternity playing and having fun.

Now that sounded like something worth fighting for.

Feeling like shit, I crept around the back of what appeared to have been the lighthouse keeper's house and peered in through the windows. It was in utter disarray.

The kitchen was ransacked, everything trashed, with graffiti on the walls and pots and pans everywhere. The cupboard doors were hanging off their hinges and clearly nobody lived there. Peering through other windows showed similar sorry scenes. People had been here, probably kids, and just had some fun and partied, but my guess was that was years ago and since then the place had remained abandoned.

The other building had been a tourist information place with a compact cafe at the front. Same as the house, it had been ransacked, trashed, then left to slowly fall apart. Many of the windows were smashed, the roofs were beginning to sag as the weather got in, and nobody had made any effort to tidy up.

All that was left was the lighthouse itself.

I didn't try to hide. I didn't try to act clever. I didn't even take a deep breath. Merely took the steps up onto the large base of the lighthouse and stood outside the door and listened. Nothing. The faded red paint was blistered and cracked, just like my skin. Knowing there was no point knocking, I turned the rusted handle and pushed the door open.

Into a winter wonderland.

I jumped back, gasping, as cool, almost frosty air hit me. Goosebumps sprang up on my arms. So unexpected was it that I just stood there, with my skin cooling rapidly, the feeling so pleasant but so shocking I couldn't seem to do much of anything.

An oversized, peculiar-looking air-conditioning unit, but not venting to the outside, sat in the middle of the bare concrete floor trailing wires into hidden places. A huge fan hummed as it rotated in the housing, the blast of cold air it spewed incredible for the size of the machine.

Not caring, and with no time to figure out how it worked, or why, I quickly took in the room then tiptoed inside and shut the door. Damn, it was truly freezing in here. The drone of the unit drowned out any other noise, so I figured the only way was up. Great, a shit ton of stairs. Just what I needed.

With no other choice than to walk out of here right now, I reluctantly grabbed the handrail and began the arduous ascent. There were no other floors, no interesting features as I made my way up, just bare stone walls and grubby steps that hugged the walls of the lighthouse all the way to the top.

I climbed, each step miserable. My thighs must have been hammered during the fighting, but I couldn't even recall how. Maybe it was from riding Tyr? I'd tensed my legs so tight against his saddle that I'd probably ruptured something, so high had the stress level been.

Pausing, I checked my legs as the pain worsened. The memory of Eleron stabbing back into my midsection and landing a decent hit into my thigh returned. The blood pouring from the wound, staining my jeans, was also a slight giveaway. Nothing I could do about it now.

Onward and upward, still no new sounds, just the receding drone of the unit. It grew warm, but only in comparison to the ground floor. My mind slowed as thoughts grew sluggish and my momentum lessened.

Was this a natural feeling, or was something else going on? I stopped again for a moment to regroup my thoughts, and only then did I feel the offness of this place, the definite magical vibe permeating the air. Awesome. Some twat with more magic than sense.

Maybe not. As I wasn't being my brightest self. Why didn't I morph? There would be pain, but not as much as climbing these bloody steps. I glanced up to the top, then without thinking too much about it I simply morphed and came to directly underneath the trapdoor I assumed led to the area that housed the light.

Before I could knock, or even recover properly from my morph, which wasn't as bad as I'd envisioned, so the power of Tyr's shit was definitely still lingering, the trapdoor was flung open. A large man, with an even larger beard, and an even larger grin, looked down at me from above and greeted me in the strangest manner imaginable.

He just nodded and smiled. Then he reached out a hand to help me up.

"I'm good, thanks," I told him, beyond perplexed. He nodded and stepped back out of sight.

Cautiously, I took several more steps, expecting to emerge at the top of the lighthouse. I glanced around quickly to ensure my head wasn't about to be chopped off, but the man kept a polite distance. This was a room beneath the open area where the light was housed. Up above, another trapdoor presumably led to outside. I emerged into the small room, taking a moment to get my bearings.

Waiting patiently until I entered, the peculiar man spread his arms wide and stepped forward as if to hug me. Like I was welcome. He frowned as I stepped back, then nodded his understanding and tried to look solemn, but he couldn't pull it off. My mark laughed instead. A deep, hearty, bellowing chuckle that echoed around the cramped space then slapped me about the ears as it returned to the source.

"Welcome, my friend. I would say this is unexpected, but I was waiting for you. Welcome. Come in. What a place. What a view. Look at it. Such majesty." He indicated the view through the tiny, grimy window. I glanced quickly.

"Very impressive. You know why I'm here?" I stepped inside and closed the door with my foot without taking my eyes off him. The loud thud went unnoticed, or he plain didn't care. He turned his back to me and stared out to sea, so I took in the room with a glance then focused back on him. He had camping gear, a sleeping bag, a small stove, a large pile of food, and even some tech to keep himself occupied. Judging by the bucket, and the smell, he'd been here for several days.

But why?

"I bet you have so many questions. I know I would. Don't worry about it, my friend. I have the answers I have sought, and now my masters have called for me to come home. Don't feel bad, don't lament, for they bring us all home eventually. I will share with you, so you too may know the truth of such things. Here, come, sit, listen to my tale and learn what I have discovered." He smiled broadly, eyes not quite right. A madness hung over him, like so many others over the years.

Some welcomed their end, others fought tooth and nail. A few believed it was right, the minority even believed it would take them to the Necro overlords. That a fantastic, wondrous afterlife, or even a second life, awaited them where everything would be wonderful.

They all died the same in the end. What awaited them afterwards was not for me to say. But I hoped it was everything they deserved. Most deserved the worst kind of purgatory, but not all. This man was deluded, clearly lost to his personal madness, but I wasn't here to cure what ailed him.

"Sit, listen. You will know the truth. I have found it."

"If you say so. But no, I don't want to know."

"You will sit," he ordered, all humor gone. He glared at me as he reached down to his side. As his hand moved to his knife, so a familiar feeling came over me. Time slowed, I anticipated his next move, and I knew what I had to do.

"Oh, for fuck's sake. I don't need this crap." I felt for the perfect weight and balance of my new knife, then flung it expertly straight at the guy with more force than I believed I had in reserve.

I was as surprised as he was when it stuck deep into his chest. His eyes widened in utter shock, same as mine, as he grasped the hilt.

"I wouldn't if I were you," I told him, not unkindly.

As tears filled his confused eyes, and he stared at me, imploring, he yanked the knife out. His bowels loosened with an unhealthy *spluuurt*. Liquid shit stained the inside of his trouser legs. His bladder gave way and a dark stain spread across his crotch.

It was no way to die.

No glorious ending, just base and embarrassing. Blood pumped furiously from his punctured heart, arcing high then splattering in a puddle at my feet, splashing my boots and jeans. He sagged, dropped my knife that clattered to the frigid floor, then keeled over forward and landed with a sick crunch on his face. Blood pooled from underneath him, spreading across the floor until it lapped at my tainted boots like an ocean of accusation.

I retrieved Bone Slicer then turned and walked from the room. It was done. Again.

I felt nothing. No remorse, no guilt, just empty inside. Truly a creature deserving of such a fate myself.

Was I even human any more?

I was. More's the pity.

Surprise!

I sat slumped outside the lighthouse with my back to the striped wall and ignored the buzzing of drones that circled this ancient, life-saving monument. How many ships had it warned off the cliffs? How many lives had it saved? And here I was, having taken one in a place synonymous with refuge, with safety. With honor and aid.

My energy was gone, my body bruised and my bruises bruised, my face smashed, my chest tight, ribs sore but thankfully not broken. The stab wounds were serious enough to warrant a few stitches and some delicate probing by careful, practiced hands, but we could clean them up at home, wash them out, then Phage could work her magic and stitch me up. I'd recover in a month or two, no problem.

All in all, I'd come out of this better than expected when I first saw Eleron strolling along the beach looking like he didn't have a care in the world. If it hadn't been for him, this would have been a simple job. Almost too easy.

The guy inside was an oddball, clearly not quite present, or aware of the reality of our twisted world, and not up to this kind of life. If it hadn't been me that put an end to him, it would have been someone else. But it was me. It felt so wrong. There had been no fight, no real risk. I needed that so my conscience could bear it.

And I kept wondering about the damn air conditioning unit. What was that all about? I would never know. And did I really care? No. I was clutching at straws, trying to find something else to think about.

There were more important things to ponder, to put into some kind of order. More information to decipher, to fit into place. How had Phage explained it? Ah, yes. Like a jigsaw puzzle but without the picture, so you don't know what you're working towards, where any of the pieces could possibly go. It was a perfect analogy. I could see the individual pieces, but had no clue where they could fit. What the point of it all was. If there was one.

Maybe just like a jigsaw, there was no point beyond merely putting the pieces in the right place. Then you simply walked away and wondered what to do with the finished puzzle, until eventually you broke it apart reluctantly and put it all back in the box again.

Would there ever be a box? Would there ever be an end to the hints and glimpses, the seemingly unrelated evidence and clues that might eventually lead me to a clear picture, but one that may still hold no meaning whatsoever? Would I ever know what the fuck was going on?

My gut instinct told me that there'd never be an end. That I was merely one amongst many who learned more as they leveled up through the Necroverse, but would never, could never, know the full picture. The true horror of what lay at the heart of the Necronotes and the silent masters running the freak show.

What did it matter anyway? There was nothing to be done but carry on as I always had, same as every other Necro who had ever lived. People kept telling me I was special, but I wasn't that special. There would be no big reveal where I could then live a life of peace. I wasn't foolhardy enough, or so full of myself, to believe that for a moment. No, as the witch bitches said, the notes endure.

Even the fucking trolls had notes. But why not the elves? What made them so bloody special? If anyone deserved such a life, it was those smug bastards.

How come they just got to watch the rest of us suffer? Maybe because they were nigh on immortal. Even the Necromasters couldn't get them to kill each other in a meaningful enough way to make it worthwhile. Not that they were the only Necro race to be excluded. Stripe didn't have to kill his kin. Fae the same. At least, as far as I was aware. Sprites, dwarves, so many other races all just went about their business unmolested by the notes.

I wondered which ones did have them. Humans and trolls, was that it? Had anyone known about trolls before? I'd never heard it mentioned, but I didn't make a habit of hanging out with those obsessed with the Necroverse.

"Hello," came a morose voice.

I turned, startled, to see a glowing, spiral horn poke around the lighthouse wall, followed by a stupid head and a dumb face.

"Aren't you going to say something? Why are you sitting there, grinning like you're trying to have a poo?"

"I don't look like this when I'm having a poo. And how do you know what I look like when I'm on the toilet?"

"I don't. But I've seen you in the woods enough times to know you look like that," Bernard said miserably.

"What's up with you? And, um, how the hell did you find me? And what are you doing here?"

"Nice to see you too." Bernard moped towards me then stood several paces away and lowered his head, almost stabbing me in the eye.

"Careful, you almost got me."

"Oh, so sorry. Am I intruding?"

"Hey, take it easy." I took a deep breath, tensed my painful abs, then heaved up and stood with my back against the wall, trying to ignore the pain, unsure if I could remain standing for long.

"So, let me guess," said Bernard, "you killed someone, and now you're going over and over what you did, wondering why you have to keep doing it, thinking about the things you've learned, wondering if they mean anything, unsure if you've heard too much and will get your name on a note? You curse those behind the notes, you lament how unfair it all is, and you repeat everything until your head's spinning and you finally acknowledge that you have no control over this, you never will, and you're just a plaything for your unseen masters."

"Blimey, that was impressive."

"Not really. It's what you always do," he said glumly, snorting.

"No, not the recap, but that you used the word lament. And acknowledge. You been reading the dictionary?"

"I'm a unicorn. I don't read."

"Okay, then what?" Bernard hung his head and mumbled something. "What was that?"

He looked at me through his thick, long lashes and said, "I'm trying to better myself. To keep up with Kayin. She knows all the big words already and is so bright. It's not fair."

"She is a clever one. But look, old friend, don't beat yourself up about it. Everyone's different, and we all have our own skills. She's bright, sure, and she'll be a true warrior when older. She's brave, almost too brave, and her and Jen are perfect for each other, but you have your own thing. Never compare yourself to others, certainly not your children. You don't want to resent your kids, and this is a surefire way to do it. Be happy for her."

"I am. I'm very proud of her. I just want to be able to keep up so I can stay interested, help her."

"You help your children by loving them unconditionally. By always being there for them. By encouraging them to follow the right path and worrying sick about them every minute of the day. Do you do that?"

"Yes."

"Then you're the perfect father." I smiled at my oldest friend and nodded. He nodded back.

"Thank you. Gosh, you've always been good at things like this. When you aren't making fun of me."

"Hey, you'd hate it if I didn't make fun of you now and then."

"Like you'd hate it if I stopped smashing windows?" he asked hopefully.

"That's a bit different. Wow, it's hard to believe that we've been together since there weren't even windows with glass. At least, not for the likes of us. Ha, can you imagine such a thing?"

"I'm a unicorn," he said, like he had so often to explain absolutely everything.

"Fair enough. Guess glass isn't high on your list of priorities. But still, mad, right? How everything has changed so much. It's been a long life, my friend. So long."

"For you. Not for me. You're like a... a... a blip! Yes, that's it. You're a blip on my life."

"Way to make a guy feel insignificant." I glanced up at the drones as they circled the lighthouse, their work inside seemingly done. Guess the dead guy was gone now, dropped through an eye into a volcano or the middle of an ocean somewhere. They swept low, catching our conversation, or lack of it now, then were gone.

"You're a human. Even Necros live short lives in comparison to my kind."

"Exactly how old are you?" I asked. A question I'd never got an answer to from my, and we all knew it, rather dim-but-handsome sidekick.

Bernard scrunched up his face, no easy thing for a creature that's basically a very shiny horse with a horn stuck on its forehead. The silence stretched out until I assumed he'd either forgotten the question or was farting. Silent but deadly.

"Old," he said, smiling like it was the perfect answer.

"Old? That's it?"

"You don't understand. Your brain is different to mine. You're human. You read and count and do maths and think your dull thoughts. I'm a true Necro. A different creature. But I am an animal. We don't go around marking off calendars or counting the days, worrying what day it is or any of that. We never have lived like that. Animals don't have deadlines, or bills, or jobs, or anniversaries, or birthdays, or Christmas, or—"

"You love Christmas. And you love presents."

"Only because I'm with you. Animals don't have years or calendars, is what I'm saying. We don't give them a thought. Why would we? We don't mark the passing of time with mental notes or try to work things out. We just do stuff. We live in the moment. The now. That's what all you humans strive for, isn't it? To not be burdened by the past. Unfettered, you call it."

"You really are trying to better yourself, aren't you?" I was impressed.

"Yes. Soph, you are old by your standards, but you humans have so much baggage. I am truly old. Ancient beyond words. I cannot die, but that means I cannot remember much of my life. How could I? I can't be expected to remember things from thousands of years ago. Where would all that information fit? Plus, I live day by day. I don't let the past affect me."

"Liar. You're always banging on about what happened to you. All the bad things. The things you hate. The state of your stable, your food, your aching legs, the hot, the cold."

"That's different." Bernard grinned wide, his thin lips spread tight against his teeth. He looked so cheesy, so daft, but once again, my old friend had surprised me.

"You are such a dark horse. Unicorn," I corrected as he glared. "You have a deep side, my friend. Shame you hide it so well most of the time. I wonder if you've been playing with me all these years and really you're a super-smart guy."

Bernard shook his long, wavy mane. "I'm not. I know what I am. I know I'm dumb. I'm just an old, dumb unicorn who can't remember where he came from or what he did when he was young. But that's the point, isn't it? Why would I? Why should I? I am an animal, not a human being. And I'm smart enough to know that I have it much better than you do. All of you. Constantly worried about things. Stressed, scared, never happy. You never accept the way things are. You always want something different. You have mental health issues and you go so far as to ruin a whole world. How is that even possible? How could you do it? Why would you do it?"

"Honestly? I have absolutely no idea. I think it's because we are the truly dumb ones. We think we can control everything, when all we do is fuck it up. You're right, we don't accept things. We dwell on the past, on things we cannot change, rather than being in the present and thankful for what we have. But you know what? We'll never change. We can't. It's how we are wired. And damn, Bernard, this is one epic conversation. Where has all this come from?"

I looked up when he didn't answer. He was fast asleep, standing there with his eyes closed, snoring happily. I chuckled quietly. He was a daft creature, but it only went so deep. Underneath the moaning, the ludicrous things he did, he was actually much smarter than me. Smarter than all of us. How freeing it would be to not mark the passage of time. Not count the days, weeks, and years. Just live. Be truly free.

I never would be. Just like he said I always did, I'd mope and lament, rage against my lot in the world, and question everything, even my own sorry existence.

Who was the stupid one really? Not this immortal creature standing before me, exhausted from the mental gymnastics he'd had to perform to have a brief, but insightful conversation with a lowly human. He truly wasn't wired that way. Wasn't meant to discuss things in this manner. Because, after all, he wasn't as foolish as me.

Several minutes later, as I slumped back down to the ground, and watched him sleep, I realized I had no idea why he was here at all.

"Stupid fucking unicorn," I whispered, smiling.

Bernard Gets to the Point

"Hmmf. Whaaa? Gaaah? Mwfff. Gah. Ugh. What time is it?"

"Nice sleep?" I laughed.

"I wasn't asleep. I was resting my eyes after having been forced to travel all this way."

"And who forced you to come here?" I asked, hoping Bernard might finally explain his sudden arrival.

"Phage, of course," he said, looking confused. "Didn't I say?"

"No, you didn't. And look, is it important? I'm assuming Phage and Jen are fine, or you'd have said, but what gives?"

"I have a note."

My heart stopped beating, my guts churned, my head pounded, and I just about gave up and rolled over. "You cannot be serious? I don't fucking believe it. I can't do this again. Not now. Fuck. No, absolutely not. I cannot. Once a year is enough, you hear me?" I raged at the clear sky, my fist clenched so tight my palm bled where my jagged nails dug in deep.

"A note from Phage," Bernard added, belatedly.

"You stupid mother... Okay, where is it? And is everything alright?"

"How would I know? I can't read."

"No, but I'm sure the last time I looked you had ears. Yes, there they are, on the side of your stupid head. What did she say? What's this about?"

"Like I said, I can't read. But she said to hurry here and bring you the note she found. Everyone's fine at home, although Jen is rather moody lately, isn't she?"

"You should talk. At least she's got an excuse. She's a hormonal young girl who just found out she's expected to go on a murder spree every year or she'll die. You just enjoy being unhappy."

"Do not. And anyway, that's just my nature."

Things were definitely back to normal. Bernard was stupid and grumpy. I was exasperated and grumpy. "Where's the note?" I asked with a familiar sigh, beyond exhausted by the sudden switch back to dim-witted from curiously smart.

"Where'd you think it is?" he grumbled.

"For fuck's sake, Bernard. Just tell me!" I shouted, overreacting maybe a touch, maybe not enough.

"Here." Bernard waved a knobbly leg. An envelope drifted from somewhere, wafted on the breeze, then settled in my lap gently.

I eyed the white mountain of idiocy before me and didn't even bother to ask where exactly he'd secreted it. But then I thought better of it and had to know. "Okay, how'd you do that? You keeping more secrets from me? Like the fact you can race around the country in seconds, rather than the hours and days like you've always done in the past, even with your super speed?"

"A magician never reveals his secrets," he said, straight-faced. Or should I say long-faced?

"Whatever." I opened the envelope and pulled out two pieces of paper. One smelled of perfume, the other of earth and damp. And beer. I raised an eyebrow to Bernard, nonplussed, but he just nodded, eager for me to read.

I unfolded the one undoubtedly from Phage first and read the short note out loud just so Bernard wouldn't feel left out or bug me about it. "Dear Soph, that sounds strange, doesn't it? Jen and I are fine, hopefully you are too. We worry about you. Come home to us soon. The phones and internet are still dead, so I had to send Bernard. Hi Bernard."

"Hi Phage."

"Idiot."

"Was that in the note?" he asked.

"No, that was me calling you an idiot. May I continue?"

"Of course."

I glowered at Bernard, then read the rest. "Bet he interrupted you then, didn't he? Sorry about that. So, we're fine, the animals are fine, we hope you are too. Jen and I went back to the Brewer's room to see if he'd turned up as we were worried, and Jen found a note in his slippers. Not so much a note as a clue, maybe. We aren't sure what to make of it, but it seemed important so I thought it best to send it in case you need to do anything before you come home. But please do return soon. It's a nightmare without phones. I worry, and I can't get in touch with you. I could try morphing, but don't think I'd be able to reach you, and I refuse to ask Mother for help. We love you. Phage."

"That's nice," said Bernard. "Wonder what the other one is? Ooh, how mysterious."

"Don't act like you don't already know. I bet you a million of whatever the fuck we use for money now that you know precisely what it is."

"Maybe I do, maybe I don't," he said smugly.

"You've forgotten, haven't you?"

"Maybe I have, maybe I haven't."

"Twat."

"Was that in the note?"

"What!? No, of course not. That was me calling you a twat. Because you are."

"You shouldn't call me names. I'll get a complex."

"There's nothing complex about you. Now, be quiet while I read it."

"Aloud."

"Yes, alright. Aloud."

"Good."

I swear I could have battered him. I was not in the mood for this. I wanted to go home. I could be there by evening if I could manage to get back to the car. And remembered where it was. Where was it?

"Hello? Are you going to get on with this, or should I just go?"

"Sorry, got distracted. Okay, let's have a look at this." I scanned the grubby piece of paper torn from a lined pad. The Brewer had not stuck to the lines, and his scrawly handwriting was hard to read, but I'd had years of practice from reading the beer menus he used to put out until he decided it was more fun for it to be a surprise and to appear in person. "Had to go and you know what. Sorry, but it's been so long. So many years. I can't stand it a moment longer. Be back when I can face you. And face myself. Don't try to stop me. You know where I've gone, so don't worry. It's always the same place. Always. I hate myself. The Brewer."

"That's it?"

"Yeah, that's it," I sighed, putting the notes back in the envelope then pocketing it.

"What does it mean? Where has he gone? Actually, who is he? What does he look like? Have I met him?"

"Trust me, you'd know if you had. The Brewer kind of keeps to himself. He's not very sociable, and he's, er, well, he's a little different."

"Bit funny in the head, is he?" Somehow, Bernard managed to lift a hoof to his head and make a circle, the universal sign for tonto.

"Aren't we all?"

"I'm not. Nothing wrong with my head." I stared at him. Hard. "Not much," he grumbled.

"Everyone's different, and the Brewer is no exception. He's a Necro, but not by birth. More, ah, by design, if you know what I mean?"

"No idea," Bernard said happily.

"I guessed as much. The thing is, he never leaves the Necropub. He's lived in the cellar there ever since we moved in. He's comfortable there, keeps busy, stays away from trouble. He's a serious addict, so does what he can to stay straight, and away from temptation. He's disappeared before, but only to stretch his legs and go check out what the world's like now. This is different. This is worrying."

"Why? What's he going to do?"

"Something terrible. Truly terrible. He's a rare creature is the Brewer, and if I could change what that means then I would. But I can't."

"He'll come home eventually," said Bernard brightly.

"He will," I agreed. "But it's what he'll be like is the concern. I need to go get him before it's too late. Before he does something he'll regret. Damn, I wasn't expecting this. I figured he'd just be off for a few days exploring, same as he has before. I thought he finally had a handle on this."

"Once an addict, always an addict."

"You mean like you and molasses," I said, chuckling.

"That is a very mean thing to say. You know I struggle with my weight. With that sweet, sweet nectar."

"Bernard, you have neither gained nor lost a pound since I've known you. Sure, you get bloated when you do daft stuff, but then you revert to normal."

"That's because I limit my carbs afterwards. It's a constant battle trying to maintain this physique."

I honestly couldn't be bothered to talk to him any longer, so leaned my head back against the warm stone and pondered my next move. Should I go after him? Should I go home? Should I have a nap?

When I snapped out of my unplanned snooze, it was to find Bernard lying next to me, his head on my lap, his horn stuck in the wall of the lighthouse. His sweet breath came in fast bursts as he whimpered in his sleep. Since when was I a bloody unicorn's pillow?

"Bernard, you great lump, time to wake up," I said softly. For some reason I was feeling nice towards him. Probably because for once what he'd told me helped to understand not only him but all animals better.

It was easy to forget just how differently they were wired when you could talk to them. Sure, regular animals were very limited conversation wise, but I spent my time talking to animals of the Necroverse for the most part, and they were either usually as smart, or way smarter, than me.

It was a reminder how different they were, that the concerns of humans were not theirs. Our struggles for fancy shelter and posh foods, expensive beverages and cars more expensive than a year's wages meant nothing to them. Talk about envious.

Bernard kicked his legs in his sleep, a dangerous thing to be so close to. Just as I readied to shout at him, he calmed, and whimpered as his nostrils flared. I smiled at the ridiculousness of my life.

What to do? What could I do? What should I do?

I needed to let Phage and Jen know I was alive, so Bernard would have to return. But could I leave the Brewer out here all alone? He wasn't a man of the world like I was. He was once, a long, long time ago. But now? Not so much. The world had changed beyond recognition for him.

Each property I'd moved to, he'd tagged along, just like Shey Redgold, although I'd actually invited the Brewer because I owed him big time. A debt that could never be repaid in full.

No way could I abandon him, even though he was just about the strangest creature I had ever had the mostly misfortune to meet, let alone make part of my family.

Nevertheless, he was family, and I had to help him if I could.

There was nothing for it.

"Road trip," I whispered, grinning despite my pain, my all-encompassing tiredness, and my confusion over the encounter with the elves. Not to mention the realization that Tyr and I had actually confronted an arena of super beings and basically told them to go fuck themselves.

Actually, we'd done more than that. We'd royally screwed them over. Ah well, they didn't seem to mind. All part of the daily entertainment for them, as far as I could tell. Maybe we'd get plushies made of us, or movies. Did elves have movies? Would we ever make new TV shows and blockbusters with big budgets again? It had been so many years since such things were allowed. Too much of an environmental impact, we were all told. All that flying to and fro, all those sets being built, the waste of resources.

And then the movie theaters wasting more energy, everyone driving to a screening. No way, that was pure indulgence. And what about all the wasted bandwidth with streaming, or god forbid, actual discs being produced?

The world was one big dictatorship, and yet how could you argue? It was wasteful, but when creativity is stifled and the masses are left to wallow in the past, what did they think would happen?

Sooner or later, and my guess was very soon, especially if the kill switch wasn't flipped back on, there would be carnage and uprising on a worldwide scale.

"Time to get the Brewer back where he belongs before he destroys all the good he's done." I got the uneasy feeling life was about to change, and not for the better, very soon, so I'd best make the most of the transport and go get our master of beer.

Bernard twitched violently. His horn yanked from the wall where it was jammed, pulling off the render as his head whipped sideways. A cloud of dust coated me in white powder as I coughed and sneezed and once again cursed my ancient companion.

"Eh? What? Who's there?" asked Bernard. As our eyes met, he grinned sheepishly.

"Time to rise and shine, sleepy head," I told him, figuring I'd been mean enough to him for one day.

"I wasn't sleeping, I was—"

"I know, resting your eyes," I laughed. "Well, they're rested enough now, so can you get up please? You're really heavy, and I'm a bit battered."

Bernard got his act together and gave me some space, so I reluctantly dragged myself up and brushed myself down. The dust had got everywhere, so I swigged some water and swilled it around my mouth, then spat it out and turned my attention back to Bernard.

"Thanks for coming, and thanks for bringing the notes. Can you tell Jen that I miss her and Phage lots, and I love them both. I'm going to check on the Brewer but I'll be back soon. Make sure you tell them I'm fine, that my note is complete and there is absolutely nothing to worry about. You got that?"

"Huh?"

"Forget it. I'll write it down." I sorted through my pack and found a pad and a pen then wrote Phage and Jen a message. I handed it to Bernard who just stared at it.

"I don't have any fingers."

"Yes, I am well aware that you have hooves. But you brought a note with you, so you must be able to take one back. Should I throw it at you? Rest it on you back? Stick it on your horn?"

"Just, er, throw it in the air then turn your back so you can't see," said Bernard cryptically.

"Whatever." I did as I was asked then waited, and waited. "Can I look now?"

"Yes, of course. I wondered why you were facing away for so long."

I turned back around and grit my teeth. "Why so secretive?"

"It's personal."

"Taking a message home?"

"No, where I put it. How I put it there."

"Hmm. Okay, suit yourself. Guess I don't really need to know."

"Trust me, you *really* don't."

I shuddered at the mental images his words formed. Did I need to wash my hands after the message he'd brought me? "I suppose it's time to go. You okay getting home?"

"Of course. I might take in the sights as I go. Maybe stop to visit several old friends. Get a snack, see a few historic monuments while I'm out and about."

"Really? That's great! Yes, treat yourself," I told him.

Bernard stared at me. And stared, and stared, and stared. "Seriously? That was my best joke ever. I'm not doing that. I want to go home. It's rubbish out here."

"Oh yes, of course. I forgot how much of a homebody you are. Be seeing you then. Drive safely. Um, run safely. You know, when you do your rainbow thing."

Bernard shook his head from side to side then turned slowly, so I was left with a closeup of his fat arse, then with a *whoosh* he was gone.

How does he get across the water?

"Time to go save the Brewer," I lamented, wishing I could just go home and see my two favorite girls, then have a snooze in my recliner.

What was the saying? No rest for the wicked.

Fun Times

The Brewer and I had a long history. I met him when I was settling into my life as a man, having owned what I'd become, the things I'd done, the things I would continue to do. I still raged against it, same as always, but I finally had acceptance, if not peace.

This strange fellow could never fight what he'd become. There was no turning back, no choice, and no alternative. Except one. Death. Oblivion. Obliteration. Even in his darkest hours, he couldn't bring himself to end it all. Most of us are the same way. We cling to life no matter how weary we are, how sick of ourselves we become. How corrupted we have allowed ourselves to be.

In that regard he was nothing special. In other ways he was the most special of beings. Far from unique, he was still a rarity. He never asked for help, never asked for anything apart from the promise he would always have a home with me. A refuge. A place of sanctuary. Somewhere safe. I gave him that, because he and I were more alike than any other person I had ever met.

Damaged goods. Beyond redemption. Bad to the bone, yet innocent enough to accept there was good there, too. Caught up in the Necroverse in ways not of our own doing, and left with only one decision. Carry on, or bow out gracefully and leave the world to continue without us.

Neither of us accepted annihilation. We chose to live with it, to battle through, and find solace in other ways. For me it was family and the animals. They kept me sane and allowed me to give back in ways that truly made me happy. They made life worthwhile. They were my calling, my vocation, my crutch, and my passion.

For the Brewer it was an altogether different, more isolated, and terribly solitary existence. Unable to mingle with the world at large, knowing he could never be accepted, always judged, kept away from humanity because of what he was, what he'd become.

There would be no family, no children, no peaceful nights at home cuddled up on the sofa, watching TV and eating popcorn. No trips, no ubermarkets, no semblance of a normal life.

And the worst thing about it all, the thing that drove him mad and yet kept him alive at the same time, was that he liked it that way.

Which was a good job, because he had no damn choice in the matter.

Some of us like large homes. Others enjoy the comfort and security of a tiny house. A few even crave truly confined spaces. The Brewer adored his stoic, monastic life, where he could pursue his passion with obsessive joy. For it truly was the one thing that brought him pleasure.

The few others like him all shared the same need for seclusion, a confined space for at least part of their life, and became so focused on a particular passion that it excluded almost all other aspects of what would be considered a well-rounded life.

I pondered his lonely existence as I left the lighthouse and made my way painfully along the headland, keeping well away from the edge and trying not to peer down at the dizzying drop.

Tyr came and somehow scooped me up, and I vaguely recollect the return ride but didn't really come back to my senses until I was on a beach just up the coast from where I'd met Eleron, that fucking elven knobhead.

The wind howled, the salt stung my face, and the gulls cried overhead. Hardy sheep ripped at the short grass and stared at me blankly. I made no conversation—sheep weren't the best for having a chat, they just talked about grass and that was about it.

After a while, and still fighting the sickness of the short flight, I found myself at my car. I'd moved on auto-pilot, hadn't even realized I was heading in the right direction, just let my feet take me where they wanted and hoped they knew something I didn't. Relief washed over me. I wouldn't have to walk home or, worse still, ask Tyr for a ride. Ugh, made me feel nauseous just thinking about it.

Happy to have found the car, I sorted through my gear and ate what little food I had left. It was more than enough. The car gave me the luxury of packing plenty of provisions, and I hadn't wasted the opportunity.

But something was missing. I was edgy when I should have been entrenched in the comedown.

I hadn't smoked! Damn, no wonder I was jittery.

Grinning, and my heart racing with anticipation, I pulled out the pouch of tobacco and stuffed Old Faithful eagerly. I hopped into the car and lit up out of the wind, feeling guilty for smoking in the vehicle even though I was alone. I cast furtive glances, like Phage might jump out and tell me off.

With the engine running and the air-con on low, I chilled in the car, letting the bitter, acrid smoke burn my lungs and ease the stress of yet another Necronote fulfilled.

Happy days. Not.

I missed Phage so much. I wanted to hug my daughter and scowl at Mr. Wonderful. What was Woofer doing? Had he settled down after his transformation? What a nutty guy he was. I smiled as I pictured him. He was a good boy, and now, hopefully, he would be with us forever. Would he still want to play ball in a century? I laughed out loud just thinking about all the aggravation that lay before me. Unending, enduring, damn annoying.

I spluttered as I choked on a lungful of smoke and ended up stuck in a coughing fit loop of amusement and pain as my lungs burned, my eyes watered, and I contemplated having to put up with my dog pestering me to play ball for as long as my sorry existence lasted.

There were worse ways to live. Much worse.

Just ask the Brewer.

Laughter and coughing finally under control, I stepped out of the car into the stupid heat and left the door open to let the smoke disperse. Then I closed it and waited for the interior to cool down again while I pondered the best route to take to go bring the Brewer home before he did anything he'd regret, if it wasn't already too late, which it most likely was.

After checking the map and figuring I'd best get back on the main road for a short spell, I recognized I was stalling and should have been well on my way.

My head was shot, and the pain was getting worse as the slight infections began to set in. Knowing proper treatment needed to wait until I got home, I nevertheless got out the medical kit and cleaned out the wounds as best I could. I used closure strips and bandages to keep the wounds in check. I would pay for this later, but it wasn't life-threatening so I could put up with it. I'd moan about it, mind you. Even if just to myself.

Then I was off, map on the passenger seat, location set, and driving away from the scene of yet another crime.

Hours later, after I'd listened to Johnny Cash on loop three times and then driven in silence with the window open and the clean air bashing my face into consciousness, I knew I'd have to pull over to rest soon. I was nearly there, though, but the trip had been entirely uneventful, which made me nervous and agitated.

The way had been clear, nothing but the odd vehicle, with no mass reclaiming of the roads as I'd half-expected.

I wondered how long it would take for everyone to say fuck it and use the bootleg fuel, or forego their other electrical luxuries to take a road trip to visit family they most likely hadn't seen for years, or just to go on a jolly somewhere.

While it lasted, I reveled in the empty roads. But I was beyond weary now and knew I should stop.

Something drove me on. A certainty that the Brewer needed me. That his note was not left to ensure I didn't worry and to leave him be, but to go after him and stop him from doing what he and I both knew he'd regret.

How did I know he'd regret it? Because it had happened several times over the centuries and each time he did it he hated himself that little bit more, ruined himself over and over again, sank into a mire of spite and hate, of despair and desperation. It took years for him to recover mentally from the horrors of what he'd done because he was a true addict and always would be.

So I pressed the buttons for all the windows, and let the warm air smash me awake as I ground my boot into the accelerator pedal and hurtled along pitch-black motorways, not another driver in sight. I sliced through the darkness like I was heading into hell itself, and that truly wasn't far from the truth. I was going somewhere no man should ever go, certainly not one that had a choice.

And there was always a choice. But what price friendship? What price your own conscience? I was willing to pay it. But only reluctantly.

Another turn, another empty wide road. Nothing to light my way but the cat's eyes on the central reservation and my own headlights. No open service stations, no drones, no cameras, at least I didn't think so, and nobody trying to ram me off the road for some bloody peaches.

My mind drifted to Wonjin. I hoped the big fella was alright and would return to us soon. How long would it take him if he was successful? Would he be gone years? Would he be at home already, standing immobile in the garden like he'd never left? Waiting another hundred years before he geared up to go kill another of his kind and become one of the few remaining of his species on the planet? Nigh on extinct because of the Necronotes and their never-ending insistence on destruction.

He'd be alright. I just knew he would. I had that feeling of certainty like I did about some things. As though a storm was coming. Something epic, something terrible. A drastic shift that would turn our lives upside down, leaving nothing the same again.

Something like, and I shuddered at the thought, having to get a "real" job. Imagine that? I couldn't. What if I had to get up every morning and perform thankless tasks for a faceless corporation just to put food on the table? Ugh, it didn't bear thinking about. But not to worry. We might not have been swimming in money, but my investments from when young and looking to the future had ensured I'd never have to work a job I hated for as long as I managed to crawl from one year to the next.

Buoyed by the knowledge I didn't have it half as bad as some, I swerved around the curved overpass, then took a left and soon I was driving sedately through winding roads and passing countless small, sleeping villages. No streetlights, no lights above people's doors, just an occasional glimmer of life from behind badly closed curtains, or people out on the front step, smoking, and taking in the warm, balmy air. A day like any other for them, but one that had been far too full of surprises for a man who wanted nothing but a hug and maybe a large glass of something strong. Screw the glass, just give me the bottle. I deserve it.

I came to a junction, but there was no sign so I turned on the interior light and checked the map. With the route in my mind, and memories coming back of the last time I came here to retrieve the Brewer, I took a deep breath then turned right and continued on my way down increasingly narrow lanes until the wing mirrors were scraping the sides of the overgrown hedges that grew tall and spindly, almost gasping for water they were shit out of luck in finding.

Several minutes later, I was as close as I could get by vehicle. I parked in a passing point, although I doubted it mattered, then wasted time checking my gear, sorting my pack out so it was as light as possible, and then I leaned against the door and began a lengthy smoking session just because I truly didn't want to have to do what I knew I had to anyway.

"Brewer, Brewer, why have you broken your promise? Actually, it's okay, I understand. You can't help it. You can't deny your nature. But you were doing so well. It's been so long, old friend. Why now?" I chuckled to myself as I became aware of how I had grown used to talking to myself out loud when alone. Age does funny things to a man, and all he can do is accept it.

My pipe was empty all too soon, so I banged out the ash on the road then pocketed it once it was cool.

No more delays. Time to go get me a fright.

Nowhere to Turn

I felt ridiculous sneaking through the fields, skirting the hedgerows so I could keep my bearings, but having to wind the lever on the torch continually so I could see where I was going. We had no batteries, they were rarer than gold, and there was no way I could find my way without some form of light. It was either this ridiculous whirring, or me getting completely lost and probably walking straight into a cow.

Even with the light, the going was rough. The path I eventually found was little more than a gap between two long hedgerows that led directly to my destination. If you didn't know what you were looking for, you would never find it in a million years.

Not quite as magical as the witches' paths, where you couldn't even enter if you weren't on the magical list, it did, however, hold its own power that stopped any passersby from accidentally following it to its destination. There was magic, and then there was magical coercion. This was the latter.

No explicit whispers or spells, but it had become so full of the intent of those like the Brewer over the years that to all intents and purposes this timeworn path between ancient hedges of oak and beach, hawthorn and blackthorn, may as well never have existed to the world at large. It didn't.

And even if anyone did know it was here and where it led, they sure as shit wouldn't choose to follow it. Only Brewer's kind ever came here. And certainly only his kind ever left. Once, it had been well-worn and wider, but over the millennia it had narrowed as the numbers dropped steadily until now visitors were few and far between. The trees had become so gnarly they resembled sculptures rather than living plants, the world blocked by twisted trunks and shortened limbs. This was not a pleasant stroll.

Some things were for the best. This was certainly for the best. There are creatures in the Necroverse you never want to meet, things that live in the other places. And that's fine. They aren't here, amongst us. But some Necros that shouldn't be here are. This is not discrimination against a race without just cause. It is because they are not only a danger to others, but to themselves. They are mostly miserable, insane, and unable to atone. Mostly. There are, of course, exceptions to every rule.

The Brewer was one such exception.

I continued to wind the damn torch, the noise grating, so I went faster and then pushed in the handle to give myself a few minutes of peace before I'd have to repeat the process all over again. Someone really needed to invent a better device.

The trail widened; I was close to my destination. I sped up, keen to get out into the open. And then, just like that, I burst from the path into a hidden world.

The moon thankfully peeked out from behind wispy clouds, giving me enough light to see, but not enough to chase away my trepidation. Coming here was a big risk, but one I was willing to take. I wished I could have told Phage where I was, just so she'd know where to come collect my bones, but maybe it was best she didn't know. This was one place I never wanted my wife to visit.

A clearing maybe the size of a five-a-side football pitch was surrounded by the same dense hedgerow as the path. The ground was little but parched, compacted earth, and it had nothing to do with the weather. Nothing much of anything grew here apart from the odd weed or a few brave blades of stunted grass. This was corrupted earth. Barren, devoid of nutrients. Sucked dry by generations of foulness.

Home to those who slept. It was a graveyard of a very unique kind. No headstones, no markers, just a series of thick planks set into the ground at irregular, unevenly spaced intervals. Inside each six-foot deep, coffin-sized hole was a body. A corpse of sorts. Waiting, listening, praying, hoping, but utterly beyond redemption. Entirely corrupted not by what they had become, but by what they needed to become.

Food.

The one I had to open was imprinted on my mind; I wasn't likely to forget it any time soon. I cursed as the torch spluttered then died, so made do without it. Now was not the time for unnecessary noise. Not because I feared for my life, which I kinda did, but because I feared for my sanity if I disturbed too many occupants and they got pissed off.

I weaved around the planks, careful not to stand on one and make my presence known. At the far end of the clearing, I counted back two uneven rows, then nine along to the right, then stood over the weathered wood that defied the process of decay. I waited. I listened. Nothing. No banging, no shouting, no breathing, no nothing. As silent as the tomb.

Full of trepidation, I reached down to pull on blackened wood to open the grave, then remembered I wouldn't be able to see. Cursing, I stared at the damn torch and wondered what to do. The noise would surely cause trouble, but what was the alternative?

I almost laughed out loud when I realized the massive error I'd made. My bloody phone! Duh. It might not work for calls and messages, but it could bloody well work as a camera or, more importantly, as a torch. I always forgot it had that function. Call it being a man of a certain age, or just me being forgetful, but whatever the reason, I thanked the makers of such mysterious tech.

Relief washed over me as I stashed the torch, pulled out my phone, removed the case, and then simply shook the bloody thing until the torch cast its cold strong light over the wood.

With a sigh, I pulled back on the edge of the thick plank, every nerve screaming in pain as my wounds split, my ribs creaked, and my arms felt fit to snap off at the elbows.

I gently lay the covering aside, then stood over the open hole and without letting myself pause, I shone the light straight into the pit.

"You came," said the young woman lying prone in the grave that was not a grave. "It's been so long. Why have you abandoned me?"

I said nothing, just stared down at the pitiful creature lying immobile on the bare earth in the foul-smelling hole. Her once white dress was almost nothing but rags. Time might have preserved her body, but her clothes were a different matter entirely. The dress looked like something a party-goer would wear in the twenties. The nineteen twenties. Filthy, rotten, hanging off her in strips, gnawed by the bugs, slowly disintegrating.

The smell was musty, but enticing. A strong female scent that had seeped into the very fabric of the earth after so long. The woman's fingernails were long but clean, her bare feet just as pretty. But it was the face that stopped me in my tracks, halted any words I might have said.

She was truly beautiful. Slightly overweight by today's standards, there was no denying the sensuous curves, the ample chest, the long limbs, and sweeping lines of her neck. Around her pale throat was a choker with an emerald held in a silver clasp. It dazzled me as the light reflected startling green.

Her features were truly arresting. Ageless, timeless, smooth and clear of complexion. If it wasn't for the clothes, you'd truly think she'd come directly from her party and been here a matter of hours. Happy to lie down and have a rest from the racy festivities she'd escaped from momentarily. Her hair nestled around her full chest in loose golden curls, oiled and lustrous. Thin arched eyebrows highlighted her kohl-lined, pale blue eyes that danced with excitement and anticipation.

Her lips were as red as Tyr's eyes when the bloodlust was upon him. Sensuous, ripe, willing to be kissed.

She didn't move a muscle. She could speak, turn her head a fraction, but the rest of her was completely immobile. I knew it was the same for every single "person" in this field of sorrow. More like a field of total insanity.

Many of the occupants had been here much longer than this poor lady. Hundreds of years for some. A few even longer. Utterly out of touch with life above ground, they were in a limbo of their own doing. Waiting, hoping, praying, but mostly just on pause.

The atmosphere of the entire area was so thick with magical emanations it was like wading through pea soup. Each person was very powerful in their own right, but combined it made their connection to the Necroverse a true marvel. A connection at the pinnacle of stupidity those drawn to this thing called magic could achieve, if they were as bloody minded as this bunch of utter fucking mindless wankers. They had taken what little good there was in being born Necro and corrupted it, twisted it, then wrung it out until every ounce of power was directed towards one goal. To become what the Brewer had become.

I had never encountered more fools in one place than on this very spot, and I'd once been to the Houses of Parliament.

They wrapped themselves in the whispers and spells they had taken decades to master, then they'd dug their pit, and when the whim took them, or they had their first taste of what awaited them, they'd often quite unexpectedly, just like this idiot before me, simply jumped right in, shut the door, and waited. Often mere days if they realized they could never handle the long wait necessary, sometimes years, more usually centuries or more.

They didn't think, they hardly breathed. They survived on the energy of the Necroverse they had trained their bodies to feed on. The witches, the wizards, the sorcerers, the seers, all those who learned to connect deeply to the true wonders of the Necroverse could perform such a feat if they so desired, but who chose to do such a thing?

Those who craved true, everlasting immortality, that's who.

Bunch of fucking twats.

"I'm not him," I told her.

"Oh, how disappointing. Is he coming?" she asked, squinting under the glare of the light.

"I thought so. He said he was, but now I'm not so sure. You haven't seen him?"

"No. Not for so long. What year is it?"

"Let's just say it's far into the twenty-first century and leave it at that," I told her, not unkindly. Vague was better. She wouldn't feel so stressed if she didn't know exactly how long it had been since the Brewer had last visited her.

"Gosh. How the time flies!"

"Yeah, I bet. So, um, you doing okay?"

"Yes, fine. Why do you ask?"

"You are in a hole. You have been for a very long time. He might never come, you know."

"He'll come. They always do eventually. And then I shall be just like him. Oh, I can't wait."

"I bet." Disgusted, I shook my phone until it went dark, then grabbed the lip of the plank and gently eased it over then lay it down again, sealing her off from the world once more.

The Brewer wasn't here, he hadn't come. If he wasn't here, then where was he? I knew there was no point waiting. If he truly had the urge, if he couldn't keep away, then he would have been and gone by now. No, he'd had a change of heart, and that meant I had absolutely no way of knowing where he was or of getting in touch with him.

I walked away, leaving these bunch of degenerate hopefuls to their limbo. The woman would have already returned to her mindless sleep, preserving herself for when the time came and she could be immortal, live until the end of time as we knew it.

They thought the price of a few years in a pit was worth paying for such a future. I couldn't think of anything worse. I may have been Necro, I may have had a long life before me, but what lives is meant to die. Always. I'd met one such ancient in my time, and I shuddered at the recollection. You simply cannot live for tens of thousands of years and still call yourself human.

And besides, even if it did give you exception from the Necronotes, it still wasn't a price worth paying. Nothing was worth the sacrifice they made, all because they wished to watch humanity finally reach the stars, or witness the sun finally burn out and leave the universe a cold, uncaring, dead place. Colder than it already was. Just like their fractured souls.

I trod carefully between the plots, caring enough to not wish to give them false hope of a visitor. Although, much of me wanted to stomp about, lift the lids and scream at them. Tell them how stupid they were, that they were wasting a life. What they wanted would never bring them satisfaction. But they wouldn't listen, would never heed my advice, so I left them alone in their dark pits and passed back along the hedgerows, out into the fields, then returned to my car.

It felt like a different world out here. Alive, and brimming with possibilities.

Maybe I didn't have it so bad after all.

That feeling lasted about five minutes while I sucked frantically on my pipe and let the acrid smoke sear my lungs and sting my eyes.

Then my phone rang.

Hello?

"Is it me you're looking for?" I sang, my heart lifting because my phone was working and from the caller ID I saw it was Phage. I was overjoyed, excited, and realized just how much my heart ached for her, for my family. For the crazy warm glow and the joy I felt when with her and Jen. I missed it so much. I pressed the speaker icon. Okay, I tried to, but pressed mute and when nobody spoke I fished out my glasses, realized what I'd done, then pressed the right icon.

"Hello, anyone there? You alright, Phage?"

"Play ball with Woofer?"

"What? Oh, haha, very funny." I laughed at her silliness. She knew just how to lift my spirits. Her timing couldn't have been better.

"Not play ball with Woofer?" I felt the sad vibes pulsing through the phone.

"Woofer, is that really you? How are you on the phone?"

"Phage left phone out. Saw symbol. Means can talk? Woofer pressed button. Woofer is talking to Soph? Is like person? What's internet? Can have own phone? Where words go?"

"Buddy, I have no idea what the internet is or where the words go. Gosh, it's great to hear your voice. This is definitely the weirdest thing ever. Er, maybe not, but damn, boy, how are you?"

"Woofer hungry. So hungry. Come home and cook sausages for Woofer?" he asked hopefully.

"Sure, I'll be home soon. Now, is Phage there?"

"Is in garden."

"Okay, don't worry then. Just tell Jen to tell her mum I'll be home soon and all is well. Can you do that for me?"

"Woofer can. Got best memory. What want Woofer to say?"

"Don't worry," I laughed. "Just tell Jen what happened. How you made a call, okay?"

"Okay."

"Now, press the red button with your nose and we'll—"

Woofer had clearly already pressed the red button.

It was most definitely time to go home. There was nothing I could do for the Brewer. He was a grown-up and then some, so would have to handle his own shit. If he wanted my help, he knew how to reach me. For now, I had to leave him out here in a world he didn't know, and hope he wouldn't do anything stupid.

Eager to get home, warm and fuzzy with thoughts of my family, I started the car.

I didn't rest, I didn't stop, I didn't even crash. I ran out of petrol instead. Fucking typical. Did I have more in handy sized containers? No. Did I find an open garage just as the car spluttered then died on the side of the road I'd stupidly thought would be nicer to drive along than the A5 where there was at least the chance, albeit slim, of getting a lift? No.

Did I shout and swear and curse the Necroverse for picking on me? No.

Did I lie about the last bit? Yes.

I had several choices. I could walk. I could morph. I could call for Bernard. I could hitch a ride with Tyr. Or I could sit and mope.

For a while I chose the latter. Then the former. I would not ride a dragon; it seemed too wizardy. And besides, I didn't want to arrive home with puke in my hair. I'd had my fill of Bernard, and I'd had my fill of moping, so I gathered my gear, locked the car, and decided to walk the remaining ten miles. If I kept a steady pace, I'd be home in five hours. That was fine by me.

So as the day broke and the temperature rose to heights I had yet to experience, I set off with my hat firmly on my head, my shirt already stuck to me, and the last remaining blobby bits of sunscreen plastered on my face so it looked like I had a serious disease in need of immediate medical attention.

At least I didn't have far to go.

After three miles, I remembered that there was a fold-up bike in the back of the car. There for just such an emergency. Should I turn around or keep going? I'd already walked three miles, so if I turned around that'd be six. But then I'd have ten miles to cycle, resulting in sixteen miles traveled. But if I carried on, that would make it ten in total, which was less than sixteen.

With my mind addled due to pain, and unable to think because of the heat, I figured ten was certainly better than sixteen, not taking into account how much easier it was by bike than on foot. But I only figured that out at the halfway mark, and by then it was far too late to turn around as that would be like admitting defeat and that maybe I was wrong. And besides, I couldn't quite recall where exactly I'd left the car.

At mile seven, I realized I could have just asked Tyr where the car was. It would take him minutes to find. Again, too late now.

Mile eight saw me standing under the shade of a large willow on the outskirts of town, wondering if I should just cut my losses and die here. But I'd promised Woofer sausages, and I never went back on my word. With a push off the trunk, I teetered forward, almost fell, but somehow managed to remain standing and stumbled onward, homeward bound.

I was undoubtedly not in my right mind. I'd somehow managed to misplace the entire night, and never did get it back.

Seven hours later, having once more misplaced the intervening time and woken up in a ditch next to a muddy, pathetic stream, I discovered I was literally five minutes away from home. My best guess was I'd been delirious ever since battling Eleron.

I was covered in mud, my hand had been resting in a patch of angry stinging nettles, and bugs had feasted on my face and neck in a most aggressive manner.

I grunted, I swore, I had a long word with the insects and made them promise to leave me alone from now on, then forged ahead, finding my knees had locked almost solid and refused to loosen up until they too had a good talking to.

But finally, oh finally, I was at the front gate. All I had to do now was recall how to put my hand through and work the latch. For the life of me I couldn't quite manage it, so I decided I'd just rest against the weathered oak gate, breathe in the heavenly mixed scents of roses, lavender, and that unmistakable aroma of home, and hang out here until someone found me, hopefully before I burned to a crisp under the ferocious sun.

"Play ball with Woofer? Cook sausages now?"

"Oh, hey. Sure, I'll play ball. Where is it? Fetch, there's a good boy."

Woofer sat there, ears flat to his head, tail thumping worriedly against the gravel. "Soph broken? Need poo?"

"Um, no, I don't think I need a poo. But thanks for asking. Why does everyone keep asking me that?" I smiled at my immortal dog, then screamed as my sun-baked lips split and the tang of iron hit my tongue. I licked the blood and lifted my hand to my mouth, forgetting my arm was helping me remain upright. I promptly fell to the ground and shrieked as my ribs snapped and my wounds poured my insides out. At least that's what it felt like.

Woofer ran off. I watched him go before closing my eyes and smiling. I was home. But I had to stop making a habit of returning in such a mess. Jen would be worried, and apart from that, it really fucking hurt.

"Dad! Are you okay?" shouted Jen as she raced towards me from the side of the house. Woofer was right behind her, barking and generally causing a fuss.

"Fine. Just slipped. Help your old dad up, will you? Can you cook some sausages for Woofer? Poor guy's starving. He called me, you know. A dog using a phone. A phone! What next? Dragons surfing the web? Pigeons going on skiing holidays? Can you imagine? They'd have to use lollipop sticks for skis."

"Um, yeah, very funny. I think you might be a bit delirious. Probably got sunstroke. Are you hurt?"

"Am I hurt?" I stared at my daughter, at her face full of concern as she unlatched the gate, and all I could do was laugh.

And laugh.

And laugh.

And laugh.

Then scream.

Tales of Woe

"...but he wasn't there, and she hadn't seen him. So I came home. Oh, but I ran out of petrol, and by the time I remembered I had the fold-up bike in the car, I'd already walked, or maybe crawled, for three miles. I tried to do the math to figure out if I should go back and get it or not, but I thought maybe it was quicker to carry on, so that's what I did."

Phage and Jen sat at the kitchen table, eyes wide, mouths open, jaws almost on the floor. Neither of them said a word.

Woofer sat, staring at me with utter confusion. I rubbed his head and smiled. He wagged, and that seemed like enough for him. He curled up beside me and settled down for some serious sleeping. It was nice to know some things hadn't changed and hopefully never would.

"What? Sorry, I know I was talking fast, but I wanted to tell you while I remembered it all. Did you say something? Um, I might have missed some things out, like about my note, as that's not allowed. Jen, we told you that, right?" Jen nodded her head, still silent. "Good, that's good. Um, where was I? Ah, right, I was finished, wasn't I? Er, did I say anything about the elves? Did I tell you that bit? I got a cool knife," I giggled, somewhat manically, even to my ears.

"Yes, honey, you told us," said Phage in that soothing tone she used for people she thought were a little soft in the head, or close to doing something extremely worrying.

"Ah, great! Er, or maybe not. Should I have told you that? Damn, my head feels so peculiar. I can't quite figure out what's wrong with me, but I feel so odd. All fuzzy and blurry around the edges or something. So strange." I rubbed at my temples but it didn't help, just hurt. In fact, every single part of me hurt. And I was hot. Very hot. Yet somehow I was cold. Everything stung, like I'd walked through a field of nettles in my birthday suit. Or was covered in carpet burns after sexy times on the murder rug, although that would be a bit gross, wouldn't it?

I cut the thoughts off with a mental snap. Damn, I was rambling even when it was an internal monologue. What was wrong with me? Ah, just the infection from the wounds. Bit too much sun. Couple of elven stabs. Nothing I hadn't experienced before. I was fine. Everything was fine. I was home. Jen and Phage were safe and happy, although they didn't look it at the moment, but I was here. I'd made it yet again. Yay me.

"Where was I?"

"You said you were feeling strange," soothed Phage.

"And you told us you rode Tyr through a portal. What did you call it, an eye? And into the land of the elves. Then you fought a battle in a huge arena where tens of thousands of elves cheered you and Tyr on as you fought that man called Eleron. And, wow, you actually rode Tyr! All of that is so cool! What was it like?" Jen leaned forward, face flushed with excitement.

"Absolutely horrible. I felt sick to my stomach. And in there, in the arena, every time I got away from Tyr I felt so ill. It was only his connection to the Necroverse that saved me. I could have died!" I flung my arms in the air dramatically, forgetting I had a mug of strong sweet coffee in my hand. It flew everywhere, but nobody seemed bothered apart from me and Woofer, who howled as it splashed him, so hid hurriedly under the table.

"And, oh, did I show you the new knife? Want to look at my Big Boner?"

Phage put a hand to her mouth as she gasped, Jen turned purple, and I laughed nervously then said, "A bit inappropriate?"

"Just a little," hissed Phage, giving me the evil eye.

"Yes, Dad, you told us about *Bone Slicer*. Can we stick to that?"

"You sure? I just thought the new name was kind of... funny?"

"No, it isn't" snapped Phage.

"Not cool, Dad. Not cool at all. You, um, you know what that means, right?"

"Course I do. But you don't. Understand? You don't."

Jen blushed again and I added, "But how mad is this? They gave me a knife that can cut through bone like butter. So awesome." I glanced at Phage then Jen and added, hurriedly, "Um, not that knives are cool, and I'm not about to go using it or anything, but still."

"Can I see it again?" asked Jen eagerly.

"Maybe later."

"Soph, should you be saying all this?" Phage shifted her glance to Jen, then back to me, and smiled sadly.

"Oh, shit, sorry, so sorry. Jen, forget everything I said. I shouldn't be telling you all these things. It's not for such young ears."

"Dad, I need to know this stuff," she insisted. "I'm Necro too, and if I have to go out there and you know, then I need to understand as much as possible. But I gotta say, it's weird you talking about it like this. You guys never share so much. You feeling alright?"

"No, I am absolutely not, but I had to tell you in case I forget or something. My head's all wrong. It's like the memories are trying to leave. Does that make sense?"

"It does," said Phage. "You went somewhere nobody is allowed to go. That nobody has gone as far as I know, and now the memories are trying to fade. So you can't tell anyone, so the elves can keep their secrets. Mother would have a field day if she knew about this. She'd be so jealous."

"Do not tell her!" I said, panicked.

"We won't," said my two most precious ladies.

Phage took my empty mug from my now-still hands and returned with a full one. "Drink it. But don't wave it around." Her eyes sparkled with mirth and concern. I guess I was kind of a state, and had shared way too much with our daughter.

"Thanks." I took the drink and sipped at it, letting the silence and the heat calm me a little from my uncharacteristic surge of energy and my motormouth. "Gosh, I don't know where all that came from. You okay, Jen?"

"I'm fine. It's, er, a bit much, all that stuff, and what happened to the guy with the peaches?"

"Oh, he just left," I told her, already having forgotten I'd even mentioned him. Had I told them everything that had happened but left out the killing bits? I hoped so.

"Sounds like a right Muppet."

"He sure was. Not that you know what a Muppet is, do you?"

"Dad, course I do. You used to make me watch it, remember?"

"I do." I nodded. Memories flooded in of me sitting with Jen when she was a small girl. I'd point out the different characters to her once I found the shows online. I'd loved them, which was curious as I was an old man when they were first shown, but something had drawn me to them. Probably because it was the early days of kids' TV. Whatever the reason, we'd spent hours curled up together on the recliner, me happy to sit there all day with my little girl snuggled on my lap, smelling of apple and milk and that young child smell that makes your heart break.

"Hey, what's wrong?" Jen got up and came over and cuddled me awkwardly. I hadn't even realized I was crying.

"Nothing. Just thinking about the Muppets," I sniffed, then broke down and wailed, and bawled, and I couldn't stop the tears from flowing.

"Dad!" Jen's eyes filled with tears, then Phage reached out and took my hand. I stared into those loving eyes, and as she smiled sadly I gained strength from her, from Jen too, and forced the emptiness down and let the love replace it.

"Sorry, just a bit emotional. I used to adore watching shows with you. So silly." I wiped my eyes and Jen took her seat. They continued to stare at me like there was something wrong with me. I knew I was acting weird, but surely it wasn't that weird.

"Okay, I have to ask," said Jen. "What is the Brewer?"

I looked at her, puzzled. "Didn't I say? Don't you know?" Jen shook her head. I turned to Phage.

"We haven't told her."

"Oh, right." I gulped the coffee, just to ground myself. It was so sweet. But it tasted wrong. Still too bitter, like my tongue wasn't working properly.

"Well?"

"Well, what?" I asked, nonplussed.

"What is the Brewer? All that with those people buried, that's horrid. Why would they do that? What's the point? So awful."

"Oh, yeah, the Brewer. Isn't it obvious?"

"Not to me."

"He's a vampire."

"Very funny. No, seriously?"

"He is."

"Oh, like he feeds off other people, you mean? Like draws their energy because he's so strange. You mean he isn't good in social situations?" I could see it in her eyes, that she knew what I meant, but wasn't ready to accept it.

"No, I mean he's a blood-sucking, needs-it-to-survive, immortal, neck-biting, and very, very rare vampire. Why'd you think he lives in the cellar?"

"Because he's odd. You said he liked it. Keeps him focused."

"It does. Because he's a vampire."

"Right, that's quite enough of this," said Phage as she stood and glared at me.

"Sorry, shouldn't I have said?"

"Yes, no. I don't know." Phage glanced around the room, looking at everything but Jen and I, giving herself time to think, then she slumped back into her chair and sighed. "Okay, if this is happening with Jen here, then let's finish it. Soph, you are acting very oddly. I know you're ill, and I'll help to fix you very soon. You have infections, you are very red, and the steam is almost coming off you. You have said way too much to our daughter, but I guess that might be for the best, but haven't you noticed?"

"Noticed what?"

"Dad, seriously? You haven't felt it? How can that be a thing?" she asked Phage.

"I don't know. You'd think he'd be aware of it."

"What are you both talking about?"

"You're, um, how can I put this?" said Phage, frowning.

"Dad, you're beautiful. I mean, you look awful with all the bruises and the sweat and the blotches on your face because I guess you're running a fever and are terribly sunburned. But you're, um, so weird saying this to you. You're beautiful."

"She's right, Soph. Not pretty, not like that. It's hard to explain. But you're just... beautiful. There's something about you. Something different. Do you feel different?"

"I feel awful. Just terrible. Like I'm getting the flu or something. It's just the infection. Some antibiotics and I'll be fine. At least I hope I will. Ugh, can I go now?"

"Go where?" asked Phage.

"Um, not sure. I feel like I have to go somewhere. Do I?"

"No, you don't. You're home. You can rest. You're safe with your family," Phage told me.

"Oh, good. That's a relief."

Phage and Jen exchanged a look. "Okay, spill it. What else? There isn't more, is there? Do I have a horn? Have I grown taller? What?"

"Well... er... you're..."

"You're glowing," blurted Jen excitably. "You've got this kind of glow around you. All shiny and swirling. It's faint, but we can see it. Right, Mum?"

"Yes. Soph, you are, er, glowing."

"Glowing? I don't want to glow. What the fuck!"

I grabbed the back of Phage's chair, heaved to my feet, then wandered over to the mirror and lifted my aching head.

What confronted me was beyond strange. Almost beyond recognition. My face was red and blotchy, I was sweating, my hair was damp and plastered to my head, but I was somehow extraordinarily beautiful. There was no other word for it. They were right. I was simply lovely. And there was a strange otherworldly glow around me. An aura. Silver and shiny and constantly on the move.

I tore my eyes away then sat back down.

"Fucking elves," I muttered.

"Dad!"

"Oh, sorry. Um, darn, those naughty elves."

"You're so silly."

I smiled at Jen, then went to say something but couldn't form the thought and forgot what it was anyway.

"Soph. Soph!" came a voice from far away. I stared at Phage, but she was receding down a tunnel growing smaller and smaller until she was a pinprick of light.

And then there was nothing.

Chatting with Phage

"Hey," said Phage with a smile.

"Hey, yourself." I handed her a cup of tea and she nodded her thanks.

We stood in the garden under a crappy gazebo to stop from frying. It was hot, but just about bearable. Never too hot for tea, though.

We sipped our drinks in silence, that comfortable peace you only truly experience with someone you spend your life with. Who you know more about than yourself, as all of us are in denial about the person we really are, but can assess the faults of another and still love them unconditionally, even if we can't feel the same way about ourselves.

The garden was in full, ferocious bloom. I'd spent a lot of time out here since I returned. Getting back to nature, feeling the earth between my fingers, hanging out with the animals, spending more time with them than I had in years.

Reconnecting, ensuring they knew I was here for them, as I knew they were here for me. Grounding me, making me feel part of this world, rather than some alien creature that didn't belong.

Plus, I hadn't been able to go anywhere. Not that I'd wanted to. I had to miss several school meetings that they'd actually decided to hold at the school rather than virtually, and couldn't even go to the shops because it would have caused so many problems.

"You look better," said Phage, eyes twinkling.

"I feel better."

"Good." Phage sipped her tea.

"So, back to being unkempt and no more sparkles."

"Thank god. It was unnerving. You were too stunning. Now you're my rugged, handsome man again, not some super hunkfest that all the ladies would have drooled over."

"They still drool. You can count on it," I joked.

"They do," she said seriously.

"I only have eyes for you, my beautiful wife. You know that."

"I do. I know that too. And I only have eyes for you. Soph, do you really think it was just because you visited the elves? I still can't believe that happened."

"Of course. What else could it have been? I must have just picked up on the vibe there or something. It was so weird there, so damn nice even though there I was fighting for my life and Tyr's. Anyway, it's over now."

"Yes, but how could going there make you look like them? Okay, minus the ears, but you were so stunning. And that aura. Ugh, makes me go all funny."

I grinned at her. We certainly hadn't wasted the temporary change. Phage couldn't keep her hands off me and I had this insatiable desire that she was happy to quench, albeit always very temporarily. Strange as it seems now, almost getting killed in front of thousands of fucking degenerate elves turned out to be a most enjoyable experience.

"You'll just have to get used to it being regular old grumpy Soph now. And Big Boner," I added with a cheesy grin.

"Great. Don't think I could handle any more of that. And no, absolutely not," she laughed. "I told you already, you are absolutely not calling your new knife that. I know you, what you're like." Phage moved close and kissed me. I licked my lips. Tea and the apple pie we'd just finished. Delicious.

"What do you mean? What am I like?" I asked, unable to stop the smile from spreading.

"You'll be making crappy jokes forever, and it's not appropriate for Jen. Plus, they won't be funny. You'll be all, 'Where's my Big Boner?' and 'Gosh, I forgot how impressive my Big Boner was,' and you'll laugh, and think it's hilarious, but within a few days you'll be out of ideas but still making the same crappy jokes. So, no. Just no."

"You sure?" I asked, eyebrows wriggling.

"See, you've started already. Bone Slicer is cool, and I still can't believe you got given such a thing, but you deserve it, my handsome, brave, fearless, damn lucky man."

"Luck had nothing to do with it. Okay, maybe a little," I conceded. "Can you imagine what Peth will say about this? She'll be fuming."

"She sure will. Imagine, you, a lowly man, being the only one to ever see the elven wonderland."

"Yeah, it was so lovely," I laughed. "Anyway, hopefully I'll never see another pointy eared twat as long as I live."

"Let's hope so. Soph, do you think the Brewer will ever come home?" she asked, saying what I'd just been thinking.

"I hope so. At least, part of me does. I wonder where he is. If I knew where to look, I would, but he could be anywhere."

"And Wonjin. It's strange not having him here."

We both turned to stare at the vacated spot. There was nothing we could do to help him, but we both missed the big guy. Jen too. Maybe he'd return one day, maybe tomorrow. His life was a closed book, but it would be nice to see him too. We'd all grown accustomed to his presence on the lawn. It felt empty without him.

"How do you think Jen's holding up?"

"She seems really good, doesn't she?" Phage instantly came alive. Just thinking of her girl lifted her spirits.

"She does," I agreed. "Ever since I spouted all that stuff when I got home and was delirious, she's settled right down."

"I know. It's hard to get used to. She's been helpful. Jen really stepped up while you were out of action that first week until you got over the infections. She cooked, and cleaned, even did her chores without moaning. And the questions eased right off too. She hardly pestered me at all about the Necroverse."

"Same for me. She's asked a few things, but nothing much, and nothing that I couldn't answer honestly. But, that makes me worried. How come?"

"Maybe she knows everything she wants to at the moment. And let's face it, there isn't much more to tell. She's getting used to the idea of it all. It's a hell of a lot to take in for a young girl. Remember when you found out? I do. It was terrible. I'd grown up always knowing more than I should, but when Mother sat me down and told me the whole truth, I felt sick to my stomach and was a nightmare for months."

"And then you accepted it and got on with things. But it wasn't until you left to kill your first person that the reality truly sank in, right?"

"Exactly! Maybe that's it. She's just getting used to things."

"The fact is, she probably doesn't want to know any more. She asked and asked, and then discovered the terrible truth. Now she's aware she might uncover more, so is keeping her head down. She's been spending a lot of time with Tyr and Kayin, so I guess our girl's accepted it and knows she has to be ready."

"Soph, why does she have to be? I hate it. I don't want our little girl doing the things we've done. I can't stand it." Phage dropped her tea and flung herself at me. I wrapped her in my arms and just held her. We needed each other now more than ever. Our daughter knew the horror her life would hold, and she'd done amazingly well at keeping it together, but the worst was yet to come.

"She's strong. Jen'll be fine."

"She's my baby. I can't bear to think of the day that she walks out the house and know I might never see her again. It's not right for a parent to experience that."

"I know. The only way I can accept it is to think of her as a soldier in training. Just like other parents, we have to watch our child go off to war. The only difference is that ours has a dragon and a unicorn, and the best, most experienced soldiers to train her. She will always return to us. Always."

"Promise?" Phage looked into my eyes with hope, but she knew better than to ask that of me.

I shook my head. "I can't make you that promise. You know that. I'm sorry, but I can't."

Phage nodded. She knew. I hugged her tight and we clung to each other, knowing that one day we'd be doing this for real. When Jen walked out the door the day she turned twenty-one, and there was a chance she'd never return.

"We just have to make every day count. Same as we always have. We've got each other, and each year it gets harder to leave, but we must. So, every day is like our last, and we must promise each other one thing, Phage, even if I can't promise Jen will always return."

"What's that?'

"That we will be together for as long as we can. That we will always be there for each other, love each other, and never, ever, let these fucking notes come between us."

"I promise." Phage smiled, and somehow I knew that everything would be alright. At least for a while.

"Throw ball now?" asked Woofer, sitting patiently beside me.

"Sure buddy. Hey, how come you're so muddy? You're filthy." Mud covered his snout and the ball, which he was gripping eagerly between his teeth.

"Found water."

"Where?" I asked suspiciously.

"Um, in tap?" he offered helpfully.

"Best I don't know," I sighed. "Hey, what you doing?"

"Soph love muddy ball rubbed against jeans," he told me, pressing the ball into my thigh.

"Honestly, I don't" I laughed.

"No? Thought Soph loved dirty streaks over clean clothes. Woofer always do it."

"Yes, I know, and we've had a million conversations about this. If I've told you once, I've told—"

"Stop messing with Woofer and throw the ball for him," laughed Phage.

"But it's all muddy," I told her, then pointed in case she'd missed it. Or the streak on my jeans.

"So? You love it." Her eyes twinkled as she smiled at me and our crazy dog.

"It's good to know you're feeling alright, Woofer. You are, aren't you?"

Woofer dropped the ball, stared at it longingly, then spoke out loud, still unfortunately nothing but a series of barks for Phage. It wasn't fair that she still wasn't inflicted with his nonsense too. "Feel amazing. Can run fast and play ball forever and morph into other places and play tag and hide with Mr. Wonderful and do all sorts. Woofer not sad now. Happy. Will be with family forever."

"I'm happy too," I told him. "Hey, is that a squirrel?" I asked.

Woofer turned and ran around the garden in a frenzy, while we laughed at his antics.

"That was mean," said Phage.

"Was it? Look, I actually got the ball. See." I held out my hand; it was empty. I stared down to find my devious mutt had the ball in his mouth, and was staring up at me with endless hope in his eyes.

"Play ball with Woofer?"

Phage laughed. "Now, I do not need to be a zoolinguist to understand that."

I tutted at the pair of them, then grabbed out quick to nab the ball. Woofer, of course, was faster. So dumb.

"Come on," I told her, "let's go see our crazy daughter. You know what she's been doing, right? I knew she would, but damn, it terrifies me."

"It's your fault," chided Phage as she punched me playfully on the arm. "You shouldn't have told her you rode Tyr. What did you expect her to do?"

"Suck it up and wait until she was at least eighteen."

"If you thought that, then you don't know your daughter very well."

"Oh, I know her only too well, which is why I worry so much."

We held hands and left the shade of the gazebo, then wandered down the garden heading into enemy territory. Otherwise known as the next-door neighbor, Job's, land. Where a dragon, a tiger, and a little girl happily played on the platforms and in the trees high up in the air, where a single misstep could result in death. But that was as nothing compared to what our little girl was currently focused on, if not obsessed with.

"Don't look, don't look," I warned Phage, as she gripped my hand tight and scrunched her eyes closed.

"I'm not looking," she squealed.

"Good, because it's damn terrifying. Ugh, christ on a bike. Argh, fuck. No, don't do that!" I screamed.

"What? What is it?" Phage opened her eyes and peered up into the clear blue sky at our daughter. And her dragon. "Get her down, right now!" hissed Phage. "She can't be up there doing that. Bloody hell, did you see that? They did a loop-the-loop. How did she stay on?"

"Sheer bloody determination, is my guess," I said, trying to sound calm when inside my heart was hammering, my throat was dry, and I was sweating and not because of the heat.

"Mum, Dad, look at me. No hands," shouted Jen as Tyr whooshed by in Job's field, well away from Sanctuary.

"Hold on!" screamed Phage.

"You look pale," I laughed. "Told you not to look."

"But you kept gasping and shouting and swearing. I thought something was wrong."

"It is. Our not even teenage daughter is riding no-handed on a dragon, and there's a tiger waiting for her when she lands." I pointed to the top platform of Sanctuary where Rocky was sitting and watching Jen's shenanigans. He was used to it, and spent most of his time up there with Tyr when he wasn't off riding with Jen or hunting.

Rocky would come down for food and for a call of nature, but he and Tyr were inseparable and became closer every day. That was good. Because it meant Jen was closer to him too, and the more strings in her bow for when the time came, the better it would be. Or was it too much?

Would it mean she was thrown in right at the deep end, rather than her first job be the one to ease her into her new way of life? I guess it was too late now, and only time would tell.

"Soph, do something," insisted Phage.

"Well done, honey. But hold on. You're still learning."

Jen waved at us as Tyr banked right, darted up high, then dropped down fast before landing expertly on the platform.

"That was you doing something, was it?" asked Phage, grinning despite herself.

"Think of it as a fairground ride," I told her. "No way can she really fall. Tyr's saddle is the perfect fit for her. She can hold on to those weird handles, although she doesn't do that enough. And even if she fell off, he'd just swoop down and catch her before she hit the ground."

"Wow, I feel so much better."

"Good, because I don't."

"Neither do I, you idiot," laughed Phage. I laughed too, because it was that or cry, and I'd shed more than enough tears recently.

"Put it this way then. At least we save money on amusement parks. Um, if there were any open. And if we were allowed to go."

"My hero. Always know the right thing to say, don't you?"

We stared into each other's eyes and then I took my wife's hands, pulled her close, and whispered, "I love you."

"I love you too, my handsome, scruffy, no longer beautiful husband."

"I'll take it," I chuckled, then I kissed Phage. It felt like the first time. Full of longing, full of hope, full of a future together. But now there was more than just the two of us, and I couldn't have been happier.

"Ugh, so gross," said Jen as she came running over, red-faced and sweaty, smiling and as happy as any kid could be.

"It's not gross. It's love." I told her.

Jen rolled her eyes. "Did you see my moves? Tyr is so awesome. He's so fast too. Did you know he can morph at least a mile at a time now? It tires him out, but he can do it. It feels so weird. One moment you're somewhere, the next you're..."

"Somewhere else?" I asked, smiling.

"Exactly!"

"Doesn't it hurt when you morph with Tyr?" I wondered.

"No, not at all." Jen shrugged. "It feels weird, but Tyr explained that it's not me doing the morph, it's him, so I don't have to feel the pain. Even he does, you know. He says it hurts really bad, but he's getting used to it. Kind of like Woofer. Soon, I bet it won't hurt either of them. Can I go again?" she asked breathlessly.

Phage and I raised an eyebrow to each other then I said, "Sure. But Jen, take it easy, okay?"

"I will." She skipped off happily.

"At least she's not watching TV, or gaming," I reminded Phage.

"I think I'd prefer that."

We watched them for a while, then left them to it. Soon it would be time to settle the animals before bed, but there was still some evening light left, so it was nice to make the most of it and be outdoors.

Past the zoo, and back at the gate that led to our garden, Phage stopped me and said, "Soph, I've been meaning to ask you, but didn't want to get into it until you were feeling properly better and the effects had worn off. But, er, okay, I'm just going to come out and say it. Do you think the whole kill switch thing was for you?"

"For me? Are you serious? It went off for everyone, you know that. Even the elves. So I'm not sure I'm following."

"Don't you think it's a bit of a coincidence? That everything turned off just as you were going? That they gave you permission to drive? That it meant you went unseen? You went to the elves and then their internet, or whatever it is that's their version of it, went down not long after. Like it was all so they couldn't watch you, or see what happened next. A punishment for them, maybe. Teach them a lesson. Show them who's boss?"

"Don't be daft. You're reading too much into it. It was just a coincidence. I mean, why would they do that? Why cut off two entire worlds just so others couldn't watch me do what? Kill another man, same as always?"

"I don't think it was for that. I think it was because they knew you'd meet Eleron and end up where you did. I assume they don't like that sort of thing, so they shut everything down in advance just to prove to us, to the elves, and to other Necros, that there are rules and certain things simply aren't done."

"We know what they do if we break the rules," I told her. "I obviously didn't break any. I followed him in, but there's nothing to say I can't. Not that anyone else ever has, but there you go. No, just coincidence. Our kill switch might be unrelated to our invisible lords and masters. I get the feeling the elves going dark was them, but only because of what Eleron did. Come on, let's go cool down. Maybe a pint?"

"I wish."

"Damn, I keep forgetting. I wonder if the Brewer's alright. I hope so."

"Me too. He gives me the creeps, and I can't spend more than a minute with him, but he does make the best beer."

"Okay, crappy wine it is," I told her. "You go up. I'll be there in a minute.

After Phage went inside, I lingered, listening to my daughter whooping in the sky. I felt bad, really bad, for lying to my wife. I did it so she wouldn't worry, but it still felt wrong.

I absolutely had thought about the kill switch, almost to the exclusion of all else. And I absolutely did believe it was all because of me. There was no more denying that I was marked out as unique for some reason, and I believed that my masters had flicked the switch on our world and the elves because they wanted to show who was in charge, who had the power, and to make sure the elves especially didn't ever forget it. But more than that. They did it to show all us Necros that they were still very much in charge and we had better toe the line.

Or else.

What could I do? Nothing. I was sure that there were other reasons for the kill switch, but as with much else in the Necroverse, I got the feeling I would never know. More than that, I didn't want to know.

I wanted peace. Home. Phage and Jen and Woofer and Tyr and all the others. I wanted to be left alone. I certainly wasn't going to go looking for answers.

Again, I knew that it didn't matter. The answers would come find me even if I didn't want them.

But for now, and hopefully until the following year, I could enjoy being home, relax a little, and improve the dent in my recliner.

"Hey Dad," called Jen as she flew by just above my head.

"Hey." I waved as Tyr and Jen darted up into the endless possibilities of the Necroverse then vanished.

The End

Will Soph get to put his feet up? Will Woofer start morphing into the neighbor's kitchens (if he hasn't already) and nick their food? Where's the Brewer? And Wonjin? Will Soph ever get rid of his Big Boner? Er, I mean Bone Slicer. Yes, that's the last time. Sorry!

But most importantly of all, will you read the next book? This time, it's personal. **Witch Bitch** is book 5 in the series, so please continue to follow along on our favorite Necro's journey.

And be sure to **get notified of new notes** so you never miss any news or new releases.

That Time Again

Soph doesn't always travel through his adventures, more like misadventures, in a linear fashion, reaching the climax of the action and then all is well and it's time to chill until next time. The usual three-act structure doesn't apply to his life, same as it doesn't to anyone else's. He often finds that the goal he's been heading towards, killing another human being, leaves him with nothing but a sense of emptiness. And then real life, the mundane, takes over and what feels like the everyday to him is nothing but.

That's what I've tried to capture as I present Soph's life and that of his family. What it's really like to live how they do. How everyone does. It doesn't go by the book. It's messy, unconventional, and just when you think it's all over, it seldom is. He never gets all the answers, not that he wants them, and there is always something else to trip him up or give you cause for concern. I mean, if you've run out of milk even after you've done the nasty deed, you pick it up on the way home, right? As long as you can walk and your fingers are still working.

Take the Brewer for instance. Talk about bad timing. But that's the way life goes. Things never happen when you're ready for them. Life is an endless series of challenges. It isn't meant to be all fun, as if it was you probably wouldn't even realize you were having any. Major events, or small ones, come when least expected, and often at the worst possible time.

If your washing machine breaks down and you're strapped for cash, you can pretty much guarantee that the fridge will stop working in a week or two and the kettle or toaster will blow the electrics. Sorry, I shouldn't have mentioned that. Please don't blame me.

Now, about the kill switch. Far-fetched you say? Hold on a minute. Maybe not as impossible as you might first believe.

I did a fair bit of research about the possibility of all internet and phone communication being cut off, and was very surprised to discover just how widespread it has already been around the globe. Numerous countries have either turned off the internet completely, or limited its usability. The same goes for mobile and landline communication. Countries like the US and the UK have laws that would allow them to force the current service providers to basically flick the switch and the whole web would go dark.

The repercussions would be far-reaching and very scary for reasons beyond social media and me not being able to publish the book you have just read. Soon, all communication will be via internet connections, landlines being a thing of the past. Ours is currently plugged in although it hadn't been for years, but that's only so my mum can call if our mobile signal is dodgy, which it often is.

From security cameras to banking to just about everything, if we lost these services it would be a very different world. I'm sure we'd cope, us humans are good at that. But it's an interesting what-if scenario.

But hey, Soph has more to worry about than the Necronet. He's gained a lot of insight into the scope of the Necroverse and the power of the notes. The elves are certainly into it. Who else could be watching apart from the invisible, all-powerful overlords that it seems can control not only his world, but even those realms all Necros believed to be untouchable?

What he'll do with this knowledge is probably try to ignore it. He doesn't want these kinds of complications. He wants to be left alone, and live quietly. He hasn't had much luck with that so far. Maybe for once he'll get some peace.

What do you think?

I think he's leveling up slowly but surely whether he wants to or not. But he'll fight it tooth and nail, like many of us would, because being known and given any form of advantage in the Necroverse will lead to only one thing: more death.

As I'm writing this, another Covid variant is rampaging through our country and restrictions are once again in place. Maybe this is what prompted the world I've found Soph living in. Or that, combined with the increasing talks about climate change and something major actually needing to be done soon before it really is too late. I guess it's all there in the back of my mind and this is how it's played out.

Following a man and his family through extreme trials and tribulations, but coping together as a family no matter what. That makes me proud. He may be a right bastard in some ways, but in others he's a true gent. A kind, caring family man. Even if he does let his daughter do things that would make the rest of us stamp our feet and refuse to allow.

But their world is not our world.

Or is it?

Soph and family are the most realistic characters I have ever conjured. They could be living next door, leading regular-seeming lives. But once a year, for the sake of their own skin, they venture forth and do something heinous.

Would you?

Could you?

Could I?

I don't think anyone can answer that unless confronted with such a terrible choice.

But I know a man who can.

Please join me for book 5: Witch Bitch. And the star of the show is...?

Stay jiggy,

Al

Don't forget to stay updated about new notes at www.alkline.co.uk.

Printed in Great Britain
by Amazon

25893193R00158